TASTE OF FATE

Taste of Fate

Vampires of Sanguine
Book 1

Sophie Ash

Content warnings

- Mentions of bullying and abuse
- Mentions of chronic medical conditions (asthma and a heart murmur)
- Blood/gore/violence
- Bloodplay/blood in sexual situations
- Death of a loved one
- Mention of animal death
- Absent parents

Chapter 1

Taria

I watched as people filed in the assembly room, tension and anxiety on everyone's expressions. Couples and families clung tightly to each other as they came through the doors and found a place to stand in the waiting crowd.

All the worried faces and hushed conversations were understandable. It wasn't every day we gathered to find out which one of us would be sacrificed to the vampires.

No, this occasion was a once-in-fifty-years type of deal, an event called the Half-Century Selection. The last time it happened was before most of us were born. The elders would have been children, teenagers at the oldest, when the leading vampire clan came to collect their blood pet.

Amy and I stood against the back wall of the large room, mostly invisible as people came through the double doors, which were propped open. A gentle breeze blew in pink and white petals from the orchard. My cherry trees had just completed their first bloom and I was eager to harvest the fruit to make my cider, wine, and beer.

Some people walking in shot us dirty looks if they

noticed us leaning against the wall. I mean-mugged them right back while Amy ignored them.

She was full of nervous energy, shifting her weight and fidgeting with her hands. Even among the low murmurs of people filling up the room, I could hear her breath quickening.

I draped my arm over her shoulders in an effort to soothe her while also keeping her still. If she got too worked up, she could have an asthma or panic attack.

While she was a bit older than me, at twenty-seven to my twenty-four, Amy was smaller and always came across as younger. She had been born premature, and life in a world ruled by vampires wasn't easy. Along with her asthma, she also had a heart murmur that prevented her from doing a lot of strenuous activity.

In Sapien, the last purely human community in the vampire territory of Sanguine, everyone was expected to work hard and contribute to our little stronghold of humanity. It didn't matter if someone had asthma, a heart condition, or a broken leg. Not pulling the correct amount of weight led to bullying and ridicule.

I loved Amy like a sister, and there was nothing I hated more than a bully.

When she was six, a boy pushed her down in the mud and made her cry. I tripped him as he tried to run away, then jumped on his back and pounded into him as hard as my three-year-old fists could manage before adults peeled me off of him.

Amy and I had been inseparable ever since.

Our birth parents had left Sapien—and us—to integrate with vampire society. At least, that was what we'd been told with lots of disapproving head shakes and mutters about abandoning your fellow man.

In Sapien, the only thing worse than someone who didn't pull their weight was someone who left to live among the vampires.

So Amy and I had been raised together like sisters by the entire community. She became known as the quiet girl who preferred cooking, reading, and knitting. As for me? I was the loud-mouthed bulldog who didn't let anyone fuck with her best friend.

"I already feel terrible for whoever's going to be selected." Amy popped her knuckles, the nervous tic she always fell back on. "No one deserves to be offered up like a sacrificial lamb. Isn't there another way?"

An excellent question I had no answer to. I lifted one shoulder, watching the elderly council members talking among themselves on the raised stage across the room. "Why change a system that works just fine for the dinosaurs in charge?"

"Tavia!" Amy hissed and smacked my side. "Have a little empathy. It can't be easy choosing who it'll be, either. Everyone in the compound will judge the council's decision. Nobody wins here."

Yeah, right. It wasn't like we were voting on who to sacrifice or picking randomly from a lottery. The council had been taking anonymous suggestions via notes in a letterbox for the past month, but it was ultimately their decision. And I would never be convinced that it wasn't a popularity contest. Whoever kissed the council's asses would be safe. Everyone else was in the running to become a vampire's next meal.

Every member on the council was at least in their fifties. Harold was nearing eighty. A cynical part of me knew that none of them had put their own names down for consideration, despite all their talk about self-sacrifice for the good of our people.

"Hey, girls." Robin slid through the throng of people and leaned against the wall next to me with a humorless smirk. "Ready for the shitshow?"

Robin was a woman in her forties with short brown hair, frizzed with gray, and the cheeriest blue eyes I ever saw. She was one of the few who looked out for me and Amy, and was the closest thing we had to a mother-slash-older sister figure. She was also respected enough to hold sway with the council and other community elders, which came in handy when I got in trouble. Which was, to say, a lot.

In my defense, the only reason I had a troublemaker reputation was because the same bullies who picked on Amy ran off and squealed when I gave them a taste of their own medicine. You'd think it would be a simple lesson. All they had to do was stop being assholes, and my fist would stop breaking their noses.

"Do you know who they chose?" I watched Peter, another councilman, close the doors of the assembly room, which meant all one-hundred-and-eight citizens of Sapien were present.

Robin shook her head. "Norma said this morning they were up late into the night discussing it, but not a word of what was decided."

The murmuring crowd quieted as Nancy, chairwoman of the council, stood and shuffled over to the microphone stand at the edge of the stage.

"Thank you for coming, everyone—" she leaned away from the microphone as a loud screech of feedback filled the room.

People slapped hands over their ears, muttering

complaints as someone adjusted sound levels. Nancy tried again, and was successful the second time.

"Thank you for coming, everyone," she said solemnly, eyes glassy as she scanned the room. "No one is happy about this day. This is the hardest decision any of us have had to make, and we did not make it lightly."

She turned to pick up a framed document on the stool next to her and held it up for everyone to see. The paper behind the glass was ancient and frayed at the edges. Whatever words that had been written were now faded to the point of being barely visible.

"This is the original agreement made two-hundred-and-fifty years ago between the human colony of Sapien and the ruling vampire clan. At the time, that clan was Carpe Noctem, but power is constantly shifting in the vampire world." Nancy set the document down and laced her fingers in front of her. "The agreement is as follows: Upon receiving a blood pet from Sapien every half century, the leading vampire clan will forbid any feedings, kidnappings, or blood rituals being imposed upon our citizens." She looked solemnly over the crowd. "Since the inception of this agreement, the vampires have always honored their end. We have been able to thrive in a world that works against us because of this sacrifice we must make."

"Here, here." Harold thumped his cane on the stage in a show of support while low murmurs of agreement swept over the crowd.

I suppressed the urge to roll my eyes, crossing my arms while I propped one foot against the wall. Robin glanced at me and smirked, knowing exactly what I was thinking. Could it be any more obvious who would sleep easily in their beds tonight, their necks cozy and safe from any and all fangs?

"No one looks forward to this day," Nancy went on. "And yet, we must look deep within ourselves to find gratitude for the Selection." Nancy took the microphone from the stand and began walking across the stage, staring directly into people's eyes like some kind of evangelist. "The clans fight amongst each other, and humans near them get caught in the crossfire. A human man, woman, or child walks down the street, and a vampire can make a meal out of them with no consequences. These poor, misguided people are at constant risk with no community to protect them."

A few people in the crowd began to cry. Roughly a third of Sapien had someone close to them, a parent, child, or sibling, leave the settlement to see what life among the vampires was like. None of them had ever come back.

Sapien's walkaways weren't the only ones either. Other human-only settlements were now ghost towns because their populations had either been fed upon or integrated into vampire society.

No one from Sapien ventured into clan territories much, but everyone knew the rumors. People whispered about humans switching to a nocturnal schedule and allowing their blood to be drunk, either freely or in exchange for money. They became neighbors, friends, employees, and even lovers of the monsters who ruled us.

Sometimes, when Amy's bullies were especially cruel, and the council did nothing to stop it, I wondered how much worse it could really be out there.

Nancy let out a shaky breath and wiped one of her eyes, not that I could see any tears. "One sacrifice for fifty years of peace. Fifty years of not having to worry about the monsters that come lurking at night."

Tell that to Amy, who got dragged from her bed by the

Hoyle brothers and dumped in the pigpen one night as a "prank", I thought bitterly. The poor thing had nightmares of being kidnapped for months after that.

I didn't have the physical strength to dish the same treatment to two grown men, but I was petty enough to dump pig shit inside their boots and all over their laundry in retaliation. Amy had begged me not to, but they left her alone after that so I considered it a success.

"Fifty years is over half of a lifetime for most of us." Nancy had reached the far end of the stage and began retracing her steps toward the middle. "What's better? Giving up one person to them once, maybe twice, in a lifetime, or losing dozens of us, maybe even more, to their fangs in that time?"

"Keep telling yourself that, Nancy," I muttered.

Robin snorted.

For all I knew, Nancy was probably right. But based on how hard she was trying to convince the crowd that this was the Only Way, it didn't *feel* right. I personally couldn't think of any solid proof that humans were any better than vampires. How did we know our walkaways didn't want to come back?

"As long as our humanity is preserved, as long as the loyalty to our species keeps going," Nancy said passionately into the microphone. "For the good of humanity, we will continue to bear the burden of this bittersweet agreement."

Harold thumped his cane again and soft applause sounded through the room. I wondered if anyone, in our two-hundred-fifty year history, fought or spoke out against the agreement. If they had, there was none of that rebellious spirit in the room now. Just quiet, reluctant acceptance.

Nancy replaced the microphone on the stand and straightened her spine. "Thank you all for listening, and for contributing to the good of our community. I've kept you all long enough. As painful as this is, I won't stall any longer."

She took a deep breath that shook a little. "The person who has been selected as the blood pet is..." Her eyes lowered, unable to make contact with anyone in the room. "...Amy Aster."

There was a beat of stunned silence. Then I heard Amy's squeak of shock next to me, followed by blood roaring in my ears.

What the fuck?

For some reason, I never expected it to be her. But once the full force of reality hit me, it made perfect sense.

"No."

I stepped away from the wall and in front of my best friend, spreading my arms as if to shield her from an attack. "No fucking way, that's not happening."

"Tavia." My name from Nancy's lips carried a note of warning across the room. "I understand this is difficult—"

"I'll go instead." The words left my mouth before they were a fully formed thought in my brain, and it took a few seconds to process the full weight of what I was saying. But there was no way I could let Amy be the blood pet.

She was treated like shit here, yes. But better the devil we knew than the devil we didn't.

And with her health conditions, being regularly drained of blood would be far more difficult than for most people. For her, it would be nothing short of torture.

"I'll be the blood pet," I said, resolute in my decision, even though I was jumping off a cliff into a massive unknown. But I'd always been an act first, think later kind of girl. "Sacrifice me, not her."

"Tavia, no!" Amy pleaded from behind me. She pushed

on my outspread arms, but physically, she had never been stronger than me.

"As I said, *Octavia*." Nancy boomed my full name from the stage like a stern grandmother. "The council's decision has been made."

"Did the council even bother to ask for volunteers?" I shouted back. Of course they hadn't, because who the hell would sign up? "You should have done that first, not this secret-meetings-late-into-the-night bullshit. I'm volunteering, so take me."

The crowd began to pick up volume as several animated conversations took place.

"We should vote. All of us should have input on this decision," someone shouted.

I shook my head. At this point, Amy would likely be selected by the majority anyway. The council already put her forth as their choice, and most people wanted to make the council happy.

"There's no need for a vote when you have a volunteer right here," I argued, stretching my hand high into the air. "Just choose me and let this be settled, Nancy."

The chairwoman stepped away from the microphone and turned to the other council members on the stage. They huddled together, whispering amongst themselves as the crowd buzzed with energy.

People shot looks at me over their shoulders, all wearing different expressions. Some with disdain and sneers. Others with muted surprise and respect. I met all of their gazes head on, daring any of them to come forward. Where was the shit-talking and insults now, huh? Who else in this crowd of sheep was brave enough to sacrifice themselves for someone else?

After a few minutes, the council members broke up their huddle

"Octavia," Nancy called from the stage, no longer using the microphone.

I swallowed the thick knot in my throat and straightened. "Yes?"

"Come see us in the council chamber." She jerked her head to the side before heading down the small steps at the side of the stage.

I turned around to find Amy flat against the wall, tears streaming down her cheeks as she stared at me. If this worked, I had saved her life. But I had also broken her heart. We would never see each other again, and I'd probably be dead before the end of the week.

As much as I wanted to hug her, rocking her gently from side to side like I always did when she cried, I forced my gaze away and looked at Robin.

"Take her home," I instructed. "Stay with her there. Don't let anyone in but me."

"You got it." Robin slid an arm around Amy, her face grim as she looked out over the crowd. She didn't like this any more than the inconsolable young woman at her side, but she was tough enough to put a brave face on, and wise enough to deescalate if things got ugly.

With a final heart-wrenching glance at Amy, I turned away and the crowd parted for me as I headed for the room where my fate would be decided.

"WHY ARE you offering yourself in place of Miss Aster?" Nancy got right down to business as soon as the chamber door closed and the council members settled in their seats.

I squared my shoulders and met her stare head-on. "Because she already suffers enough as it is. She's given all that she can to Sapien, and her reward for it is to be kicked around like a dog. It's honestly abhorrent that you would make her suffer more by choosing her for this. You *know* she would suffer more than the average person."

Nancy leaned back in her seat, putting down the pen she'd been twirling. "You know, I remember the last Selection. I was twelve years old and I'll never forget that terrible scene." Her eyes locked on mine. "They didn't just drink her blood. As soon as the vampires received their blood pet, they tore into her like a pack of animals. They ripped her apart and ate pieces of her in front of the whole community."

My stomach turned, but I stood firm. She was trying to intimidate me, to make me back down and save my own skin. It would never happen, though. When it came to protecting Amy, I was bullheaded to a fault.

"I remember it as well," Peter chimed in. "I was oh, maybe fourteen. Threw up all my dinner that night and couldn't help Pop butcher meat for months after that."

I turned a disgusted gaze to him. He'd watched one of their own get violently slaughtered, her life cut short for no reason, and recalled it like any story from the good ol' days.

"The silver lining was," Nancy went on, "that poor girl didn't suffer long." She gave me a pointed look. "It was a brutal, terrible thing but she went quickly."

She went quickly. Like a lame old goat that had been taken out to the pasture and shot.

The suffering aspect wasn't even the point. It was the fact that the Half-Century Selection existed at all and was never questioned. It was the fact that they used it as an excuse to get rid of people they saw as less worthy.

The council overlooked everything Amy was great at doing, and saw her as the weakest link in the community. I'd bet my entire batch of cherry cider that was the reason they'd chosen her to be the blood pet. In their eyes, they were cutting dead weight.

In mine, they were heartless fucking bastards and Amy was worth more than the whole room of them.

Standing as tall as I could, with my chin high and my hands clasped behind my back, I willed my voice to not shake as I met each of their gazes.

"My decision remains the same. Select me in place of Amy as the blood pet."

I couldn't handle them sending my best friend, the sweetest and most selfless person I knew, out to slaughter. At least this way, I knew I'd be preventing her from a premature death. It would hurt like hell to never see her again, but I took comfort in knowing I stood up for her one last time.

Amy would be devastated. But at least she'd live on. She had to.

"Why are you really doing this, Octavia?" Nancy asked after a long silence.

Because Amy is the one person who deserves a better fate than this. Because no one in this godforsaken community has a shred of empathy, so who else is going to? Because I hate all of your games and your politics, and I'm fucking tired. There was no simple answer to that, and especially not one that they were prepared to hear.

"It's just the right thing to do," I said.

"And you're absolutely sure about this decision?" Harold peered at me with his beady eyes.

"Yes."

I was likely in shock and not fully processing the consequences of what I'd done, but that would come later. My mind was made up. And there was simply no option but to keep Amy safe.

Well, safer.

"Alright, then." The council members all looked at each other. "We are not barbarians or murderers."

The ones who didn't speak nodded their agreement.

I held back a snort. *Whatever helps you all sleep at night.*

"Since she is standing here, of sound mind and giving her full consent, it's decided." Nancy brought her hands together. "Octavia Franz will be given to the ruling vampire clan as the next blood pet in the Half-Century Selection."

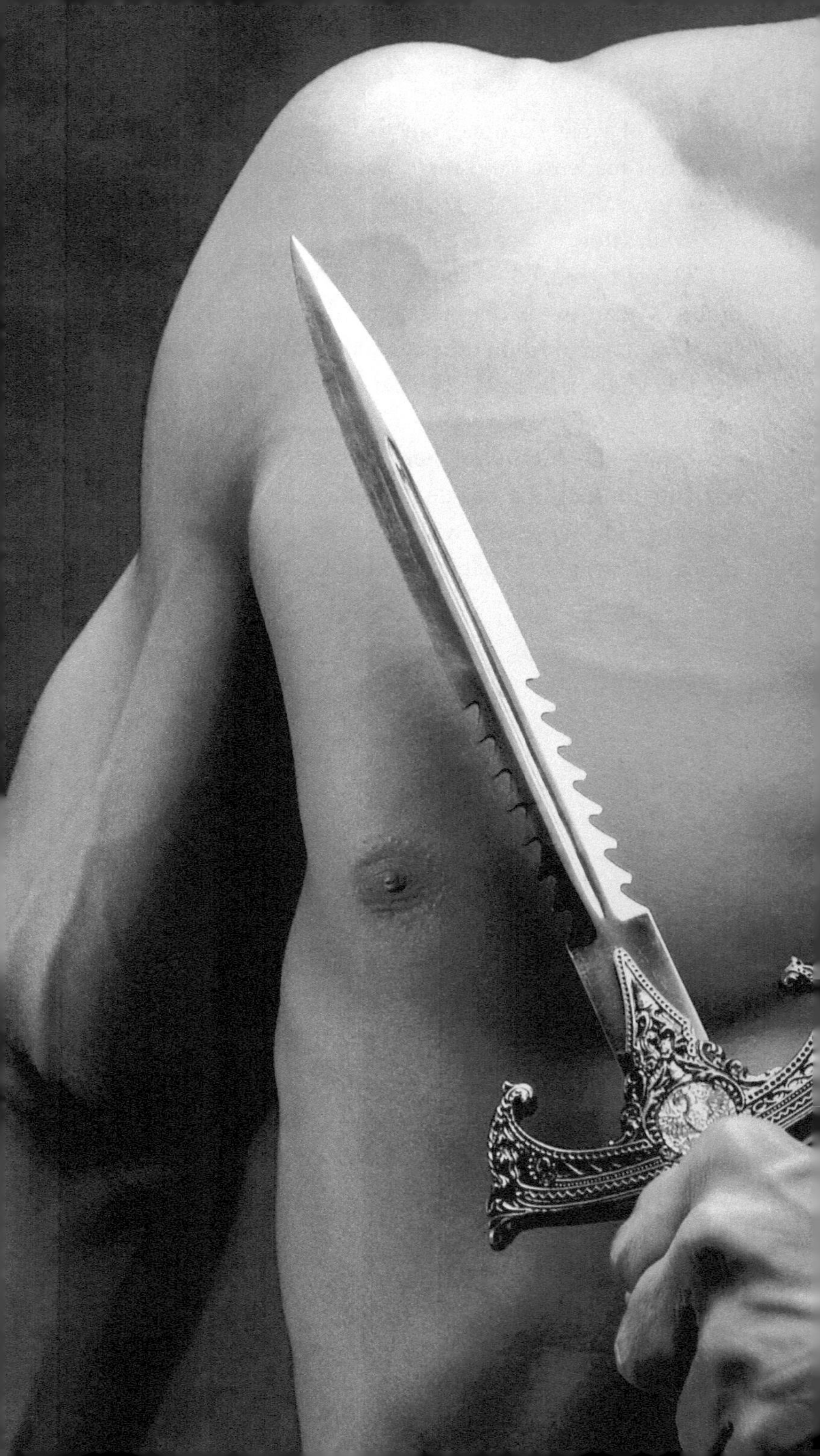

Chapter 2

Cyan

I stared at the dried stick between my fingers and groaned. It sucked being the guy who drew the shortest straw, especially when it came to something like taking on a responsibility I didn't even want.

A blood pet was the last thing I needed. I didn't even want to care for a pet hamster.

"Congratulations, buddy." Desmond slapped me on the shoulder, his fangs poking through his lips as he tried not to laugh. "I wish you and your blood pet a long, happy life together."

"Man, fuck you." I dropped the inch-long piece of straw and scraped my boot over it until it was dust. "This agreement is bullshit. Why are we still doing this with the humans, anyway?"

"They need to remember whose territory they're in." Thorne, our clan leader, lit up a cigarette, his cheeks sinking in as he dragged on it. The scent of darakt, a fine mixture of powdered blood and herbs for flavor, filled the air. "Humans are funny creatures. They insist on declaring their independence, then in the same breath, cry for safety and protection." He exhaled a cloud of red smoke that matched his eyes. "This is the price they pay for being spoiled children who get everything they want."

"Why do *we* have to take their offering though?" I ran a hand over the short buzz of my hair. "Why not let the Marrowers or Carpe Noctem have the blood pet?"

Thorne huffed irritably. "Because we're the ruling clan now. Their sacrifice is ours to take by right. It's been that way since before you were around, pup." He stuffed his hands in the pockets of his leather jacket, then kicked my boot on his way to the garage. "Let's go," he said around the cigarette in his mouth. "Time to collect our due and get this over with."

I got up from the couch with a groan, following him. Desmond came after me, still chuckling at my expense. Rhain was already in the garage, the big long-haired fucker topping off the fluids in his motorcycle. His face was so stony, I didn't think it was possible for him to crack a smile.

It was just the four of us riding out. No need for the entire clan to bring home one human. An entire fleet of bloodthirsty vampires on motorcycles would probably scare them into doing something stupid, like offering up ten more of themselves as blood pets. No, thank you.

The roll-up door lifted smoothly as our bikes roared to life. It was a clear night, the sky dotted with stars and a sliver of crescent moon. It was a perfect night to go out to Pulse Point, our club in the downtown strip just off the Heart region, maybe drink from a fiery dragon shifter or that sexy little brusang that always flirted with me.

But no. Instead, I was riding out to the North Ribs. To the last-remaining all-human settlement to retrieve what was essentially my human wife. Or husband, if they offered up a male.

Not that it was exactly that kind of thing. Relationships with blood pets sometimes turned sexual, but not always. Males of any species didn't interest me that way. Strictly speaking, blood pets were long-term suppliers of blood. In addition to feeding from them, I would be expected to keep and care for them, like I would any being living in my home.

But the part that really pissed me off about the whole exchange was the expectation of exclusivity.

That was exactly why I'd never claimed a blood pet before. I was a young vampire, only one-hundred-and-fifteen, and had zero desire to tie myself down to a single blood source. Why would I when there were so many different flavors to sample? And if tasting happened to lead to sex, well, that was just a bonus.

In another three, maybe four hundred years, maybe I'd consider settling down. Hell, the vast majority of our clan didn't have blood pets or the far more rare and sought-after, blood mates. So yeah, I was pretty damn sour on losing hard in our little lottery. I felt like the humans in the old TV shows that got forced into marrying young because they got caught making out in a barn. What a sad life.

As the four of us rode through the night, I was already thinking of how to get rid of this burden I'd been saddled with. *Maybe I can pass the pet off to someone else. It shouldn't be too hard to find a vampire with a boring palate.*

Humans were common enough in Sanguine that I'd already sampled a good number of them, either at the blood bank for a quick fill, or one of our clubs in a more salacious setting. What I'd found out, and most vampires agreed, was that humans tasted bland.

Their blood didn't taste *bad* by any means, but there was nothing to be excited about from those veins. From what little I knew about human food, their blood could best be compared to a bowl of rice with no seasonings, or a plain slice of bread. It could sate hunger for a time and contained enough nutrition to survive for a while, but that didn't mean the experience of having it was *good*.

Sure, there were small flavor variances here and there, but nothing compared to the wild spiciness of a dragon shifter's blood. Or the warm, comforting mouth feel of a fellow vampire. Werewolf and angel blood were only available in black market channels, but those were said to be a near-religious experience. I had made it a personal goal to try them at least once.

But instead, here I was giving up my variety-loving palate for the same boring meal every day. Kill me.

The ride could have taken all night and it still would have been too short. The lights of Sapien, the human settlement, appeared on the horizon after only two hours. I squinted at the increasing brightness as we got closer. It was easy to forget humans were diurnal creatures and needed a ton of extra light to see at night. Most of the ones living among us in Sanguine had adapted to nocturnal schedules and they always had lights with them.

The community was spread out over several acres with many mobile-looking homes set up on wheels. The more permanent structures consisted of squat, single story buildings. Many of our buildings looked similar. Considering vampires spent much of their days underground, we didn't need more than a single story at ground level.

Unlike us, the humans had multiple rows of fenced-in beds with plants growing in them, along with several pens containing animals such as chickens, ducks, goats, and pigs.

I wasn't the only one who stared at the animals as we slowed the bikes on our approach to the compound. Rhain looked like he'd never seen a chicken before.

"Keeping live animals is fucking weird," he muttered with a shake of his head.

Someone must have spotted us and alerted the other humans then, because they started pouring out of the large center building in droves.

"Alright. Guess we stop here." Thorne cut his engine a good fifty feet away from where the humans were gathering, and the rest of us did the same behind him.

It was like watching ants emerge from a single hole in the ground. They came out and then went to the left and right, spreading out thinly in front of their building. Some small groups, probably families, stuck together. One older human had her arm around a much smaller, younger woman who was red-faced and hysterically crying, trying to stifle her loud sobs.

I frowned. The younger one looked utterly stricken with grief and fear. Was she the blood pet?

As much as I tried to ignore it, discomfort itched up my spine. Humans were weak, short-lived, and tasted boring, but they were just as sentient as any species in Sanguine. They were capable of joy, suffering, and everything else in between. It didn't occur to me until now that giving up one of their own wasn't just inconvenient, like it was for me.

It was having a loved one ripped away, suddenly and unfairly. This event would shake their community for months, if not years. The blood pet's family and friends would mourn as if they had died, but a situation like this was worse than death. It was not knowing if they were dead or alive, well or suffering, that was the most persistent poison. The absence of knowledge haunted worse than any ghost. At least you knew a ghost was dead.

I knew that poisonous, never-knowing feeling all too fucking well, and didn't wish it on anyone.

Strangely, the small woman seemed to be the only one truly visibly upset. The one holding her blinked away tears and seemed to be biting the inside of her cheek. Everyone else looked to be a mixture of afraid, nervous, or curious.

A much older human woman strode out of the building and walked straight toward us. Despite the fear pinching her lined face, she carried herself as a leader.

"Hello," she called out, stopping about twenty feet from Thorne's headlight.

"Good evening," he returned, lighting up another cigarette. A few humans gasped and muttered to themselves at the puffs of red smoke from his nostrils and mouth. He paid them no mind. "We represent Blood 'til Dawn, ruling clan of Sanguine. We've come to collect the blood pet per the Half-Century Selection agreement."

"Welcome, ah, Blood 'til Dawn." The elderly woman repeated our clan name clumsily and brought her hands together in front of her. "We're honored to, uh...honor the agreement between Sapien and the ruling clan."

"Have you chosen a blood pet?" Thorne drawled in a bored tone.

"Ah, yes. We have."

He stuck the cigarette between his teeth and waved his free hand. "Then let's get this over with. It's a long ride back. Cyan." He jerked his chin at me. "Come up and collect your pet."

With a resigned sigh, I pulled up alongside him and dismounted my bike. Might as well stretch my legs first if I was about to ride home with a passenger.

"The blood pet is mine," I said to the human woman. "I'll take them now and we'll be out of your hair for the next fifty years."

The woman blinked at me, the lines around her eyes deepening as her forehead creased. "You? I mean, *just* you?"

"Yes," I said with a hint of annoyance. "We don't share."

"Right, of course." She flashed me a nervous small before turning to the open doorway behind her. "Come on out, Octavia."

A figure appeared, her white dress a stark contrast to the dark interior behind her. She stepped across the threshold and approached us stiffly, shoulders tense and her hands clenched into fists at her sides.

Something about the tension in those fists screamed danger, like she'd used them as weapons before.

Her hair was loose down her back in reddish brown waves moving slightly in the breeze as she walked forward. The white dress was a ridiculous get-up, honestly. Were they going to happily inform me she was a virgin too?

It was her expression that intrigued me the most. Her clenched jaw, lips pressed tightly together, brow furrowed over alert, stormy gray eyes. With her face like that, along with her clenched fists and stiff movements, it looked like she was tensing every muscle in her body, bracing for something. Or holding herself together so that she wouldn't fall apart in front of everyone.

She was pretty in an unexpected way, keeping all the wild intensity in her posture like a tempest in a tea cup. It suited her, like she had been shaped and molded by holding lashing winds and a fiery temper within her.

This woman would not be easy prey, and my fangs throbbed with a dull ache. Despite knowing she was human, knowing her blood would be bland and plain in my mouth, the predator in me wanted the challenge of melting that steel from her spine. I wondered what it would take to make this storm-filled woman calm and compliant in my arms, baring her neck for my taking.

I swallowed on nothing, ignoring the pulse in my fangs as I stepped forward. To taste this woman would be to commit myself exclusively to her blood alone, and I'd do well to remember I was not signing up for that responsibility.

"Octavia, is it?" Remembering the human custom of a handshake, I stuck my palm out. "I'm Cyan of Blood 'til Dawn. It's a pleasure."

She stared at my hand and then at my face, eyes narrowing. I swore she clenched her fists even harder, and said nothing.

I dropped my hand and tried to offer a smile that looked comforting. Fangs had a tendency to make that difficult, though. "As you are my blood pet, I'm what's known as your *verakt*. Roughly, it translates to protector. You don't have anything to fear."

Verakt was an ancient term that had no real translation in English. Protector was the closest match, but it also carried the weight of something like *master*. Not exactly in an ownership sense, but more as the more dominant, stronger one in the relationship, which circled back to protector.

The woman, Octavia, continued to squint at me wordlessly. This time seemed more out of confusion than fear or hate.

"Alright then." My hands clapped together awkwardly and one of the guys, probably Des, snorted behind me. Ignoring them, I asked my new pet, "Do you have any personal items you'd like to bring with you?"

She blinked, seeming taken aback by the question. "Why?"

Now I was confused. Did we or the humans misunderstand something? I slid a glance at the older human woman, who seemed intent on avoiding eye contact with any vampires. I then looked over my shoulder at Thorne, who offered up a helpful shrug.

Turning back to Octavia, I said slowly, "Because you'll be living with me?"

She blinked several times as if fighting back tears, then took a slow, shaky breath. "No. I don't have anything."

I found that hard to believe. Humans and vampires were both fond of having sentimental things. There were also basic necessities like clothing and toiletries that all people needed, but my blood pet had been offered to me empty-handed. I scanned the faces of the gathered humans, wondering why they were handing over this woman with nothing but the clothes she wore.

"Okay, then," I relented and angled my head toward my bike. "Let's go."

"Go?" Octavia stayed rooted to her spot, her brow furrowed again with confusion.

"Yes." Maybe she just wasn't fully there mentally. In which case, no blood from her would ever touch a vampire's lips. Our clan had strict laws about informed consent from any living blood source we took from. "You're my blood pet now, my responsibility. I'm taking you to my home where you will be cared for and looked after. Do you understand?"

"You mean," she frowned. "You're not going to just drain me of all my blood right now?"

My fangs throbbed like that was an excellent idea, which didn't make any sense. I went to the blood bank right before we drew straws. I wasn't hungry. But the thought of tasting this woman was a temptation I couldn't seem to shake.

"I'm not sure what happened during the last Selection," I said. "But that's not how we do things." I leaned in close, until my mouth nearly touched her ear. Her little gasp at my nearness had my teeth aching.

"Look, this is enough of a circus as it is," I whispered. "Being chosen as a blood pet is a privilege. Feeding from one isn't a spectacle. It's personal. Intimate. Not something to gawk at." Her pulse accelerated in her neck and it was so damn distracting that I had to pause for a breath. "After casting you out, they've gawked at you enough, don't you think? So let's get out of here and settle you into your new life."

When I straightened, her expression had relaxed somewhat. Her jaw and lips remained tense, but there was an understanding in her eyes. A calm in her storm.

"Can I just say goodbye to someone first?" she whispered.

"Of course." I nodded and took a step back. "Take all the time you need."

She turned to face the gathered crowd, and it was no surprise that she went straight toward the small, crying woman who burst into a fresh wave of tears. They embraced tightly and I found myself looking away from the scene I had no right to be watching.

Octavia hugged the older woman who had been with her crying friend, but no one else approached to offer affection or well wishes of any kind. I scanned faces and they all looked mildly uncomfortable. Inconvenienced. The fear and nerves seemed to have passed, and now they all wanted to return to their lives.

It was all very strange to me. Maybe humans didn't get as attached to each other as I had thought. In a vampire clan, every single member would be devastated at losing one of our own. The humans' reactions made me wonder about Octavia's relationship with the two people she *was* saying goodbye to.

After a few more hugs and hushed words, my blood pet reluctantly stepped away from her fellow humans and returned to where I stood. Her face was dry, although her eyes shone with unspent tears.

"Okay," she said. "I'm ready to go."

I dipped my head in a nod, but said nothing as I led her to my bike. This whole ordeal was fucking strange and my head was spinning.

Thorne tossed his finished cigarette on the ground, then returned his grip to the handlebars. "See you in fifty years," he said to the human leader before revving his engine.

My bike roared as I took off after him with my new blood pet seated behind me, and my fangs itching for her blood.

Chapter 3

Tavia

I could almost convince myself that this was a nightmare. I had the eerie feeling of being suspended in space, not truly going anywhere. That I hadn't actually left the only home I'd ever known, nor said goodbye to Amy for the last time. Her tear-streaked, heartbroken face wasn't real, because we were still together. I wasn't traveling across a dark landscape at high speeds, wind whipping at my skin while I clutched for dear life onto a vampire's leather jacket. I was just floating, disconnected from it all.

I'd never been on the back of a motorcycle before. It must have been freezing, tearing through the windy night while holding onto a vampire's waist, wearing nothing but the stupid white dress the council had put me in. But I felt so numb to the bone that I couldn't truly feel anything at all.

At some point, the out-of-body experience ended and everything felt real again. Biting winds gave way to stagnant air. Instead of the constant roar of motorcycles in my ears, silence poured in, then echoing voices and footsteps. I blinked and realized I was in a garage. Concrete floors, a high ceiling with florescent lights, and a sea of motorcycles stretched out before me.

Reality hit me like a brick wall then. I was completely alone in a den full of vampires, and I would never see Amy or go home again.

"Shit. You're freezing."

I turned stiffly toward the voice and saw *him*, the vampire I now belonged to. Despite living in Sanguine my whole life, I had never seen one this close. And like a rare wild animal, he was fascinating to look at.

He appeared mostly human, but a little different. It wasn't something I could put my finger on, even before I had noticed his red eyes and elongated canines. He was dangerous in a way that set my instincts on edge. His dark hair was buzzed close to his scalp, nothing hiding his incredible bone structure. He was beautiful in a masculine way, his face boyish with full lips, prominent cheekbones, a straight nose, and dark lashes framing those ruby eyes.

Even his pinched frown was painfully gorgeous.

"I should have given you my jacket," he said. The tips of his fangs flashed in the overhead lights as he spoke. "I forgot that your kind is more susceptible to cold temperatures."

Looking down, I saw his hand around my upper arm and found myself curiously inspecting the differences in our skin tones and textures. I had a bronze tan from years of working out in the sun, plus plenty of small scars and freckles dotting me all over. His skin was completely unmarked, smooth like it was airbrushed, and much paler with reddish undertones.

"Come inside." His tone was commanding but held a warmth I didn't expect. "We'll get you warmed up and settled in."

He didn't pull me off the motorcycle, but waited with his hand firmly around my upper arm.

My insides felt like a gated horse just waiting to bolt. I wanted to run back to Amy, away from him, his fangs, and this strange place. But the metal door had since dropped closed behind me, and my legs were cramped and stiff after hours of riding. I would never make it even if I tried.

Plus, this was the fate I signed up for, after all.

I slid from the motorcycle's seat to the floor with his assistance. Once my feet hit the ground, he released my arm and proceeded to lead the way.

We left the garage through a door, entering a massive, open room. The ceilings were high and vaulted at steep angles, with the only windows being small rectangles near the tops of the walls. A small, elevated stage with a stripper pole stood in the center of the room. Classy. I'd heard stories that vampires enjoyed their debauchery on a whole other level.

My protector, or whatever he was, Cyan, cut a path straight through the room, bypassing the many couches, bars, large flatscreen TV on one wall, stripper pole, all of it. The opposite side of the room contained a huge, ornate kitchen, even bigger than the community kitchen in Sapien. This looked much nicer and more updated than ours, but Cyan walked quickly and I hustled to keep up. When he crossed the room, opened two heavy and intricately carved doors on the far wall and kept walking.

There was a spacious landing and then a staircase leading down. I followed Cyan carefully down the steps, noting how much cooler the air felt as we descended. This level had to be underground. I could vaguely remember from my early education on vampires that they preferred to be underground when asleep during the day. It was more comforting to sleep under the surface where the sun's rays couldn't reach them.

I once thought going underground would feel incredibly claustrophobic, like being buried alive, but the corridor we landed in was spacious and well-lit. The angled ceiling continued on the second level above us, so there was no sense of being crushed under the weight of the earth.

Cyan marched down the corridor, his booted footfalls echoing. The walls were lined with doors, with sconces placed between each door. The wall lights were warmer here, giving off a yellow glow that was almost soothing. There were also side tables holding plants and portraits on the walls between the doors.

When Cyan stopped at one door to unlock it, I touched the plant at the nearest side table. It felt real and looked like some kind of fern.

The portrait on the wall below the light was of Cyan and another vampire I didn't recognize. He hadn't been part of the small group that collected me. Their arms were around each other, mouths open and grinning with laughter. The other vampire had longer hair brushing the tops of his shoulders, and his eyes were a darker shade of red, almost brown.

"Here we are," Cyan said brusquely. He stood aside and gestured the way through the open door.

I didn't exactly want to be in a confined room with him, but what other choice did I have? I stepped through.

To my surprise, the room was far more spacious than I imagined. It was more like a small apartment, or a hotel suite. There was a small living room with two couches and an armchair, a TV, and a bar overlooking the room. Not much of a kitchen besides the bar and sink, but I supposed vampires didn't do much cooking.

"There's a second bedroom through there." Cyan pointed to a door off the living room. "It's a bit small, but it's all yours. The bathroom is shared."

"Um, thanks," I croaked, realizing it had been hours since I said a single word.

Standing in the entryway, I turned to look at him, my confusion only growing. First he didn't want to kill or even bite me in front of everyone back in Sapien, now he was showing me a bedroom like we were going to be roommates? What had I actually signed up for here?

His shoulders sagged a little at my expression, the youthful boyishness of him suddenly looking much older and weary. "Have a seat." He gestured to the couch. "Would you like anything to drink? Water?"

I wet my cracked lips, only then realizing how thirsty I was. "Sure, thanks."

If he was planning on drinking my blood at some point, he wouldn't give me anything poisonous, right?

Cyan took his leather jacket off, dropping it over the back of a barstool before he opened a small, countertop refrigerator on the bar and pulled out a sealed, plastic water bottle. He handed it to me, then seated himself at the opposite end of the couch with a strained smile. I started entertaining the radical thought that maybe he didn't want to hurt me.

"If I may take a wild guess," he began. "You weren't exactly jumping for joy to become the Half-Century blood pet."

As he spoke, I unscrewed the cap on the water and gulped down half the bottle. "What gave it away?" I wiped my mouth.

He let out a soft chuckle, propping an arm on the back of the couch. His T-shirt sleeve rode up with the movement, exposing a flexed bicep. "I'm not sure how you were selected, and you don't have to tell me. But we drew straws and I got the short one. That's the only reason you ended up with me. Nothing against you personally, but I didn't want a blood pet. Still don't."

I blinked at him, my confusion mounting. "You don't want my blood?" The question I didn't dare ask screamed loudly in my brain. *Does this mean I can go home?*

"It's not that. I'm sure your blood is perfectly fine." Cyan's eyes narrowed. "What do you know about being a blood pet?"

I shook my head. "Nothing really, aside that I belong to you and you drink from me."

He let out a long breath, running a hand over the short fuzz of his hair. "Right, okay. Well, here's the thing." He sat up taller. "A blood pet has to be claimed by a vampire. This means no one else can feed from you, and likewise, it's frowned upon for a verakt to feed from anyone besides their blood pet. There is," he gestured between us, "supposed to be a commitment here, on both ends."

My mind reeled as I sucked down the rest of my water. "So it's like...a relationship?"

"A type of one, yes. Blood pets and verakt often end up with romantic or sexual feelings, but that isn't always the case. There are plenty of platonic situations as well."

I took in his posture on the couch, the way he settled into the cushions. He was like a tiger at rest, beautiful and alluring but deadly even when relaxed.

"If I were to drink from you, that would be seen as making the relationship official," he went on. "Sort of like a consummation. Not exactly, but similar idea."

"And this kind of relationship," I hedged. "Is not one that you want."

"You get it," he said with a fanged smirk and approving nod. "I like variety in my blood meals, and have never felt the need to claim a pet. So, yeah." He scratched at his temple, his smile charming. "We both got kind of screwed on this, didn't we?"

"Then what does this mean?" I tried to smother the hope brimming in my voice. "If neither of us want this, then what's the point? Why do this at all?"

Cyan's smile dropped, his eyes sharpening. "Because this agreement is the only thing keeping up your people's so-called independence. If it weren't for this, nothing would stop the vampire clans from moving in, gorging themselves on blood, and dismantling everything you've built for generations." He shrugged. "It doesn't make a difference to me, but I'm guessing that's not what you want."

I shrank back against the couch. "Right, sorry. Forget I said anything." My head was so scrambled, I'd forgotten what Nancy had been beating into our heads the moment before she announced Amy's name up on that stage.

Cyan's expression softened. "You're already here and I'm not completely heartless. I'm also never one to go back on a deal."

Neither was I. I didn't want to imagine the kind of stress Amy would be under if she were here instead of me.

The vampire rubbed his chin, looking thoughtful. "The deal is done, and there's no undoing it. But," one of his fangs dug into his lower lip, "maybe we can make our own deal."

I didn't know whether to feel suspicious or hopeful. "What kind of deal?"

"I can release my claim on you as a blood pet at any time. But you're in an unfamiliar place where you don't know anyone, so for now it's best that I continue to claim you for your own protection. But," he stared at me intently with that ruby gaze. "It will be as a verbal claim only. I will never take your blood, and continue to sample variety like I always have. Just...more discreetly than I have been, I guess."

"So..." I took a moment to process his words. "I'll still be yours outwardly, to the vampire world. But you won't drink from me."

"Correct." Cyan nodded. "And no one else will try to drink from you as long as they know you're mine." He gestured once again to the bedroom door. "You can stay here as long as you like. I'll never go in your room and your privacy will be respected." He flashed another smile, one that I was certain worked in his favor when he *sampled variety*, as he put it. "And hopefully my...daytime activities won't disturb you."

I snorted. "None of that bothers me." The walls of our mobile homes in Sapien were thin, and people often left windows open on hot nights. I was pretty sure there wasn't a sexual noise I hadn't heard before.

My nerves were relaxing by each passing minute. Cyan had only touched me to help me off the motorcycle and was respecting my personal space now by keeping to the far side of the couch. He had no desire to use me as a drinking fountain, which had been my main concern in the beginning. I hadn't completely let my guard down yet, but my instincts were no longer flashing in fight-or-flight mode.

Cyan laughed a little, the sound low and rumbling almost like a purr. "As you get comfortable here, maybe meet a vampire you'll actually want to attach yourself to, I'll release my claim so you can become their blood pet instead. Just let me know when that time comes."

That instantly soured my mood. "Do I *have* to be someone's blood pet?"

He gave me a sympathetic look. "You, yes. Because those are the terms of the Half-Century Selection. Humans in general have a lot of freedom here, but there is safety and security in being claimed by a vampire."

I could see how some people tolerated having their blood drunk in exchange for guaranteed basic necessities. But outside of dire circumstances, who would want a life like that?

"While you're under my claim," Cyan said, "I can arrange visits to your human settlement, if you'd like that."

Like a yo-yo, my mood soared with hope at the thought of seeing Amy again, but the cautious side of me activated as well. It felt like a dangling carrot and I did not want to be manipulated. "You will? You really mean that?"

He grinned. "I thought that might make you happy."

"Sure, it does." I tried to keep my tone casual, leaving hope out of it. "But you don't know me. What do you care about my happiness? I'm not giving you blood or...anything else. I'm just an extra mouth to feed here. Why *are* you being so accommodating to me?"

"Like I said, I'm not heartless." Cyan cocked his head, studying me. "To be perfectly honest, I think the Half-Century Selection is fucked up. You seem like a nice enough human, and brave as hell. I can't imagine any clan sacrificing one of our own like that, and yet you handled it with dignity." His head tilted in the opposite direction. "I don't know you, true. But I can sympathize with being thrown into a fucked up situation that's unfair to you and out of your control."

Cyan's jaw clenched and I wondered if that last part referred to some specific experience he'd had.

"I actually volunteered for the Selection," I admitted. Why I thought he should know that, I had no idea. Maybe it felt good to tell someone who didn't have any preconceived of me as Amy's guard dog.

Plus, he had called me brave and said I had dignity. I couldn't pretend those weren't nice things to hear.

"Really?" Cyan's eyebrows went up in surprise.

"My best friend was actually selected first," I hurried to explain. "I believe she was targeted for, well, fucked up reasons. I volunteered to go instead of her because..."

"Because you didn't want to send her into the pit of bloodthirsty monsters," Cyan filled in for me.

"I mean, I didn't know you would—"

"Relax," he said, smirking. "I'm not offended. We certainly *are* bloodthirsty monsters, depending on who you ask." He gave me an appraising look. "But you're even braver than I thought, Octavia."

Having his respect felt good. At this point, I was pretty sure it would keep me alive as well. And if I could visit Amy too? That was more than I could ever ask for.

"I go by Tavia usually. Or Tavi."

Cyan grinned, fangs on full display like a smiling cat. "Tavi. I like that. My name isn't short for anything, but the guys call me Cyanide sometimes."

"Why's that?"

He rubbed a palm over his head, looking almost bashful. "They say I'm a smooth talker. I smooth out a lot of our conflicts with the other clans. Some say I'm so good at getting the upper hand in negotiations, the other side doesn't realize what hit them until too late. Like sneaking a cyanide pill."

"And is that true?"

He winked at me. "You'll have to let me know."

Heat surged within my body, the sensation just as overwhelming as it was unfamiliar. Was he...flirting with me? And the bigger question, was it actually affecting me?

"So, uh, what you said before." I looked everywhere but at him, smoothing my palms, which felt sweatier than a moment ago, over my knees. "Did you mean it, about being able to visit Sapien?"

"I did." Cyan dropped the charm and became serious. "It's clear this friend means a lot to you. She was the crying one you said goodbye to?"

A lump formed in my throat. Fuck, I missed her already. "Yeah, that was her. Amy."

"Good friends are priceless," he said softly with a sympathetic nod. "I don't want to be the person who tears two friends apart."

His voice thickened on the last part of that sentence and I wondered again if something happened that caused him to feel that way.

"If you're serious, I appreciate that more than I can express." I laced my fingers and then released them. "I just don't know if I can trust you."

Cyan leaned away from the couch's backrest, sitting up straight. "Here. Let me show you how serious I am." Before I could react, he whipped off his T-shirt.

And drew out a long dagger from his boot.

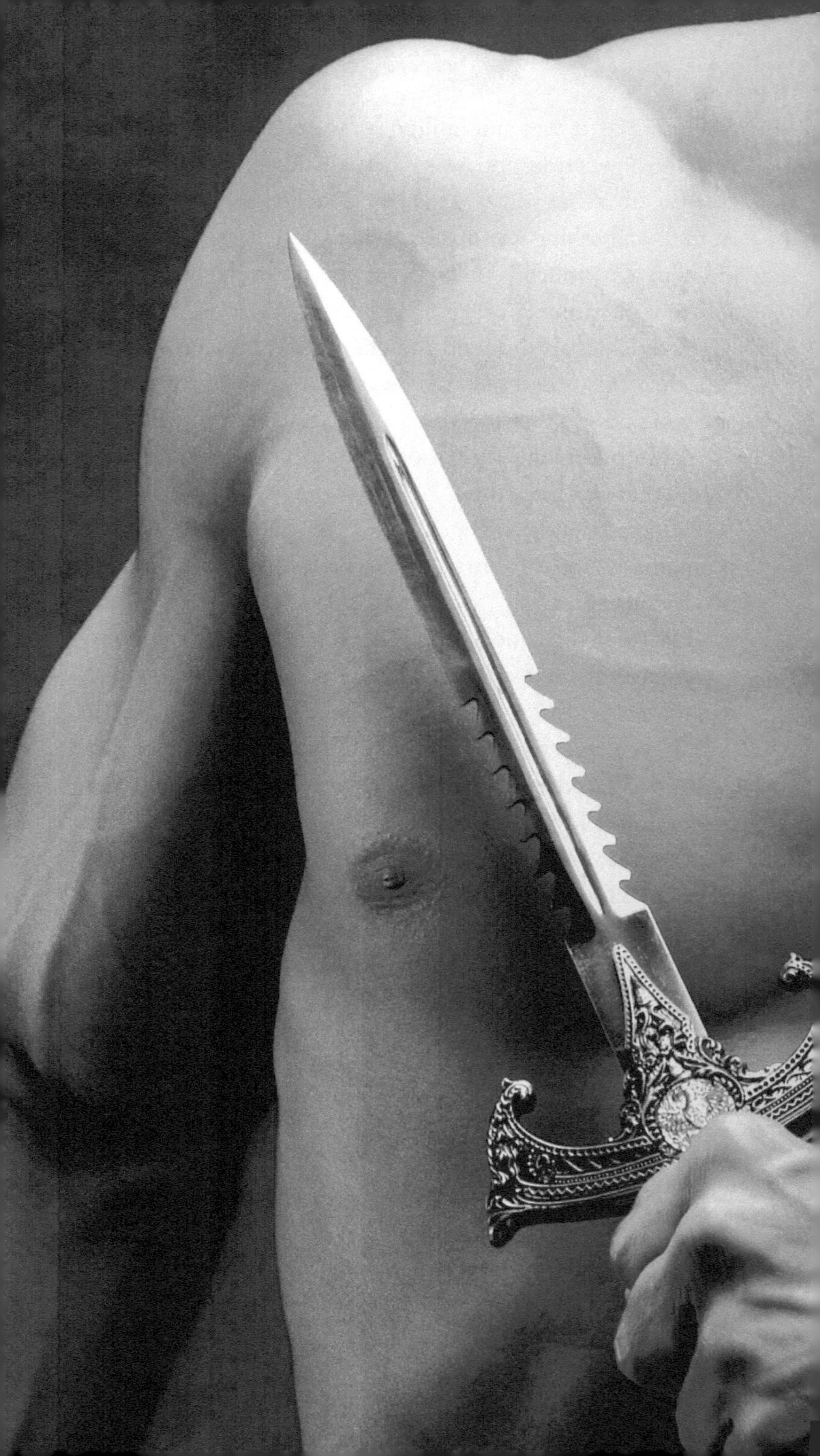

Chapter 4

Cyan

Tavi's eyes widened at the long, silver dagger I drew out of my boot sheath. She backed up until she hit the arm of the couch. I didn't even notice she had begun inching closer to me until she backed away.

Her once calm heartbeat ratcheted up to a rapid thrumming that made my mouth water. I swallowed the groan of hunger that yearned to escape my throat, stabbing my fangs down into my lower lip. It was annoying really, how much the movement of her blood affected me. I had never craved someone's blood this much without tasting it first. It was fucking distracting, especially when I was trying to make her believe that I would never feed from her.

"Relax," I said, twirling the dagger's handle between my fingers, careful to not touch the blade. "This is for me, not you."

Her eyes didn't move from my weapon. "I don't understand."

"Look." I ran my hand over the raised characters carved into the right side of my chest. "Silver is the only thing that can scar us, you see. When we make a vow, oath, any kind of promise, we write it into our skin with a silver blade. This makes it permanent and unbreakable. If a vampire isn't willing to bear his word in silver, he's not someone you can trust."

Tavi's shoulders and breathing relaxed slightly. Her heartbeat slowed from a frantic rhythm to a sensual one, still elevated but without the spark of fear kicking it into overdrive.

"So what does that mean?" She lifted her chin to indicate the scars I already had.

"This is the oath I made to my clan, Blood 'til Dawn, when I came of age. They're my family, and when I reached adulthood, I vowed that my life and loyalty would always remain in service to them."

"And that?" Tavi's eyes drifted lower, her cheeks flushing red. Her dark gray eyes dilated and she was enjoying looking at me.

I wanted to tease her, to flirt and make a joke about how closely she was inspecting my body. But the lower markings on my ribs brought no sense of joy or pride. The vow attached to them was simple—to remember who I had lost.

"That's a vow I will never speak of, out of respect to the person I made it to." I kept my voice light, grinning as I said it despite memories creating a knot of dread in my stomach.

"Oh." Tavi pulled back again, a frown of embarrassment crossing her face. "I'm sorry."

"Don't be. You didn't know."

She rubbed her face, giving a sheepish little laugh. "When humans want an oath made in writing, we usually just use pen and paper."

"My kind tends to live longer than those materials," I said. "Which is why we use our bodies. We also find significance in carrying our vows everywhere we go, and being able to see them in a mirror. A vow is not something to be shut away in a drawer and forgotten about."

Tavi leaned forward slightly, her fingers lacing together. She was inspecting me again and I liked her gaze roaming over my skin. I liked any attractive female appreciating how I looked, but this wasn't just lust in her eyes. Her eyes lowered to the markings on my ribcage again. She seemed curious. Had she ever seen a vampire up close before?

"So this is what you're preparing to do for me, someone you hardly know?" Her brows knitted together. "Cut yourself with silver to prove you won't feed on me and will allow me to see my friend?"

"Yes." It truly was that simple. "We barely know each other at this moment, but whether you're my blood pet or someone else's, you're part of Blood 'til Dawn now. I want you to know I'm someone who keeps my word. Someone you can depend on if shit goes sideways." I flipped the dagger with a smile. "As a friend, of course. Nothing more."

Tavi let out a breath that sounded like she'd been holding it a while, and a small smile played on her lips as well. "I think I can handle being friends."

"Good, me too." I flipped the dagger once more, the blade's sharp tip pointing directly at my sternum. "Shall I begin?"

She stiffened. "You don't have to, Cyan. I appreciate your willingness, but I believe you'll keep your vow."

"I *do* have to. I said I would." My grin widened, probably looking a little unhinged with a sharp edge pointed at myself. "I'm not going back on my word now."

For some reason I couldn't explain, it felt important to do this. The ritual needed to be carried out, and not just to follow through on what I said. Carving our vows with silver was a sign of integrity and honor, partially because it was a painful, uncomfortable process.

No amount of pain would make me honorable, not even if I was covered in head to toe in vows to keep. Maybe it was punishment I craved, the burn and hiss of the silver cutting apart my flesh like no other weapon could. Some days I wondered why I didn't drive the silver dagger straight through my heart.

And then I remembered that I simply didn't deserve such an easy exit. If Kalix had to suffer, so did I.

But he was gone, and right then I had to think of how to write out my promise to Tavia. Not dwell in the past.

The vampire written language was made up of characters and pictographs based on phonetic sounds as well as concepts. There was no direct translation of her name, so I'd have to combine characters to make a single depiction that symbolized her. It came to me quickly with a rightness that could only be attributed to inspiration.

"Do you want to see your name in our language?" I smirked and pressed the silver point to my skin before she could react.

The pain of the first cut had me hissing in a breath. It had been fifteen years since I made my vow to the clan, and I'd forgotten how much it burned. The surrounding skin turned bright red, but no blood fell. Silver cauterized surface wounds like these, and I would heal in minutes, but it always left scars behind.

And it hurt like a bitch, but no more complaints would slip past my lips. I continued drawing the character for *Octavia*, a combination of the symbols for *brave* and *human female* into the left side of my chest.

When I finished her name, I held the knife aside so she

could see. Tavi looked pale and not as impressed as I'd hoped.

"My name?" She swallowed and met my gaze. "You have *my name* as a permanent mark on your body forever?"

"Well, yes. You are the subject of my vow," I explained. "It wouldn't hold much weight if I didn't name who I was making the vow to."

She blinked. "Right. It just seems...significant."

"It is."

"I know, but not in the sense that you're making a vow, but..." She brought a hand to her mouth, gaze drifting to the side like she was thinking. "Do vampires get married?"

The sudden change in subject threw me for a loop and I narrowed my eyes. "It's not exactly the same as a human marriage, but many of us do have long-term romantic partners, yes."

"And do you make vows to each other? When you find that person and decide to become partners for life?"

I laughed. "No, it doesn't really happen like that."

"No?" Tavi cocked her head.

"Long-term is not the same as a lifetime for us. We live for eight hundred, a thousand years at best. Nobody expects to stay together for that long because any multitude of things can happen in that time."

"Oh." Tavi looked thoughtful, and from what I could tell, a bit disappointed. "I guess that makes sense."

"When vampires get together as a couple, they just...do that, get together. There isn't really any pomp and ceremony over it. They'll stay together for fifty, a hundred, maybe two-hundred years. If they can conceive, maybe they'll raise a child or two to adulthood. And then eventually they get bored, drift apart, and see other people."

My chest had finally stopped burning and I looked

down to see her name rising from my skin in delicate, new scar tissue. The cuts had already closed up and it looked damn good, if I did say so myself.

"The only exception to that is blood mates, which *is* a lifelong thing and subject to pomp and ceremony." I scoffed. "It's incredibly rare, and thank Temkra for that. Being shackled to one person for the rest of your life sounds like a fucking prison to me." I rubbed gingerly over the fresh scar tissue, which itched slightly. "Sorry, how did we get on this topic?"

"Oh, no reason. I was just curious." Tavi let out a long breath and raked a hand back through the long waves of her hair. "You may, uh, continue with the vow, I guess. Unless all you need is my name?"

"Oh, no. The whole thing needs to be spelled out." Bracing myself with a breath, I pointed the blade to my skin again. "Here we go."

I started above her name to ensure I gave myself enough room. With each symbol I carved into my flesh, I spoke my vow out loud.

"I will protect and honor Octavia, but shall never take her blood." The last half of that statement was especially too painful to carve out, like my body was protesting the notion of never tasting her.

My words were tight, voiced through a clenched jaw as I refused to make any sounds of pain. My skin was on fire, redness covering my entire left side, and yet I had to push through.

"As long as she is my blood pet, I will ensure she maintains contact with her kin in whatever manner she wishes." Finally, I held the knife away from my chest, breathing hard. "May Temkra hear my vow and hold me to its bond for as long as blood sustains me."

With a weary smile, I returned the dagger to its sheath inside my boot. "There you have it."

"That looks...really painful." Tavi leaned forward, the closest she had gotten to me yet. A sudden mental image of her touching her name on my chest sent my blood surging.

"What?" I asked, realizing she'd said something.

"Can I get you ice or a cool towel maybe?"

She wanted to ease the pain of my vow? It was such a strange thing to offer, but she didn't understand it was important to bear the pain. Vows in silver were so ingrained in vampire culture, no one else I knew would ever offer pain relief.

And yet, I was touched that she asked.

"No, thank you. I'll be all healed up in a few minutes."

She leaned even closer, and another image invaded my brain. This time it was of her mouth on my scars instead of her hands.

Fuck, I couldn't think like that. Sexual attraction and blood feeding were so closely intertwined, and I just swore that I wouldn't do the latter. Better to not have any suggestive thoughts, no matter how attractive she was for a human.

"Wow." She squinted a few inches away from my chest and it was pretty fucking adorable. "Your skin is closing up right in front of my eyes."

"We heal fast. Even from silver if it's just surface wounds." I grabbed my T-shirt that I'd thrown over the back of the couch but was in no hurry to put it on. Not while she was looking at me like that.

"Satisfied?" I asked, unable to suppress my smirk as she watched my skin heal. *Wait until she finds out our saliva closes wounds too.* The thought almost tumbled out of my mouth then, but I remembered I wasn't supposed to be flirting.

Tavi leaned away and straightened, her curiosity giving way to a neutral mask. "When can I see Amy?"

You just got here, I wanted to say. *I just made a silver vow to you.* I had to remind myself that she wasn't here by choice. She didn't understand the significance of the vow, so I had no right to be annoyed. But for some reason, I was.

"I don't know yet. I'll have to clear it with Thorne to take you on one of my nights off."

"Who's Thorne?"

"Clan leader. The one with the cigarettes and neck tattoos." I pulled my shirt on, feeling the need to clear my head and get outside. "I'll get you a phone to call your friend in the meantime."

"My own phone?" Tavi blinked up at me. "Like what you have?" She pointed at the device I had taken from my jacket pocket to put on a side table.

"Yeah. You've never had one?"

She shook her head. "No one in Sapien has personal phones. There's a closed landline system for all of the buildings to communicate, but the council says personal phones are a distraction from work."

What kind of backwards-ass world did these humans live in?

"I'll get you two phones, then. One for you and one for her." I stood from the couch, straightening my shirt. "You're not nocturnal yet and probably exhausted, so feel free to rest, relax and make yourself at home. I'll send someone over later who can get you situated with all your human needs."

"Oh." She seemed taken aback, like the fact that she was living among vampires for the rest of her life had just hit her. "Okay. Thank you, Cyan."

I gave her a quick nod, retrieved my jacket and was out

the door in seconds. Now that the scent and rhythm of her blood wasn't all in my senses, I took a moment to pause in the corridor.

A deep sigh left my chest as I rested the back of my head on my door. For the time being, Tavi was my responsibility and I had to keep my shit together.

But responsibility was not my strong suite. The care and protection of a naive human was the last thing that should have been placed in my hands. The best I could hope for was someone else in the clan wanting to claim Tavi as a blood pet before I could fuck this up too badly. The fact that her blood called to me like siren's song was just the fucked up cherry on top. But surely that temptation would fall alway when someone else fed from her.

Right?

I pushed off the door and headed for the stairs, not looking back at the portrait of me and Kalix on the wall. I could feel his heavy gaze on me as if he were actually here, judging my new lot in life.

But because of me, he wasn't.

Chapter 5

Tavia

I slept deeper and longer than I expected. Cyan's spare bedroom was pitch-black without any lights on, and the bed more comfortable than anything I'd slept on in my life. When I woke up, I fumbled around for five minutes looking for a light switch.

After a shower, I took in my new surroundings with fresh eyes and less panic. There were no windows in the suite, probably none at all on this underground level. A clock on the wall noted the time as four-thirty, but I had no idea if that was morning or afternoon.

I puttered around Cyan's empty place for only a few minutes before a soft—way too soft to be any of the male vampires—knock came to the door. A spark of fear jolted me at the sound. Should I open it? I had just been considering snooping through Cyan's bedroom when the knock came, like I was being watched and had been caught.

Were blood pets even allowed to open the door? Could I leave the suite and just explore? With zero notion of what I was supposed to do, I just froze.

"Hello!" A feminine voice called through the wood,

followed by more soft rapping. "Cyan's blood pet, are you awake? I'd just like to introduce myself, one human to another."

Human?

My body shot into action, rushing to the door like it would self-destruct if I didn't get there in time. When I flung it open and met the gaze of the woman standing across the threshold, a small part of me wanted to slam the door shut again.

She was not human.

What were supposed to be the whites of her eyes were completely black. Her smile showed fangs and her olive skin had that perfectly smooth, unblemished look of a vampire. Her irises though, were not red as all vampires seemed to be. They were an aquamarine, shining bright like gems against her black sclera.

"Ah," she said, taking in my reaction. "First time you've seen a brusang, huh?"

"A what?"

"Is it okay if I come in?" She held up a plastic bag with styrofoam containers inside. "Figured you'd be hungry, so I brought breakfast."

The scents from the bag hit me then like a slap to the face. Cheese, meat, grease, salt. My stomach didn't so much as rumble as it roared. I hadn't eaten since the morning of the Selection, and that was at least a full day ago.

"Um, sure." I stepped aside, not caring if this person was permitted inside Cyan's place or not as long as I got fed.

She breezed in gracefully, her long black hair barely fluttering from her movement. Even with the jarring black eyes, she was pretty. After setting the bag on the small, high-top table, she turned to me.

"I got you two breakfast burritos. Wasn't sure how you

felt about avocado, so I had them leave it off. Dig in and I'll explain everything." She made herself comfortable on one of the barstools, pulled out a small paper bag of tortilla chips and a container of what had to be salsa.

"Mexican food in a vampire world, huh?" I went to the barstool across from her at the small table, reaching for the bigger container.

The woman laughed before crunching down on a chip. "I know, right? The market is supposedly near one of the borders to the human world, specifically somewhere in LA. So, the humans who stumbled their way into that area love their Mexican food. The deli specializes in it because of that."

I paused in my unwrapping of the burrito. "There's an entrance to the human world all the way out here?" The only one I knew of was a half-day's hike from Sapien. A barely-marked, winding trail through a woodland area dumped out into a small town called Jacksonville, Oregon.

No one was completely sure how our worlds connected, or if they overlapped in some way. But we'd always known growing up that there was a world full of humans with no vampires, angels or any shifters at all. Crossing between the human world and ours was tricky, and only done when absolutely necessary.

I'd been to Jacksonville a few times to help buy essential supplies for Sapien, but Oregon always felt different in a way I couldn't explain. Robin said it was because there was no magic in the air, which was probably true. It would explain why no one over there believed in vampires.

"Oh yeah!" The woman's eerie eyes flashed excitedly. "Like all of 'em, it's hard to find. I heard you gotta walk down this maze of alleyways, give a drop of blood to a bat statue, say a prayer to Temkra, and if you're lucky, she'll show you the way. All the market suppliers know, but they're keeping it under wraps."

"So wait, there's a market?" I chewed and swallowed the most heavenly mix of tortilla, potato, egg, cheese, and sausage I'd ever eaten.

"Mm-hm. It's the only place in Sanguine that sells human-specific grocery items. It's not big like a Wal-Mart or anything but they make so much of their own stuff." She pointed at the salsa as she chewed. "Mmm, I watched Alejandro blend this up himself before he sold it to me. Can't get any better or fresher."

I got up to retrieve two water bottles from the fridge. "So you uh," I tried to phrase the question in a way that wasn't offensive, "eat food?"

The woman licked her lips and laughed. "Sorry, how rude of me. I'm Bea, by the way. And yes, brusang do need to eat, although not as much as you unturned humans. I need to eat human food about every other day. For the rest, I feed on blood."

"Unturned humans?" I had so many questions, but the burrito was so damn delicious and I couldn't stop taking bite after bite. It was hard to talk without my mouth full.

Bea nodded. "Brusang are humans who have been turned by vampires. So we're a bit of both, but don't fully fit into one species or the other."

Since putting food in my stomach, my brain seemed to get better at connecting dots. "Wow, so that has to be where the human-world myth comes from. The one about how vampires are made."

"Correct. I suspect brusang have tried to integrate back into the human-ruled world in the past, but were ostracized as monsters." She shrugged and popped another salsa-dipped chip into her mouth. "I've never been to the human-only side, but that's my theory."

My throat tightened and I took a big gulp of water. "So, is Cyan going to want to turn me?"

Bea stared at me for a moment before her eyes went wide with horror. "Oh Temkra, no! He would never. The turning process is extremely risky and it fails something like fifty percent of the time." She tucked a piece of hair behind her ear, her gaze lowering to the table. "It's a um, last resort kind of thing. Most vampires won't turn a human unless they're already dying. You could say it's a last-ditch effort to save a human's life."

With how serious her mood turned after being so full of laughter moments ago, I could only surmise that was exactly what happened to her.

"Oh, I see." Awkwardness settled in. "I'm sorry."

The corner of her mouth quirked up and she gave a flippant wave of her hand. "It's fine! I got turned over twenty years ago. Sometimes I forget I was human at all. Then I get a craving for peanut butter or something and it's like, oh yeah!"

My stomach now felt like it was near bursting, and I leaned away from the table. "Thanks for the food, and explaining things to me. I'm Tavia, by the way."

"My pleasure, Tavia. You feel like walking off that burrito baby? I figured we could go to the market and you can start getting the lay of the land. You're welcome to my food of course, but you should probably stock up on groceries for yourself."

"That sounds good, thanks." Bea was bubbly and friendly in a way that made me feel at ease. It was hard for me to feel unguarded around anyone besides Amy and

Robin, but I could see her being added to that list. "So, do you live here? In this, uh…"

"Mm-hm, I live in the Blood 'til Dawn compound." She crunched on another chip with a nod. "I'm just across the corridor from you, actually."

"Are you uh, somebody's blood pet? I'm sorry if that's rude to ask, I truly have no idea how things work here."

"Ah, you're good, girl. And nope, I'm unclaimed." Her smile twitched in a way that I didn't know how to interpret. "Want to digest that deliciousness in your belly first, or you ready to head out?"

I looked down at the single piece of clothing I'd brought with me, the stupid white virgin sacrifice dress Nancy had stuffed me in. At least I didn't have to die in that hideous thing after all. I wasn't even a virgin, not that Nancy knew that.

"I would like to explore, but I don't have any money for groceries," I admitted. "Or a change of clothes."

"Oh no, babe! Don't worry about money." Bea waved both palms at me with a shake of her head. "All our necessities will get billed to Blood 'til Dawn. As for clothes, I probably have some things you can borrow for now. But we can go clothes shopping too, if you're up for it. We're near some great boutiques."

"The clan will cover everything?" I stared at her skeptically. "Are you sure?" Cyan certainly could have mentioned that as a perk, but maybe he took it for granted.

"Oh, they're flush, believe me. And they take care of their people, which is what you are now."

I never thought I'd see the day I'd be part of a vampire… faction? Extended family? I still wasn't sure what a clan was.

But, first things first. Groceries and new clothes.

"Alright, then." I slid out of the barstool, my gaze landing on the clock that now read 5:02. "Is it early morning or afternoon?"

"Morning," Bea said. "We brusang can function fine in daylight as long as the sun isn't at its strongest. So I can hang with you until about ten am, then I'm useless until about six pm."

"Okay, good to know." I drummed my fingers on the back of the barstool. If it was morning, was Cyan already asleep in bed? Or would he be getting in soon? What was the typical bedtime for vampires? I had so many questions.

"Guess I'll get cleaned up." Earlier, I had seen a brand new hairbrush and toothbrushes in Cyan's spare room, which I probably should start calling *my* room.

"You do that." Bea gathered up the food containers as she headed for the door. "I'll come back with some clothes for you to try on, and then we'll go out. 'Kay?"

"Sure, sounds good."

After brushing my teeth and detangling the mess on my head, I stepped out of the bathroom to find neat stacks of clothes folded on a chair just outside the door. The folded pants and shirts smelled of fabric softener when I held them to my chest. A wave of emotion came over me to the point where I was almost blinking away tears. Bea was being so *nice*, and I wasn't used to anyone helping me out this much.

I composed myself quickly, tried on a few different things, and settled on a jeans and T-shirt combo that fit me best. With a final check in the mirror, I figured I was decent enough. Bea was lounging on the couch and glanced up from her phone when I walked out of the bathroom.

"You look much better," she said with an approving nod and smile. "Rested, refreshed. A woman of the twenty-first century instead of a Victorian ghost child."

The laugh that burst out surprised me. "Thanks. I guess it was time for an update."

With a grin full of fangs, she stood. "Ready?"

"Uh, yeah. Only I don't have a key or anything. Do I need to lock up behind us?"

Bea jerked her chin at the side table against one wall. "Already taken care of."

I went to look at what she was talking about, and found a note under a simple, ordinary-looking key. In blocky, masculine handwriting, the note said,

> TAVI,
>
> THIS IS FOR YOU. YOU ARE NOT A PRISONER, SO COME AND GO AS YOU PLEASE. THE KEY IS MADE OF SILVER SO ONLY YOU CAN TOUCH IT DIRECTLY. I'LL SEE YOU AROUND. —C

I picked up the key, continuing to stare at the note while feeling oddly sentimental about it. He had this made for me and me alone, apparently while I'd been asleep. That, along with literally carving a vow into his flesh for me, seemed oddly...sweet?

"You can't touch silver either?" I looked at Bea as I slipped the key into my pocket.

"It doesn't burn me as badly as pure vampires, but it's uncomfortable to touch, yeah. Imagine sticking your hand in a colony of fire ants and they're stinging you all over."

"Ouch."

"Tell me about it," she snorted. "I found out the hard way. I used to love my silver jewelry." She traced one of the hoops in her ears with a sigh. "Now it's stainless steel forever for this bitch."

"Is that common around here?"

"Oh yeah!" she chirped. "Stainless steel jewelry and accessories are huge. Actually, I think it was a human metalsmith who started the trend, then the vamps caught on."

We left the suite and while locking the front door, I noticed Bea staring at the portrait of Cyan and the other vampire on the wall. She seemed to have gone somewhere else in her mind, her intense, strange eyes full of emotion as she touched the glass with one finger.

A sudden thought hit me like a kick to the chest. Did she have a thing for Cyan? Was that why she was being so nice? She could be trying to make me lower my guard and then manipulate me with whatever ulterior motives she had. It was the same treatment I'd expect from anyone in Sapien.

The only question was, why would I care if she wanted Cyan? I didn't. I definitely didn't. The sight of him with his shirt off and carving my name into his skin did absolutely nothing for me. Not at all.

But when I moved away from the door, a sigh of relief escaped me when Bea rested her finger over the face of the longer-haired vampire, not Cyan.

"Who's that?"

Bea pulled her hand back, blinking like she was returning to the present, then turned to me with a sad smile. "That's Kalix. Shall we go?"

"Oh." The abruptness didn't seem like her. Her expression was neutral as we started down the hallway, but her eyes still carried that sadness. "He's another Blood 'til Dawn member, I assume? I haven't met him yet."

"You won't meet him," Bea said quietly as we went up the stairs. "He's gone."

"Oh. Shit, I'm sorry."

We entered the main, high-ceilinged room with all the couches, stripper pole, and luxurious kitchen off to the side. No vampires were in sight, probably because daylight was approaching.

Bea gave a sad smile as we crossed the room, heading for the exit. "So am I."

Chapter 6

Cyan

When I woke up in the early evening there were subtle, but noticeable, changes to my apartment. The first was the scent in the bathroom. Along with the hint of moisture from a shower taken hours earlier, there was something feminine and lightly sweet in the air.

Tavi's scent, I realized. Her natural scent, untainted by fear and stress. It was rich and tart. Something between an apple and a cherry. I wondered if her blood would taste the same.

"Nope." I spoke out loud to myself, heading into the living room. "No, actually. I don't wonder that at all."

My note to Tavi and the silver key were gone from the side table, so she and Bea must have gone out. That was good, I had a feeling those two would get along. Bea had been turned for twenty years at this point, but she still knew human needs and customs better than any of us born vampires. And as the only brusang in the clan, I got the sense that she still felt like a bit of an outsider. I hoped she and Tavi could connect and help my new platonic blood pet settle in.

I rummaged through cabinets in my small kitchen, looking for rolling papers and a canister of darakt to make some cigarettes. Instead, I found boxes of dried human goods. Curiosity got the better of me, and I picked one up to inspect.

"Goldfish crackers, huh?" I mused at the foil-lined bag. Did humans enjoy eating goldfish that much?

After a few minutes of poking at the new items in my kitchen, I jumped in the shower and found myself enjoying Tavi's scent a little too much. The thick, humid air enhanced her flavor, making it an almost tangible taste on my tongue. And the air wasn't the only thing thickening in that room. The fresh scars on my chest still itched a little, and I absently ran my fingers over her name in my skin.

I needed to get a fucking grip, and not on my cock, which I pointedly ignored as I scrubbed myself clean. Tavi lived here now. It was just a matter of time before her scent covered the whole apartment.

Eventually I would get used to it. Become nose-blind and stop noticing it. The same with her blood. Every living creature had blood. That didn't mean I was distracted by thousands of heartbeats every single time I walked outside.

Tavi was just new. And new things often piqued my curiosity. That was all this was.

As I dried off and got dressed, my thoughts turned to how she was faring. She had been in shock, guarded and a little defensive last night, but seemed to be taking things in stride. That had been nearly a full day ago, and reality must have sunken in by now.

Tasting and fucking her were off the table, but she was still my responsibility.

Once decent, I left the apartment and headed up to the great room. The moment I hit the landing and opened the door, Tavi's scent immediately hit my nose. It was fresh and bold this time, not the faint lingering hours after a shower.

I clenched my teeth, stopping all thoughts of piercing through a vein, despite the gnawing ache in my fangs. I had just been to the blood bank, for fuck's sake. I wasn't hungry, despite the overwhelming urge to find out what Tavi tasted like.

It's curiosity, nothing more, I told myself. One that if I indulged in would surely lead to disappointment. She was just a human, after all. Chances were she'd taste like the thousands of others I'd had. If only my damn fangs would get the memo.

"How long you plan to keep standing in the way, Cy?" Someone shoved at my back, making me stumble forward into the room. Rhain came out from behind me, muttering like a curmudgeonly old man.

"Aw, woke up on the wrong side of the coffin again, Rhain?" I teased, taking my sweet time making room for him to pass through.

"Fuck off." The grumpy bastard hated all jokes, but the vampire stereotypes were his least favorites.

"I'll take that as a yes."

A few other clan members, the early risers, were milling about. In a few hours, some of them would ride out on patrols to make sure all was well in our little kingdom of Sanguine. Since becoming the ruling clan, we had more territory to cover than ever before. Our compound here was in a central location, the Heart of Sanguine, and our tenure had been an overall peaceful one. Even so, there were clans on the fringes, such as in the Crown and the Ribs, that were less agreeable with our position. Even with outposts and allied smaller clans, we had to ride out far and wide to constantly put out fires.

Fortunately for me, it was a night off.

Tavi and Bea sat at the large island counter on the kitchen side of the great room with a few bottles lined up between them, like they were doing a tasting of some kind. Laith sat on the stool next to Tavi, leaning in close to her in a way that made me want to bare my fangs at him.

"Hey." I came up to the adjacent side of the island. "What kind of party we got over here?"

"For what it's worth, I told her not to." Laith smirked and I suppressed a growl.

"We're tasting blood chillers," Bea supplied. "Someone got curious."

"These are awful." Tavi made a face as she set a bottle down. "These are really supposed to mimic what blood tastes like to vampires? It's like someone dumped a bunch of sugar into cough syrup."

"I told you it was a total gimmick." Bea laughed and pushed forward another bottle. "You sure you don't want to try—" she paused to read the label "—Tastes Just Like Real Angel?"

"No way." I picked up another one of the bottles to examine. "Who would make this?"

"Someone with the brilliant idea of trying to market vampire things to humans." Bea shot a teasing look at Tavi. "Targeting those suckers who go, 'Ooh, what's this?'"

"I was just curious," Tavi moaned, lowering her face to her palm.

Something we have in common, I thought, watching the delicate pulse flutter in her neck.

I took a tentative sip from the bottle and nearly spat it

back out the moment it hit my tongue, much to Laith's cackling amusement. "Oh fucking Temkra, that is awful."

The label said it was supposed to resemble werewolf blood. That could have been accurate, if it had sat out in the sun for a few weeks and then was mixed with mud and moldy fruit.

"See? It's criminal." Bea laughed. "No one should be allowed to bottle and sell that."

"In the human world, they have all this government red tape you have to go through before a product hits a store shelf," Tavi explained. "There's the FDA, USDA, and probably more. Everything is tested to make sure it's safe to be consumed and doesn't contain any harmful ingredients."

"Maybe we should have something like that here." Laith's eyes slid to mine. "If there's a high risk of humans getting sick from whatever they buy at the market."

"Most of the market's stock is smuggled in from the human world anyway," I reminded him. "So they already go through those regulations Tavi mentioned. Only a very small amount of things sold are actually made here."

"It was a very interesting trip," Tavi said. "I never expected to see preserved dragon scales sitting next to the peanut butter."

"Don't get us started on dragon products." Laith and I exchanged a glance and a groan.

The dragon shifters were technically our allies, so they had free rein to move in and out of Sanguine from their neighboring territory, the Shadowburn Cliffs. Some of them even lived in Sanguine full time.

Our alliance began nearly a thousand years ago, when it was discovered that vampires who ingested a small amount of draitrium, a mineral found only in the Shadowburn Cliffs, allowed them to walk in daylight unharmed. After that discovery, dragons couldn't mine draitrium fast enough, and business flourished between our two species.

Unfortunately, draitrium turned out to be incredibly addictive and came with terrible side effects. To this day, we were battling an epidemic in Sanguine and our clan especially wanted it gone from the streets. We were Blood 'til Dawn, after all. Not Blood 'til Noon.

Eliminating the draitrium trade would not happen easily though. Our people's relationship with the dragon shifters had become deeply intertwined after all this time. Cutting vampires off from the drug would not only make enemies out of the dragons, but could turn our own people against us.

In other words, it was way more than I wanted to explain to Tavi in that moment.

"What else did you think of the market?" I asked her. "Does it have everything you need?"

She gave me a nod and a small smile. "It should work, I think. It's definitely more convenient than Sapien. We had to make or grow almost everything ourselves. Sometimes we went into the human world for essentials but that was rare, maybe once a year."

A sad look crossed her face. Even though my scars were healed, I felt a burning sensation in the vow I carved into my chest. She missed her friend, that much was obvious. Soon, I'd have to fulfill my promise to take her back for a visit. I would never go back on a vow I made, but the idea of it made me uneasy.

What if she refused to come back to the clan compound with me? It was alarming how much that thought distressed me. I barely knew this woman and yet I already enjoyed her presence in my space. At the same time, I liked and respected her too much to rip her away from her friend, especially a second time.

"If I had to complain about something other than these..." Tavi waved her hand over the blood chillers and hesitated.

"Tell me," I urged, leaning forward over the counter. "If the market is missing anything, we can source it for you."

In my peripheral vision, Laith's eyebrow lifted in surprise. Was I too eager to make my new blood pet, who I wasn't feeding on or fucking, happy and comfortable in her new home? Maybe, but I didn't care. Nor could I explain where such a desire came from.

Tavi brought her hands to her face, an adorable flush creeping up her neck and into her cheeks. "It's nothing, really. It's dumb, actually. You're going to think I'm a snob."

"Tell. Me." I growled the two words, flashing fangs as I leaned into her personal space. "Or I'll bite you."

It was a joke. Honestly. I was smiling as I said it. But part of me wanted to see how she'd react, wanted to see if she'd take me up on it rather than voicing whatever complaint she had about the market.

Tavi's lips parted and her pupils blew wide. Her pulse accelerated to match the beat throbbing through my fangs. In that moment, I forgot that we weren't alone. My whole world shrank to her plump mouth, her pretty face flushed with strong, healthy blood beneath the surface. She went still, so still for me like a good blood pet. She would not move while I decided which blood vessel to drink from.

Just as my hand lifted to push her hair away from her neck, she broke eye contact with a laugh. "Okay, fine! I'll tell you."

I leaned away, hiding my aching hunger for her under a smirk. "I'm waiting."

"So, the market has a terrible alcohol selection. Especially wine." Tavi picked at a label on one of the bottles. "All the wines barely took up one shelf and they were all terrible brands that looked decades old. It just made me a little sad, that's all."

"You like good wine? That shouldn't be hard to get." I looked at Laith to confirm and he nodded. He had human-world connections most of us didn't.

"I do, but it's not really about drinking the good stuff." She hesitated again. "Back in Sapien, I used to make it. That was kind of my thing. My art form, you could say."

"Shut up!" Bea exclaimed. "You know how to make wine?"

Tavi nodded shyly. "Wines, meads, ciders, and beer too. Seeing that crappy selection makes me miss my hobby, you know? It was something I enjoyed and kept me busy."

She had barely finished talking, and startled when I slammed a notepad and pen in front of her.

"Make a list of all the supplies you'll need. I'll make sure you get everything."

Everyone's gaze fell on me, but hers was the only one I focused on.

"Cyan." She breathed my name out so sweetly. "You don't have to do that."

"I know." My index finger tapped down on the paper. "Start writing."

"Why?"

"Because I can't read your mind and find out what goes into winemaking if you don't write it down."

"No, I mean," she laughed, picking up the pen. "Why do you want to get me winemaking supplies?"

I shrugged. "Everyone needs hobbies."

She needed something to do, something to stay busy in

the day-to-day so she wouldn't get bored or depressed. Better to make it something she already enjoyed than throwing random hobbies at her. That was what I told myself anyway, as I watched her write her list.

Dark eyelashes swept over the tops of her cheeks, and her blunt teeth sank into her lower lip as she focused. A lock of hair fell forward, covering more of her neck, and my hands itched to push it back, to let my fingertips trail over her pulse.

I jerked my gaze away with a clench of my fists. Laith's red eyes met mine with a knowing smirk, and I shook my head at the implication.

Not fucking her. Not feeding from her. We're just going to be friends. That's it.

Once Tavi received her supplies, *my* new hobby would be keeping the hell away. With any luck, she'd be busy enough that we would barely run into each other. The newness of her would wear off and my curiosity would eventually disappear. It would be so much easier if only she would stop being so attractive. Interesting. Intoxicating.

But no matter how much of a temptation she was, I would never claim her. Whether romantic or platonic, there was an intimacy between blood pet and verakt, an expectation of openness and trust.

And I had no intention of letting Tavi find out what kind of person I really was.

Chapter 7

Tavia

"You sure that's it?" Cyan loomed over me, eying my list as I wrote down the supplies I'd need to ferment some good quality alcohol.

"These are the basic essentials." I capped the pen and slid the notepad across the counter to him. "Anything more would be fun to have, but is not necessary."

"Like what?" Cyan barely glanced at the list before he flipped it around and slid it back to me. "You've got room at the bottom, add some fun stuff."

"No, really. This is good." I started to push the pad in his direction, but he stopped it in the middle of the counter with a slap of his palm.

"I want you to have everything you need, not the bare minimum." He lowered his chin, but a smile tugged at his lips and his eyes were bright with mischief. "Don't worry about cost or convenience, Tavi. I'm extremely resourceful."

"You're also pushy."

The jab made his smile grow wider, like he was pleased. "For my blood pet to be content while she practices her art, absolutely."

My whole body heated with that declaration, although I couldn't explain why. We'd agreed for him to publicly claim me as a blood pet. He was just playing his role so that no other vampires would try to sink their fangs in me. Even so, there was a warm playfulness to Cyan. He looked at and smiled at only me. I could almost believe he was actually flirting with me, that I was the only woman he was interested in.

In the brief moment where I forgot that he was just pretending, the attention had actually felt nice.

"I don't want to take advantage of your generosity," I argued.

"I want you to," he retorted, fangs poking through his smile. "You can take advantage of me all you want."

My face grew even hotter. Jesus, was he trying to get me flustered? Even though he didn't actually want to seduce me, he was good at it.

"Get a room," groaned Desmond.

"Get a blood pet," cracked Laith, elbowing the other vampire.

Des huffed and shook his head. "No, thanks."

It seemed Cyan wasn't the only one who didn't want that kind of responsibility, apparently. He and Desmond looked alike, possibly related. From what little I was getting to know about Des, his default mood was serious, if even broody. It took Laith and Cyan to loosen him up and start cracking jokes.

Laith had a similar sense of playfulness as Cyan, but his pale blonde hair made him stand apart from the others. Come to think of it, almost all of Blood 'til Dawn were dark-haired except for him.

"So how are you settling in, Tavi?" Laith's tone and

expression were friendly. His eyes were unique for a vampire, almost more purple than red.

Before I could answer, an odd noise, almost like a growl came from Cyan, but his expression had already smoothed over when I gave him a puzzled glance.

"You can call her Tavia," he said to Laith in an eerily calm voice. "She's Tavi only to me." His gaze slid in the opposite direction. "And to Bea, I guess."

Laith chuckled, the sound laced with nervousness. "I get the picture, didn't mean anything by it, Cy. Anyway, *Tavia,* you must have questions. Have you seen many vampires before coming to live with us?"

My brain felt like it was being whiplashed. What was Cyan's deal? He was possessive over my nickname now? And Laith just accepted it and moved on? I felt like I was a few steps behind and hurrying to catch up with the conversation.

"Um, well. I had seen vampires before, but only from a distance. Not up close. Like I knew you all had red eyes, but not that there were different shades."

"We're actually born with eye colors very similar to humans," Desmond said. "Once we start feeding on blood, that's when the change to red starts happening."

"For real?" Bea piped up. "I didn't know that either."

"If you look closely," Cyan leaned in until his face was mere inches from mine. "You might be able to see specks of my original eye color."

His eyes were captivating, I had to admit. A pure, deep red, just like a ruby. He shifted the angle of his head and I stifled a gasp. It looked like he was angling his head to kiss me, and I could also see the flecks he was talking about. Warm, golden brown hues circled his pupil.

"I see them," I murmured, only then realizing how close my lips were to his.

"I like your eyes," he said, breath fanning gently over my mouth. "They remind me of storms."

"Stop rolling your eyes, Des. They're having a moment."

Laith's chiding voice had me pulling back, flustered and hot again. Cyan smirked as he straightened, thoroughly pleased with himself. He really was a shameless flirt, this was so effortless for him.

"Can you guys uh, tell me about the clan?" I asked, swallowing my embarrassment. "How Blood 'til Dawn came to rule Sanguine, what makes up a clan exactly. Are you all family?"

"Ooh, she wants a history lesson." Laith slapped the back of Des' shoulder. "Go on, Des-nerd. This is your wheelhouse."

"Huh, well." Des cleared his throat and settled into a barstool at the counter. "How much time you got?" He shot me a crooked smile and I noticed one of his fangs was chipped and blunt at the end. "Remember, we live for a very long time compared to you. There's a *lot* of history."

"Make it quick." Cyan snapped his fingers. "Brief overview of the last age. Humans were still living in caves before then, so she doesn't need to know about all the earlier stuff."

"To be fair, so were a lot of vampires," Laith said.

"She's asking about the clan, not our evolutionary history," Des corrected.

"Well, don't make it boring at least."

"Leave him alone." Bea shoved at Laith's arm. "Go ahead, Des. I'd be interested to hear too."

"Alright, well." Des cleared his throat again. "Generally speaking, our clan is a family unit. But we're all more extended family to each other. Cousins, nephews, and such." He reached up and ruffled Laith's blonde hair. "And along the way, we've picked up a few strays like this guy."

Laith wrapped his arm around Des's shoulders and nuzzled the side his face. "You're basically my daddy."

"Get off me." Des shoved him off and continued explaining to me. "A couple of the other clans are like us, the Marrowers and Carpe Noctem, primarily. But the rest are more, hm, what's the word." He rubbed his chin. "Political factions, I guess? Followers of a certain idea with a leader at the helm."

"You can call them cults. No one here will be offended," Cyan said.

"Hey, Temkra's Blood isn't so bad," Laith piped up. "They're a deeply religious bunch but never give us any trouble."

"So, where are your immediate family members?" I asked. "If most of Blood 'til Dawn is extended family, where are your parents and siblings?"

"All of our parents are dead," Desmond stated bluntly. "As for siblings, that's actually rare for vampires. Because we live so long, the flip side is that our species has difficulty conceiving. Most families only have one child, if they have any at all."

"But your parents?" A chill crept up my spine as the vampires exchanged hard looks. "None of you are so old that your parents have already passed on, right?"

"Not of natural causes," Cyan said cautiously.

"We were at war with the werewolves for a few hundred years," Des said in a low voice. "It was mostly our parents' generation. Thousands of them were killed as a result."

"They're called the lost generation," Laith said. "Most

vampires alive now were children during that war." He gestured around the great room. "That includes just about everyone in Blood 'til Dawn."

"Rhain was grown back then." Des crossed his arms. "So was Kalix."

Cyan stiffened at the mention of Kalix's name, which I might not have noticed if I hadn't been hyperaware of his presence. He didn't move or say a word, but I could sense his energy change. The warmth of him became a block of ice.

I glanced at Bea, who was more of an open book. Her expression became distant and saddened. I knew Kalix was the guy in the photo next to Cyan, and they both clearly had some connection to him. But it seemed neither was eager to talk.

"I bet Rhain just fuckin' bulldozed some werewolves." Laith laughed. "Kal did too, probably."

"Why were you at war with the wolves?" Even I'd known about the animosity between werewolves and vampires. The species' mutual hatred of each other was common knowledge, but I never knew the origins of it.

"That's a great question," Des said. "What actually happened is lost to history, but if you ask me," he rubbed his chin, gaze flitting over his fellow vampires, "I think we started it."

"Ugh, slander," Cyan complained.

"Werewolf blood is supposed to taste like liquid gold or something," Des explained to me. "So the most common theory is one of us drank from a wolf, their pack retaliated violently, we answered with more violence, the wolves retaliated again, angels sided with wolves, dragons sided with us, and so on."

"For hundreds of years, that's all it was," Cyan tacked on.

"Anyway, going back to the clans." Des steered the conversation back on topic. "There weren't really vampire clans back in those days, about five hundred years back. Family units sure, but we were all just vampires, right?"

"Except for the Marrowers," Laith interrupted. "They've always kinda done their own thing."

"Sure, but the clans started because everyone disagreed on how to handle the wolves. Some wanted to invade their territory and enslave them and shit. Others wanted to move into the human world and carve out a space for us there. So there were lots of divides, lots of factions. And despite werewolves already killing plenty of us, the clan disagreements never stopped. So we turned to fighting our kind."

"We do love spilling blood almost as much as drinking it," Laith mused.

"Don't scare her," Bea chastised.

"It's fine, really." I brought a palm up. "Humans love going to war on each other too. That's part of why Sapien's founders left the human world. It's a big part of our history too, so I get it."

"Shortly after the clans formed, one of them—probably an extinct one, the details have been lost—declared themselves the ruling clan of Sanguine." Des spread his hands out to the sides, a wry smile on his lips. "And their leader said if anyone didn't like it, they could fight for the title. Well, someone did and won. So then they became the ruling clan."

"That didn't last long," I muttered.

"And that's basically how it went for the last four hundred years," Des said. "Clans got wiped out or absorbed into alliances. Leaders were crowned and then toppled. For centuries, it was a bloody, violent mess for power. And we were actively at war with the werewolves until about a hundred years ago."

"But something changed recently?" My gaze swept over the vampires, who each stood a little taller. "How does Blood 'til Dawn fit in to all this?"

"Our ancestors were violent when necessary, but the founders of Blood 'til Dawn were a more diplomatic sort," Cyan said. "Our generation learned to work quietly from our forebears. Thorne and his inner circle negotiated with smaller clans and gathered support in the shadows, rather than vye for the ruling seat in the spotlight. When we made our bid for the top spot, it was nearly a hundred years in the making. By then we had set up the blood bank, restored businesses, and made the streets safer for our resident vampires and humans. Over half of Sanguine supported us but the leaders still had to battle."

"And you won it?" I asked eagerly. He and Des were equally good storytellers, but I was fixated on Cyan. "Thorne fought and won?"

"He did." Cyan grinned. "Get him drunk enough and he'll show you the scars from the fight."

I laughed. "I think I'll pass. So how long has Blood 'til Dawn been in power?"

"Fifteen years," Des said. "And it's been the most peaceful and prosperous time in our recorded history, which says a lot."

"Fifteen years?" I repeated. "That doesn't sound like very long, considering how long you live. How long you'd been at war."

"It's not," Laith said. "It's a fuckin' flash in a pan. And yet it's the longest, continuous amount of time a clan has ruled Sanguine. No one else has lasted this long."

"That's..." I didn't have words for it. Couldn't imagine the instability and violence that had plagued this world for centuries. An average vampire lived long enough to see all of it too, if they were lucky enough to survive the carnage. What kind of life was that, to live so long and never know a peaceful period?

And yet, Blood 'til Dawn had shown that peace was possible, even among a bloodthirsty species.

"Has Thorne been challenged since taking over?" Bea asked.

"A couple times," Des answered. "Nobody who's a real threat, though." His chipped, blunt fang dragged over his bottom lip. "He doesn't expect to hold power forever, though. There's always someone who comes along who's stronger than you. At least, that's what he believes. He's just waiting for it to happen."

"What happens then?" I asked. "What would happen to Blood 'til Dawn, everything the clan has built?"

Cyan let out a low chuckle. "Nothing lasts forever, Tavi. And nobody knows that better than vampires."

Chapter 8

Tavia

I opened the door to find Bea grinning at me from across the threshold, her aquamarine eyes glittering like jewels set in their black depths. "Hi! I'm taking you out."

"Out?" I blinked at her, still a little disoriented from my late afternoon nap. I was having a hell of a time trying to make myself transition to a nocturnal schedule.

"Yes, out. You know the market and where to get your essentials. Now it's time for fun." She made a shooing motion at me. "Get dressed. I'll wait here."

She left no room for argument, so I did as she said. In fifteen minutes, I was put together enough, and left the suite with a quick glance to Cyan's closed bedroom door. A few of my winemaking supplies had shown up, but I hadn't seen him since that night in the great room three days ago.

It almost felt like he was avoiding me, which threw me for a loop. I thought we'd had a fun night getting to know each other. As friends, of course.

Bea turned to me with that bright grin as I locked the door behind me, but I caught her staring longingly at the picture of Cyan and the other vampire, Kalix, a moment before.

"Ready, sunshine?"

"Yeah." I nodded at the picture. "Are you ever gonna tell me what happened to him?"

Her smile drooped, tinged with sadness. "Over a drink, sure. It's not really a conversation I can handle sober."

"Oh, I'm sorry. That sounds heavy." We started down the corridor together.

"It is, but you might as well know." She gave me a little nudge with her elbow as we ascended the stairs. "Human or not, you're Blood 'til Dawn now. Kalix is part of our history, and now you are, too."

I gave a little laugh as we crossed the great room, waving to the few vampires milling about. "Blink and you'll miss me, right? I won't live long enough to be any significant part of vampire history."

"Not true, necessarily." Bea led me through the garage and then a side door, a different one from our route to the market. "You could be someone's blood mate, fall hopelessly in love, and gain a vampire's lifespan through the mating ceremony. It's extremely rare, but there's always a chance."

"Blood mate?" She made it sound much more appealing than the disgust Cyan had used when he mentioned it. I shoved my hands into the pockets of my sweater, the chilly evening air a sharp contrast to the warmth inside the compound. "That does sound like a step above blood *pet*."

"Oh, it's the ultimate goal." Bea sighed dreamily, her face turned up to the sky as we made our way down the sidewalk. "When all the chemistry and proteins in your blood fulfill the needs of one vampire or brusang perfectly, they'll be insatiable for your blood alone. Everything else will taste like garbage once they've had their perfect match. It's like a switch flips in their biology. They will be driven to feed from the perfect source and nothing else."

"Wow. That actually sounds kind of romantic."

"Doesn't it?" Bea's eyelashes fluttered. "It's pretty rare, to the point where the whole territory celebrates if a blood mate pairing is found, and an elaborate ceremony is conducted to seal the bond. The last one was maybe fifteen years ago."

"And the ceremony would make the non-vampire half live as long as the vampire?"

"If they're human, yes." Bea smirked. "But if they're another vampire, a brusang, or a shifter, they already have the long lifespan. So the magic at the ceremony is more symbolic in those cases."

"What was the last pairing?" I couldn't stop peppering her with questions. No one in Sapien ever talked about vampire culture. What else did I not know?

"Two vampires, which is the most common, I think." Bea's smile grew wider. "But the best part was that it was two females. The first gay blood mate ceremony ever publicly celebrated in Sanguine, so it was quite an event."

"Aw, how sweet! You were there?"

"Oh yeah, everyone turned out to see it. And it shut up a lot of the ancient bigots who claimed same-sex blood mates was impossible because it went against biology."

"Were you a brusang then? Or still a human?"

Bea's smile dimmed just slightly. "I had been a brusang for about five years at that point. It felt like I was still getting used to the experience. Seeing that ceremony was definitely a highlight during that time."

"I'm sorry." I'd been asking questions so fast, I didn't stop to remember what she'd told me. The turning process was a traumatic experience, and she'd been near death before waking up in her new life.

"All good," she chirped before pointing at a red-bricked building up ahead. "That's where we're headed."

I'd been so absorbed in asking her questions that I hadn't truly taken in my surroundings until then. The street was lively, with humans and vampires alike going about their business. Tall street lamps illuminated the sidewalks and roads. Businesses were open with bright neon signs affixed to their buildings.

There were multiple clubs, lounges, and restaurants on this strip with their large windows open to the street, along with a smoke shop, a motorcycle mechanic, and a butcher.

It reminded me a bit of Jacksonville, the town in the human world we had sometimes visited for supplies. Apparently it was a popular tourist destination in the summer, and the streets would be teeming with people at certain times of day, primarily lunch time. Those trips had felt exactly like this, only during the day.

"Busy night," I mused to Bea as we squeezed past people walking in the opposite direction. A vampire exhaled a spicy red smoke that made my eyes water.

"Locals call this area the Cap," she said.

I looked at her. "Cap as in hat?"

She laughed "As in, short for capillary. We're just off the Heart of Sanguine. Vampires can't resist blood analogies, so this neighborhood with all its little side streets and alleyways resemble capillaries. Or just the Cap. It's one of the most popular areas of Sanguine, which is especially impressive considering these buildings were all ruins decades ago."

"Someone put a lot of money into this place, huh?"

"Yes," she agreed softly. "Blood 'til Dawn did. They own every building you see."

"Whoa." That *was* impressive.

I took in all the details as we walked to our destination. The smoke shop had a sign in the window that said, *No drae here! Walk into the sun and burn, assholes.* Seemed a little harsh, but okay.

Down a side street stood a square, white building that resembled a small hospital. BLOOD BANK was written on the side in bright, red letters. Above the door was a painted sign that read *Donor Entrance.*

Before I could ask Bea about it, she shoved a paper menu in my hand. "Let me know what you think of the human menu. If it sucks, we can go somewhere else."

We were standing in front of the restaurant she'd chosen, a place called Carnassian's. Upon scanning the menu, I realized that they specialized in meat dishes, many of them rare or raw. Nothing looked too intimidating to me though, and they had some seafood options as well, which I felt better about eating raw than say, steak.

"No, this is good," I told Bea.

"Great! Let's grab a seat."

We got a table next to one of the large open windows facing the street. Our server was a vampire who looked young enough to be a teen. I knew better than to ask if she was old enough to work, but the agelessness of vampires never ceased to fascinate me.

I ordered the ceviche and a Mexican lager. Bea settled on a blue rare strip steak and a blood sangria.

"So vampires do eat food." I subtly looked around at the other clientele, which I estimated to be seventy percent vampire or brusang, thirty percent human.

"For pleasure, yes. Out of necessity, no." Bea leaned

back and smiled pleasantly while our server placed our drinks in front of us. "Eating raw or rare meat satisfies blood thirst for a short time, so that's what we usually prefer."

"Do I ever have to worry about being on the menu?"

I said it jokingly, but that was the main thing the council had drummed into our heads when it came to keeping ourselves separate from the vampires. Truly integrating into their society was impossible, because drinking blood was a slippery slope to having our flesh torn away and eaten.

"No." Bea shook her head, her expression serious. "Vampires understand humans are sentient and self-aware. The vast majority only take blood with consent, whether that's from a human, fellow vampire, any being with the capacity to give consent." She took a sip of her blood cocktail. "I won't deny that it has happened, and that there's a small minority of vampires who believe it's their right to treat humans as literal livestock, but vampire society as a whole has come a long way from that. A huge part of it is because of Blood 'til Dawn. They've made sweeping changes over the last few decades."

My fingers drummed on my beer glass. "We were told that the last blood pet given at the Half-Century Selection was ripped apart in front of everyone. Basically eaten alive by a mob of monsters."

Bea winced. "That's awful. You must have been terrified when you were selected."

I nodded, then chuckled through my next sip of beer. "Cyan was not what I expected, that's for sure."

Bea smiled across the table. "Vampires are capable of change. If anything, I think their long lives make them more adaptable to it."

It was only after our food came out and we ordered our

second round of drinks that I dared to ask what burned my curiosity the most.

"So, are you not sober enough to tell me about Kalix?" I crunched down on a chip loaded heavily with ceviche.

"Ha, not nearly." Bea's smirk was cheeky, but her eyes were sad. "It hurts to talk about him, if I'm being completely honest."

Guilt sliced through me. "It's okay, you don't have to—"

"No, no." She downed the remainder of her first drink and pulled her second one closer. "I should talk about him, even though it hurts. Cyan never brings him up, but Kal deserves to be remembered." Her eyes flicked up to me. "I know you're wondering and the answer is yes, he's the one who turned me."

I let her words sink in with a long pull of beer. "He saved your life, then."

She nodded. "I didn't grow up with Blood 'til Dawn. As a human, my family and I were employed by another clan. We were the housekeeping staff, and..." She swallowed, nervously rotating the stem of her drinking glass. "That clan *did* see us as inferior, little more than working animals."

The protectiveness that I usually reserved for Amy rose up like a tidal wave. "Fuck, I'm so sorry."

Bea gave a small nod before continuing. "My sister had it okay. She was the pretty, charming one. Once she became of age, she was claimed as a blood pet by the clan's heir. She's one of a few, I've heard. Rumors say he has a harem of pets. But anyway, once she got that cushy life, she never had much to do with me. Our parents died pretty young, they were so overworked. The clan had a few other staff members, but the bulk of the work fell to me."

My heart tore open for Bea. Her story made me wish I could have traveled back in time and been there for her. She reminded me of Amy, vulnerable and pushed around for no reason other than existing. It sounded like she really needed a friend back then.

"A little over twenty years ago, Cyan and Kalix started coming by the estate where I worked." A dreamy smile touched Bea's lips as she recalled the memory. "I had an instant crush on Kal. Cyan's cute too, don't get me wrong. But there was something about Kal that was just magnetic to me."

"What was he like?" I waited as she took a delicate sip from her drink.

"Tall. Big." She smirked. "Almost as big as Rhain, but not quite as scary."

My eyebrows went up. I'd only seen Rhain, Thorne's second in command, in passing a few times, but that vampire was massive. Tall enough that he had to duck through most doorways and built like a bodybuilder. He also had a permanent scowl that guaranteed most people stayed out of his way.

"There was a warmth to Kal," Bea continued. "He seemed like a gentle giant type, but he wasn't soft. He was quiet. Solid. If he wanted to be intimidating, he could be. Maybe I imagined it, but he always seemed to be polite and gentle with me. I answered the door whenever they came and he would say hello with this little smile when he saw me."

"Sounds like you weren't the only one with a crush," I mused.

Bea waved that off with a girlish giggle. "I would lead them through the foyer, offering refreshments and snacks. Cyan jumped to accept but Kal always politely refused. Though he always made small talk with me, asked me how I was doing like he genuinely wanted to know."

"Returned crush confirmed," I teased.

"Stop." Bea waved her hand again but this time, her smile faltered. "I was never present for their meetings with my employer unless I was called in to serve drinks or something. And one day, I..." She paused, taking a slow breath. "I brought in a tray of blood cocktails. They were iced, so there was condensation on the glasses. I picked one up to give to my employer and...my fingers slipped. I dropped it."

I remained silent during her next pause in the story, not wanting to encourage her to keep talking nor tell her to stop. Whichever she chose to do, this was clearly difficult, and my support would be best given by listening, not trying to sway her either way.

"It spilled all over his desk, on the documents he had out." Bea's gaze had fixated on some spot on the table, her voice going low and flat. "He was furious, calling me stupid, useless. I was so scared that I froze like a statue. Then he got even more angry because I wasn't doing anything to clean it up. He took a letter opener and slashed it across my throat."

"Oh my God, Bea."

Without thinking, I reached across the table for her hands. She didn't return my grip, her slender fingers limp in mine and slightly cold from her chilled drink. The poor woman was somewhere else now, in that horrible memory.

"I didn't even feel the pain of it, but I could feel myself dying." Bea swallowed, and I noticed the faint scar across her throat for the first time. "I don't think the shock ever fully registered. I remember feeling confused like, how can I be dying right now? I was fully alive five seconds ago."

I squeezed her fingers in a silent, gentle urge to rise out of that awful, traumatic scene. "But Kalix saved your life, didn't he?"

It worked. Clarity returned to her eyes and a faint smile

returned to her lips, but there was still so much sadness there.

"I must have fallen to the ground, because I remember looking up at his face. He looked so worried about me. I remember feeling so embarrassed. No one wants their crush to see them bleeding to death, it's so undignified."

A laugh choked out of me. She was definitely back in the present.

"Kal asked me one question. 'Do you want to live?' I immediately said yes, or I must have mouthed it because I couldn't speak. I was so scared. My life hadn't been great, but I wasn't ready to die. The last thing I remember before waking up as a brusang was his wrist against my lips and the taste of his blood in my mouth."

Bea paused there to finish off the rest of her drink, throwing it back and setting it down dramatically. "When I woke up, I was in the Blood 'til Dawn compound looking like this." She gestured to her eyes then touched her tongue to one of her fangs, which I realized were a bit shorter than a vampire's.

"Thank fuck you got through it." I polished off my beer, then hesitantly asked, "And Kalix?"

"Gone."

I almost thought she would leave it at that until she said, "Imprisoned by that clan, Carpe Noctem. Blood 'til Dawn was not the ruling clan at the time, so they didn't have the power to overrule it. Cyan took me in and made sure I was taken care of. He said that was what Kal wanted."

"Wait, back up." I held up a palm. "Imprisoned, why? Because he turned you?"

"That's my assumption, yes. My old employer would be petty and cruel enough to demand retribution for giving me a second life when he wanted me dead."

"What the fuck?" I shook my head at the table. "So, he's imprisoned for how long?"

Bea lifted a shoulder in a shrug. "Vampires don't take half measures when it comes to these things. Punishments are either executions or imprisonment for life."

Fuck. No wonder she talked about him like he had already died. As she said, he was simply gone.

"It hit Cyan hard too, he and Kal were close. Aside from telling me the most basic details after I woke up, we've never spoken about it." Bea released a sigh. "I'm glad I talked to you, though. It's a heavy thing to keep in your mind for twenty years. So, thanks for listening, Tavia."

"Yeah, of course. I just, wow. That *is* heavy." I rubbed my forehead. "It's hard to imagine how Cyan would react to that kind of loss. He seems so...carefree. I had no idea he'd ever lost anyone."

"Between you and me." Bea's voice lowered. "I think it's a mask. He adored Kal, so I think he shoves that day far down that he doesn't have to deal with the pain of it."

"Was he there? I wonder if he blames himself."

Bea nodded grimly. "I'm sure there's an element of self-blame. There certainly is with me."

"Hey." I flattened my palms on the table, making sure I had her attention. "I'm really glad you're here, okay? I would be so lost if you were dead. I'll never meet Kal, but he sounds amazing. He saved you and I'm so grateful to him because he allowed me to have you as a friend. Live your new life, it is what he wanted. That's why he gave it to you."

"I'm usually good about gratitude, positivity, all that shit." Bea sniffed and delicately wiped her eye. "But I have my moments where I wish I could talk to him for five minutes. Ask him why he did that for me. Or just been able to get to know him, you know? See if there was anything there, or if it was just my crush giving me false hope."

There was nothing I could say to comfort her, except to commiserate in the fact that those unknowns absolutely sucked. Before I could say anything else, a presence loomed over our table. Thinking it was our waitress, I looked up with my mouth open for another round of drinks.

But it was a different vampire, a male. Someone I didn't recognize. He was almost certainly not from Blood 'til Dawn.

"Hi, ladies. How are we doing tonight?" His grin was cocky as he grabbed a nearby chair, turning it around so he could straddle the back of it.

I glanced at Bea, who looked just as perturbed as I felt.

"Can we help you?" Her tone was snitty, a clear signal to buzz off.

Naturally, like with human men, the signal went over this guy's head.

"Just seeing what you're up to, seeing if you're in need of anything more fun than booze." The moment I realized something was off about this guy, he produced a slim vial with a golden liquid inside and a squeeze dropper top. "You ladies ever tried drae?"

Bea sucked in a sharp breath. "You're trying to push that here, really? Do you have a death wish or are you just stupid?"

"Come on, little brusang. Don't act like you don't miss the sun from your human days." He turned his gaze to me, and I noticed his red eyes had a tinge of yellow that didn't look good. It looked like sickness, like something wrong. "And I know you're human, but give it a shot. You might see beautiful things when the sun comes out. Ever try LSD? I hear it's like that for your kind."

"We're not interested." I said it firmly, like I was shutting down a pushy salesperson in the human world, but the vampire was not deterred.

"Don't be scared, ladies. It's just a little sunlight. It gives life to every living thing except us. Why should we be excluded?" He gestured to himself and Bea, who was still staring daggers at him. "This lets us see the world the same way all of Temkra's other creatures do. Equality, finally! And all it takes is a little drop in your eyes an hour before dawn."

"Oh, thank fuck." Bea muttered.

"Yes, exactly! That's what I said when I first tried it and felt the sun's light on me..."

The rambling, probably-still-high vampire didn't notice she was actually looking past him, at the furious Cyan storming directly for our table.

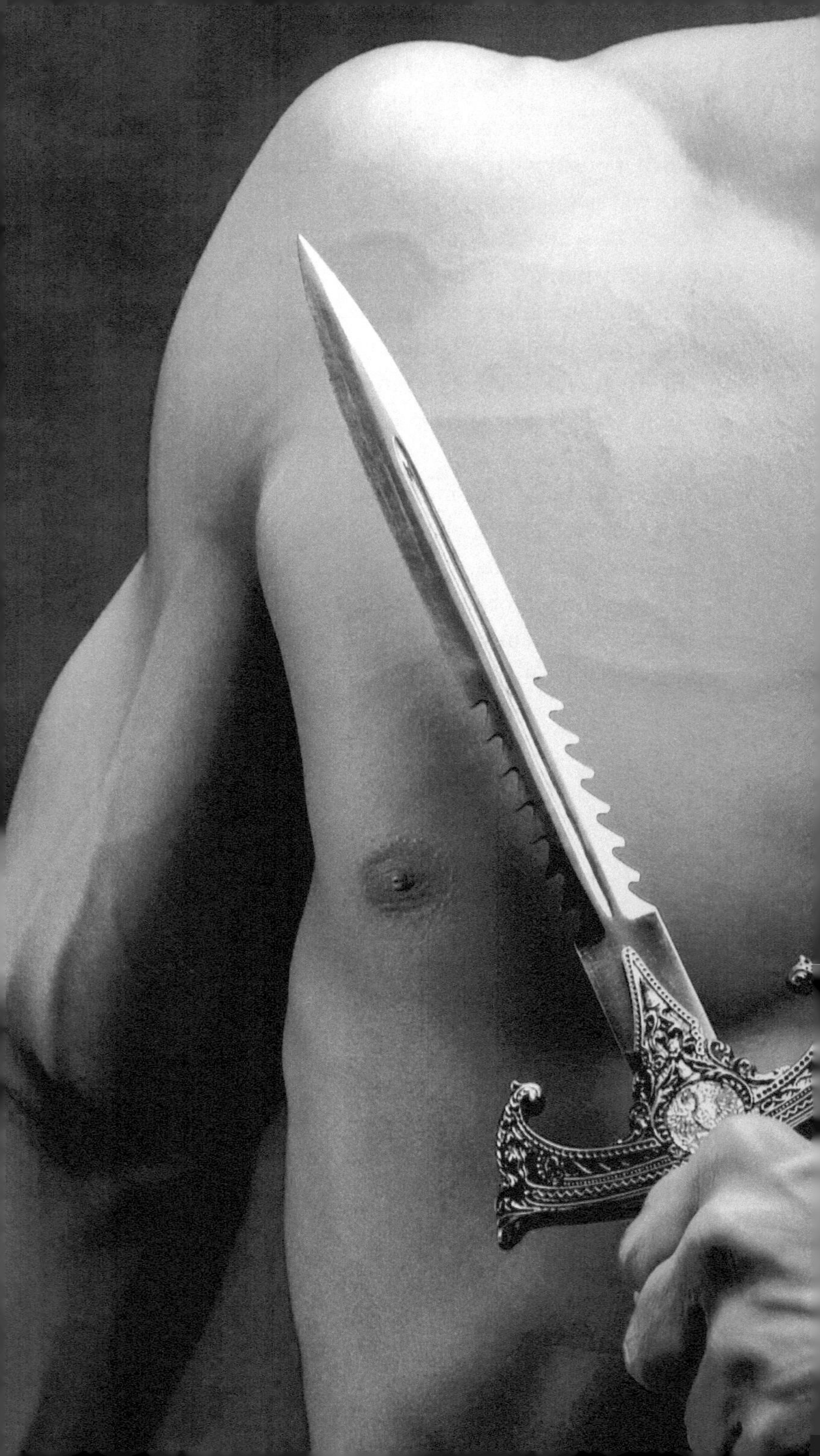

Chapter 9

Cyan

My next day off had me antsy as hell, buzzing with restlessness. I sure as hell couldn't stay home so I hit the street heading toward the Cap, opting to walk instead of riding my motorcycle.

It was no mystery why I was on edge. A certain human woman was the culprit, one that I couldn't touch or drink from, lest I shackle myself to her and only her. The answer to handling that was the same way I handled most stresses in life—a pulsing neck at my mouth and a pretty ass in my lap.

Tavi had been haunting me like a ghost since she arrived, and not an entirely unwelcome one. Her scent always hit me like brisk, fresh air when I entered my apartment. It smelled like coming home, not just crashing in my bed for the day. Even when I left my place, small hints of her presence lingered in the hallway and great room.

It felt like witchcraft, some strange magic that I began associating her scent with home and comfort. And it unnerved me.

After a few days, Tavi seemed to be settling in well

enough. She and Bea were attached at the hip, always together. My clan mates were starting to talk about her, referring to her in casual conversation like she was one of us. And technically speaking, I suppose she was. This arrangement was not temporary. She was staying with us for the rest of her natural life. That thought always gave me strange feelings. Not bad exactly, but feelings I wasn't used to.

She was my blood pet in name only, and yet I felt oddly possessive of her. I got twitchy and a little snarly when someone else referred to her as Tavi. Only *I* called her that, Temkra damn it.

Why did she have to be so...interesting? Why couldn't she be a typical human who made themselves small around us, trying like hell to not to draw attention to themselves? No, she had to have that tantalizing scent, had to bravely volunteer for the Selection to save her friend. She even had the cool winemaking hobby, which was especially unfair for making her even more interesting. On top of all that, she had to be appealing to look at too.

All of those factors combined made me insatiably curious about the taste of her blood. But the moment I tasted her, I'd be claiming her. Which was absolutely not an option. And so the vicious cycle of pulling away began again.

Eventually, I would get bored of her. I inevitably got bored of every female who came my way. Until that happened, I had to settle for distraction.

I weaved my way through the crowded streets of the Cap before walking into Pulse Point like a man on a mission. It wasn't the only club Blood 'til Dawn owned, but it was my personal favorite. The VIP lounge in the loft was always reserved for our clan members only, roped off to anyone else except our personal guests.

With a nod at the bouncer at the base of the stairs, I went up to the loft to find it empty. Perfect. A night out was usually best enjoyed with friends, but I was about to drink from someone who was not my blood pet, and I didn't want any of their disapproving looks killing my buzz. The waitress coming over to serve me, on the other hand, was exactly what I needed.

"Cyan," she purred, orange eyes lighting up. "What can I do for you?"

Irina was a dragon shifter, and a gorgeous member of the species. More importantly, her blood was spicy, rich, and satisfying. Her forked tongue often lent to a good time as well.

"Blood." I held out a small wad of cash and gave her my most charming smile. "And the pleasure of your company, of course."

She smiled back, plucking the cash from my hand with long, slender fingers. "I'll be right back. Should I send over a drink while I get ready?"

"That would be great."

I settled on one of the plush couches while she left to wash off any make-up, sweat, or perfume that might affect her taste. The neck was an area where scents tended to concentrate, so a quick wash or rinse was standard procedure.

Another waitress brought over a drink on a tray, my usual, a Sazerac with a small dash of blood. I left a generous tip on her tray, and she was forgotten the moment I picked up my drink. Absently, I watched the light show and the DJ on the floor below as I took a sip, and the taste that hit my tongue immediately pulled me out of any relaxed state.

I grimaced, holding the glass up to examine it. Something was off in the drink. It wasn't awful but not the taste I was used to. I made a face as I swallowed, then sniffed the inside of the glass for anything amiss. Nothing that I could detect.

"Everything okay, Cy?" Irina's deep, honeyed voice floated over, closely followed by her hand landing with gentle weight on my thigh.

"You change up your blood source? Or your whiskey?" I set the drink aside.

Irina frowned, a crease forming between her reptilian orange eyes. "No, they're both the same as we've always used. Why?"

"Something taste's off, but it's not a big deal." I slid an arm around her waist, bringing her to my lap.

"I can get you another." Her arm came around my shoulders, lips ghosting over my ear.

"Nah." I held the nape of her slender neck, angling her for a comfortable bite. "This is what I really want."

She arched with a soft sigh, giving me more access, and I wasted no time in sinking into her vein.

When her blood hit my mouth, it was all I could do to not let out a groan. Of disappointment, that was. Something tasted off about her too. The spicy, rich taste that I'd enjoyed in the past was now bland, almost watered down. What the hell?

I'd barely drawn two mouthfuls when I unlatched my fangs and flicked my tongue over the two points to seal the wounds. It was quick, perfunctory, not the playful neck licking that I was known for. I pulled away, not meeting Irina's eyes with the confusion I knew would be in her stare.

"Cy, what's going on?" She dragged her nails over my

scalp, an affectionate gesture I used to love, but now made my skin crawl with wrongness.

"I don't know," I admitted. "Maybe I'm coming down with something. Everything I taste is just...off."

"Aww, getting the vampire flu?" She touched the back of her palm to my forehead. "Can your kind even get sick?"

"It's rare, but it happens." She wasn't getting off my lap, so I pushed her off as gently and non-offensively as I could. "I should get some fresh air or something. Sorry we couldn't have more fun."

Her lips curved in a coy smile, accepting my apology. "Call me when you feel better. It's been a hot minute since I came to the compound."

My immediate reaction was no, hell no. I did not want to bring my casual fuck-slash-blood source around where Tavi was. And then I felt something like guilt. Shame. Like Irina was a dirty little secret I didn't want Tavi knowing about.

But I gave her a tight smile in return. "Sure. See you, Irina."

I couldn't leave the club fast enough. And yet the cool night air didn't feel any better. My mind was back in that cycle of missing Tavi, wondering about her taste, then chiding myself for being tempted to fall in that trap. The more I avoided her, the greater the temptation seemed to get.

I hit the pavement, going nowhere in particular, just needing some movement. It was busy tonight in the Cap. People crowded the streets and storefronts were bustling with activity. A pair of motorcycles rolled slowly down the road, taking care with the pedestrians. I recognized Desmond and Laith, and gave a quick wave, which Des returned.

We patrolled our turf in rotating pairs, so that everyone could watch over different areas, have different days off, and work with a different partner. My clan mates were family, and of course I loved them all. But no one had made a better pair than me and Kalix.

"Fuck," I muttered aloud, watching Des and Laith's tail lights get smaller as they maneuvered down the street. Guess I was feeling sentimental about all kinds of things tonight.

Kal would've slapped me upside the head over how hard I was avoiding Tavi. He'd encourage me to accept my responsibility, to jump headfirst into taking care of my blood pet. To provide her with protection and a comfortable life.

"It's the least you can do when you're taking her blood, her life force. When she's trusting you not to drain her dry," he'd say.

"Well, I haven't fed from her once so how's that for a loophole?" I'd retort. And he'd snort and call me an idiot.

He was always right, of course. I was an idiot. And a coward. I let him get imprisoned when it should have been me, after all.

Fuck, I wished he was here. I knew exactly what he'd say, but I'd give anything to hear it straight from him.

My aimless walking brought me to the restaurant district. The night was warm enough that most places had their windows open to the street. Scents of food, alcohol, and all kinds of species poured out of those establishments. Human, brusang, vampire, and dragon shifter. I drew in a deep breath and nearly gagged. None of it appealed to me.

Except...one.

One scent that was light, sweet as dark berries, and comforting like home.

I followed the direction it came from, turning toward

the restaurant window as if manipulated by a puppet master, and almost laughed at the cruelty of the universe. Tavi was sitting right there, at a table directly next to the window, with Bea across from her.

Of course the human I was trying to avoid and forget would pop up right in front of me.

Their heads were turned away from the window, focused on some third person who I assumed to be their waiter, until another scent drifted across my path. One that made me gag. Sunlight and rot with an undercurrent of burning.

Fuck. If the scent wasn't enough, the vampire's face confirmed it. His red eyes were tinged with yellow and his skin looked dry and faintly blistered. All signs of coming off a draitrium high. When he pulled out a vial and held it out to the women, I didn't think. I just acted.

My feet carried me through the restaurant's entrance, and once I spotted the back of his head, no one could unlock me from my target. I headed toward him like a bull after a red flag. He was so out of it, he never even heard me coming.

With my hand around the back of his neck, I slammed his face down on the edge of the table with enough force to call attention to the whole restaurant. Good. He needed to be made an example of.

Despite his shock and pain, the addict managed to keep hold of the little vial in his hand. He even resisted when I pried it from his fingers.

"What is this?" I forced his head to turn and look at the vial in my hand.

"Nothing!" he cried.

"Mm, try again." I squeezed harder around his neck. Sun exposure had made his muscles weak and soft.

"It's drae!" he whimpered pathetically. "It's drae, okay? Fuck, I'm sorry."

"And you were trying to sell it to these two? Out in public, huh? And on a busy night in the Cap, no less?"

"I mean, I was gonna let 'em try it for free, but—"

That only pushed my anger into dangerous territory. I dropped the vial on the floor and crushed it under my boot, which made the addict flail in panic.

"No, no! I spent my whole month's salary on that! I need to work overtime during the day and, ahh—"

I lifted him up from the table and, with a flipped grip, used the same hand to lift him off the floor and slam him against the wall.

"I should fucking eviscerate you," I hissed. My fangs fully elongated, not in blood thirst, but in a surge of seething anger and violence. "For not only trying to sell drae in Blood 'til Dawn's territory, but to *my* fucking blood pet as well."

The vampire's eyes widened and not just because I was slowly suffocating him. He'd been trying to sell an outlawed drug to a blood pet of the ruling clan. The same clan who outlawed the drug in the first place. Now he realized how fucked he was.

"You're going to tell me who your supplier is," I said, deadly calm in my fury. "And then you will never come anywhere near my blood pet again. If you see her coming down the street, you go the opposite way. If she comes into a bar, you get up and leave. If she says hello, you apologize for existing and get the fuck away. You get me?"

"Yeah! Yeah, I'm sorry! It won't happen again."

I released his throat only enough to let him breathe and talk. "Your supplier. Now."

He hesitated and I squeezed again, making him flail in panic.

"Cy, don't kill him."

Tavi's voice cut through my haze, reaching through to the real me underneath all the fury. It was only because of her demand that I loosened my grip by a hair's breadth on the dealer.

"Vlad," he choked out. "I'm a middleman for Vlad, in the south Ribs."

"Huh." I grunted, keeping my grip steady. "You're pretty far north from home."

"I'm visiting family and uh—ugh..."

"Scoping out new customers?" I drawled.

His shaky nod was all I needed. Well, fuck. The draitrium problem truly was a beast with dozens of heads. We cut off a few, and new ones grew back to sniff around for new territory.

"The whole Heart of Sanguine is off limits to your business," I hissed in the dealer's face. "If I see you or anyone associated with you in Blood 'til Dawn's home turf, we're sending you to Vlad in pieces. Understand?"

Again he nodded shakily. I drew him forward, then shoved him back just hard enough for the back of his head to hit the wall. "Say it."

"I understand," he sputtered. "I'm l-leaving the Heart tonight."

Only then did I open my fist, and then watched him scurry out of the restaurant like the vermin he was.

I took my first deep breath in ages, looking at the two women still sitting next to the window. "Are you two alright?"

Slow, tentative nods from both of them. Bea understood we had to get rough sometimes to keep drae and its pushers out of circulation. But it was the first time Tavi had seen me do that, and I couldn't read the expression on her face.

One thing was certain. I had to make sure she was always safe, especially if I was hellbent on avoiding her and wouldn't always be at her side.

"Time to come home, ladies," I said. "Tavi, meet me in the apartment in a half hour."

I got out of there, heading straight for the compound. My blood cooled after a few minutes of walking, and I could think rationally again.

"Fuck," I bit out to myself at a sudden realization.

What I was about to do would make resisting Tavi so, so much worse.

Chapter 10

Tavia

I didn't wait in the apartment for long, but nearly paced a hole in the floor by the time Cyan arrived. He came through the door looking grim, his eyes still alight with rage, all the angles of his face sharp and tense.

"Sorry to keep you waiting. I had to brief Thorne on what happened." He looked around the living room and made a broad, sweeping gesture with his hand. "Let me move the furniture out of the way, then we can get started."

"Get started?" I turned, watching as he shoved the couch, coffee table, end tables, and lamps to the far corners of the room, creating a large, empty space.

It was impossible to read his mood. I'd never seen him so pissed off like he was in that restaurant and I still couldn't fully reconcile what happened. Cyan had always been so relaxed and easygoing until then. The confrontation was a stark reminder that I truly didn't know him at all.

The vampire who'd come up to us had been pushy, but after watching Cyan deal with him, I almost felt bad for the guy. He was scared out of his mind. Now, Cyan's anger was no longer explosive, but this quieter rage was almost more unsettling. He didn't say a word as he stepped into the center of the newly-cleared living room, just put his hands on his hips and gave a small, satisfied nod as he looked around.

"This should work," he muttered.

"Work for what?" I demanded, only then realizing I was inching toward the door. "What are you going to do?"

He met my eyes, his hard expression softening ever so slightly. "Relax, Tavi. Take a few deep breaths."

"Tell me what you're going to do." My fists clenched at my sides, every muscle bracing for the unknown.

Was he pissed at me for some reason? Bea gave no indication that I'd be in danger when we returned to the compound, just that he might want to lecture me.

Cyan gave a crooked smile, flashing one fang. "I'm going to show you how to defend yourself, silly human. Here." With an open palm, he reached down into the side of his boot and withdrew a silver dagger, the same one he used to carve his vow into his skin. Careful to avoid touching the blade, he held the handle out toward me. "I'm going to show you how to attack me using this. It's your best defense against any vampire, regardless if they're sober or on drae. Take it."

I hesitated for a moment, feeling exactly like a silly human, before tentatively accepting the weapon. "Was that guy really dangerous?"

Cyan's expression darkened. "He could have been. Drae addicts are unpredictable, and like with alcohol, their inhibitions are lowered. They may try things that they wouldn't normally do while sober."

"And they can go out in the sun while on it?" The dagger felt heavy and awkward in my hand, so I examined the intricately carved handle.

Cyan sucked in a harsh breath when I touched the flat side of the blade, then looked relieved when he remembered that silver didn't burn me like it did him.

"Yeah, that's the whole point of taking it," he said blandly. "The draw of feeling sunlight for the first time is all it takes to entice any curious vampire. Brusang fall for it too when they get nostalgic about their human lives. No one gives warnings about the side effects and addictive qualities until it's too late. And that filth," Cyan snarled, pointing toward the door, "doesn't care about the lives ruined, the vampires burned to a crisp because they miscalculated a dose, the dependency that makes them sell everything for another fix, as long as he's getting paid. Him, his supplier, and all the others like them, are what's gonna be the downfall of vampires. Not the clans, not the werewolves, but the scum of our own kind taking advantage of people."

Cyan took a deep breath, shoulders sagging like the explanation exhausted him. Like this whole quiet war on the streets was a constant, unwinnable churn.

"I'm sorry," I said after some silence. "I can see why Blood 'til Dawn outlawed the drug."

He let out a dry laugh. "If only that were enough." Straightening, his gaze returned to the silver dagger in my hand. "Now, to learn how to use that thing. Getting out of any confrontation alive is more mental than physical. Remember that vampires can sense your heartbeat. Work on breathing deeply so your pulse isn't going too fast. If you're mentally calm and in control, your body will follow."

"Is an aggressive vampire going to give me time to do breathing exercises?"

"No, but just something to keep in mind." He smirked. "I know you're being cheeky, but if your pulse is steady, it's going to throw your attacker off *his* game. He's going to want a spiked pulse, a fearful response. Don't give him that, and you're already ahead." Cyan curled his fingers at me in a beckoning motion. "Come at me with the dagger, try to stab me."

"What if I hit you?"

"You won't." His smirk became a full-on grin. "Let's see what you got, brave little human."

I was no stranger to physical confrontations, even fist fights, but my body felt encased in cement. I was a defensive brawler, always standing over or in front of Amy. I couldn't just rush Cyan unprovoked, even if there was no risk of me hurting him. Running to attack someone unarmed or undefended was just not in my DNA.

"No," I said, and the vampire arched a brow. "I'm defending myself. So you need to come at me."

"Fair enough."

Cyan's shrug barely registered in my vision before he was on me. I felt a sharp pain in my scalp as he jerked my head back by my hair. His fangs hovered just above me and I reacted on instinct, slashing upward with the dagger.

He closed a hand around my wrist to halt the attack. The blade didn't even touch him.

Immediately he released me and took several long backwards strides until he was against the far wall. "Not bad, but keep your arm tight to your body, don't swing wide with it. Protect your vital organs and your throat. You also need to have the dagger up before I reach you."

The next thing I knew he was on me again, his fist gripping the hair at the base of my skull, teeth pulled back and fangs hovering over my neck. My slash at him was just as slow and uncoordinated as my first attempt. He'd moved so fast, his advice hadn't even registered before I reacted again.

He didn't even grab my wrist this time, but simply deflected my strike with a lift of his elbow.

"I wasn't ready," I panted when he released me again. His arm had wrapped around my waist this time, and I swore his fingers lingered there before he walked across the room again.

No, I had to be reading into it.

"You'll never be ready when a real attack comes," was his only reply.

Cyan came at me again. And again. And again.

By roughly the 8th time, I started anticipating his strikes and incorporating his advice into my defense. He didn't do the exact same thing every time, but I quickly figured out that he would always go for my neck. When I started catching on to one technique, Cyan would switch it up and rush me another way. We practiced over and over so many times, I started to see the similarities and differences for each situation.

Cyan didn't talk much except for brief pointers. "Tuck your chin. Keep a slight bend in your knees, let gravity help you. If I come from the side, cross your arm over your body and slash downward."

Mostly, he allowed me to figure it out on my own, which I appreciated. I wasn't used to fighting with a weapon, but I knew how to target weak spots and break holds when being grabbed. After he encouraged me not to hold back, I had to admit it was satisfying jabbing my elbow in Cyan's stomach.

"I'll heal in minutes," he said against my ear while capturing me in a hold from behind. "Only silver can permanently damage me, remember?"

I made sure to kick the inside of his knee, but stopped myself from shoving the heel of my hand into his nose.

Broken noses could heal badly, on top of being painful as hell.

The dagger felt unnatural at first, but after so many repetitive rounds it began to feel like an extension of my arm. I held the blade outward when I slashed up to protect my neck, kept it facing my attacker as I rotated my body away from him.

We went through pretend attacks so many times that my arms and legs ached with exhaustion, but I also felt like a well-oiled machine. I could sense Cyan's movements and even anticipate his fake-outs. He was always faster than me, but I knew he was doing me a favor by not taking it slow and easy. He wanted me to be prepared for anything, and I appreciated that from him.

I liked that he respected me enough to not coddle me.

"You're doing well." After hours of drilling, he didn't even breathe hard. I, on the other hand, was fighting for air and dripping with sweat. "Let's take a breather, go through it a few more times, then call it a night. Dawn's approaching."

I nodded, lacing my fingers behind my head as I sucked in mouthfuls of air. Across the room, as far away from me as possible, Cyan made a face. It looked something like a grimace, but he looked away and smoothed his expression in the next instant.

"Do I smell bad or something?" I ask through my panting breaths.

"What?" He stared at me, facial muscles tense like he was trying to not make that grimace again. "No, you smell...fine."

"It's okay, Cy, you won't hurt my feelings." I gave him a knowing smile. "I'm a big girl. And I've been sweating for the past hour. I badly need a shower."

"No, seriously. Your scent is...it *really* doesn't bother me."

"Cy." I shot him a withering look. "You've been standing as far away from me as possible every moment you're not attacking me. I'm sweaty and ripe, I get it."

"No." The word came out more forceful, tinged with a growl. "Nothing's wrong with your scent. You know what it is? It—" He cut himself off abruptly, rubbing his jaw. "Nevermind."

"No, tell me." I took a few steps toward him and immediately noted how he flattened against the wall. "If it's not how I smell, then what?"

"Don't come any closer," he snarled. "I can only handle it up close in small doses."

"Handle what?"

"Your pulse," he snapped. "Your heart's been hammering like a drum the whole time we've been training and it's," he inhaled a harsh breath and forced it out, "it's fucking distracting."

"Oh." While I pondered on that, I took a few steps away from him.

"What was the first thing I told you?" Cyan groused. "Breathe deeply. It will slow your heart rate and lessen your fear response. Not only will you be able to defend yourself without panicking, your blood won't be so...alluring."

"I get that, but," I laughed softly, "we've been training for over an hour, Cyan. This is the most exercise I've had in a while. You do realize my heart is going to be beating fast as a result."

"Learn to control it."

"I can't just slow my heartbeat at will."

"Well, find a way how," he snapped.

"I don't know if that's a vampire thing, but for humans it's pretty much impossible—"

"Figure it the fuck out!" he bellowed.

I startled at the sudden raised volume of his voice. I wasn't afraid, but never expected that reaction from him. He hadn't even yelled at the dealer at the restaurant like this.

Cyan pushed off the wall with a muttered curse, heading for his room. With a slam of the door, I found myself alone and wondering what the hell just happened.

Chapter 11

Taria

I barely saw Cyan over the next couple of weeks, despite the two of us remaining roommates. He seemed to be keeping his distance, even avoiding me, since the night we drilled together. I only caught glimpses of him in the corridor, hanging out in someone else's apartment, or across the great room.

The last of my winemaking supplies appeared at my bedroom door two nights after we'd drilled. But no sign of Cyan. Not even a note.

His distance confused me, and it bothered me more than I liked to admit. It seemed like such an overblown reaction to my having an elevated heart rate after moving nonstop for over an hour. I couldn't help but wonder if that was the real issue or if it was something else.

I wished we could talk it out. I thought we were becoming friends, after all. And at the same time, I would never beg for attention from someone who yelled at me over what I couldn't control.

So I threw myself into my favorite hobby for the next three weeks, making some homemade wine. I hung out with

Bea, became acquainted with the other vampires of Blood 'til Dawn, and worked on becoming active at night.

Switching to a nocturnal schedule proved to be one hell of a pain in the ass. After some time, it seemed the best I could do was wake up between noon to one in the afternoon and go to bed around four in the morning.

My "mornings" were the quietest part of the day. Since the sun was at its highest, Bea and all the vampires were dead asleep. That was when I tinkered with my wine-making experiments.

Fortunately the human market had a good selection of fruit in their produce section, so I had plenty to play with. Grapes were the obvious choice for wine, but I also loved experimenting with citrus, berries, and other fruits. One of my biggest hits back at the compound had been a blackberry wine aged in an oak barrel for eighteen months.

I had thought about adding a barrel to my original supplies list for Cyan, but it wasn't so much a *need* as a *nice-to-have* and I didn't want to be too greedy. He'd been too generous to get me all the essentials anyway.

That morning, which was actually early afternoon, I paused to stare at his closed bedroom door like I always did. I hoped he pulled his head out of his ass and talked to me soon. I still needed a phone, and to find out when he'd take me back to Sapien to see Amy.

And as much as I hated to admit it, I kind of missed him.

I didn't dare let those feelings linger. Amy was my priority, not Cyan.

Despite having complete faith in Robin, I was worried about Amy. Robin couldn't be glued to her side all the time, and I wondered if the bullying had gotten worse without my being there to shield her. I needed to know if she was okay. Once we had phones, it would be so much easier to check on her.

It was jarring to find out that all the vampires in Blood 'til Dawn had phones. Almost all of the other humans and brusang I saw at the market had them too. While growing up, Amy and I had been told that personal phones were a luxury. No one in Sapien had one because we couldn't afford them. Not when we had to buy rice, lumber, fabric, work boots, fencing wire, animal feed, and everything else needed for survival.

I dragged myself away from staring at Cyan's door like a weirdo and headed for the great room.

Most of the cabinets in the huge kitchen were empty, considering vampires didn't need to store a bunch of food. Bea, as the only brusang residing here, claimed two cabinets and one shelf in the refrigerator for her cooking supplies and few eating needs. I stored most of my stuff in Cyan's place, and used the rest of the cabinet space for my wine-making experiments, most of which were in 1-gallon glass jars.

After helping myself to a cup of coffee from Bea's machine, which she always encouraged me to do, I set to checking on my creations.

The first one I checked, a standard red grape wine, I knew I had screwed up somewhere.

"Oh boy." I took a gravity reading and winced at the number. "I sure overpitched you, didn't I?" The batch would need more sugar and a secondary fermentation, otherwise it would taste entirely too dry.

My two other batches thankfully had normal readings, which meant they were ready to bottle and taste. I was dying to try them and see if I still had my touch, but first, I wanted to buy fresh grapes for the first batch.

I looked at the door heading out to the garage, feeling hesitant. It was two in the afternoon, which meant the vast majority of Sanguine was asleep. The market was open twenty-four hours to accommodate humans on all schedules, but I had never gone there myself before.

Come to think of it, I had never stepped foot outside of this compound without Bea at my side.

Come on, I pep-talked myself. *They've made it clear you're not a prisoner. It's a short walk and all you need are some grapes.* Sanguine was still a foreign territory to me, but the walk to the market was an easy, straight shot. There was no way I'd get lost.

Fighting the nervous flutters in my stomach, I put shoes on and headed outside. The moment I stepped into the sun, I had to stand and just let my skin soak up the golden light like bathwater.

It was *so* warm and felt heavenly on my face. I'd never been much of a sunshine addict like some people, but after three weeks of barely seeing it, I'd forgotten how much I missed those warm rays.

I started on my walk, feeling a little glum about my new life. Unless they took that drug, draitrium, vampires would never feel this energizing warmth. The sun was lethal to them, and I found that sad. I could definitely understand the temptation to try a drug to feel the sun for the first time. Or in the case of a brusang, the first time after years of darkness.

I wouldn't take sunlight for granted anymore. Now that I lived among vampires, these midday walks would probably become few and far between. I'd savor them when I could.

While enjoying each sunlit step, I made it to the market and bought my grapes without incident. On a whim, I also bought a few avocados that weren't quite ripe yet. I'd been craving guacamole for a while, which was also a luxury I rarely indulged in back in Sapien. But here, money seemed to be no object for the ruling vampire clan.

My mind was on the wine I'd be bottling soon, and the guacamole I'd be eating in a few days, when I left the market and turned the corner, nearly running straight into a man who came out of nowhere.

I shrieked and nearly dropped my shopping bag, which drew his attention from the sky toward me. The sight of his face sent my heart hammering and I backed up a step, thinking I should run back inside.

His eyes and skin had a sickly yellow appearance. There looked to be tear tracks down his cheeks but instead of water, it was a thicker, gooier substance. His skin and lips were also incredibly dry and blistered like he'd been sunburned. The man's mouth hung open and I saw the tips of fangs.

A vampire out in broad daylight could only mean one thing. This man was high out of his mind on drae.

He looked truly out of it, and so much worse than the guy trying to push on me and Bea at the restaurant. That vampire barely had a yellow tinge in his eyes compared to this man. He had control of speech and seemed cognizant of his surroundings. This poor vampire looked extremely sick and I couldn't begin to imagine what his state of mind was like.

I took another step back, trying to gauge him from a safer distance.

"Are you okay, sir?" I asked, against my better judgment.

His head cocked at the sound of my voice. He was

already facing my direction, but his eyes couldn't seem to focus on me.

"Beautiful sunny day," he mumbled, more to himself than me. "So beautiful, the sun."

I began side-stepping, making a wide circle around him. He followed the sound slowly, looking extremely unsteady on his feet. If it came to it, I could maybe outrun him.

"Blood," he said, his voice a dry rasp as he wiped the gunky tears from his face. "When did I last have any blood?"

He lifted his nose to the air and sniffed, and I walked faster in my attempt to get around him, my heart hammering.

"Can I have some blood?" He seemed to forget about me, talking to someone he couldn't see. "I need blood and… and drae. I'll pay you back, I swear."

His mutterings faded to nothing as I speedwalked back to the Blood 'til Dawn compound, constantly checking over my shoulder to make sure he wasn't following me. I didn't relax until I crossed the garage full of motorcycles, entered the great room and shut the door behind me.

I leaned against the door for a moment, catching my breath with my eyes closed. When I opened them, my heart sped up again for an entirely different reason.

Cyan sat on the central island, shirtless and in sweatpants, his bare feet swinging slightly as he sipped from a coffee mug.

"What are you doing up?"

"What happened to you?"

Our questions burst out at the same time, but he was quicker to act. Hopping down from the counter with feline grace, he strode over to me, took the shopping bag from my shoulder, and gently pulled me to a barstool with a hand wrapped around my arm.

"Are you hurt? You look like you saw a ghost." His nostrils flared, probably scenting me for a bleeding wound, as his fingertips ran from my shoulders to my wrists.

The closeness of him, and the circumstances of how we last spoke, made me painfully aware of my pulse thrumming through every blood vessel. Damn him for making me self-conscious of physical responses I had no control over.

"I'm okay," I said, forcing deep breaths to make my heartbeat slow down. "I saw another addict. Someone in really bad shape and it spooked me."

Cyan pulled away, crossed the kitchen to grab an empty glass, which he filled with water and set in front of me.

"Thank you." Damn him for being thoughtful. If even sweet.

"Tell me what happened. Where did you go?" Cyan crossed his arms over his bare chest, his tone leaving no room for argument.

"I needed more grapes for one of my wines, so I went to the market. On my way back there was this guy, a vampire out in the middle of the street in broad daylight."

Cyan's face fell. "Fuck. How did he look?"

I described the state I saw him in and Cyan looked more exhausted with each passing second. "That's the draitrium, right? The drug that other guy was trying to push."

"Yeah, that's it." Cyan blew out a long breath and scrubbed a hand down his face. "I know exactly who you're talking about, and I'm sorry you had to see that. His name is Pyke. The clan has tried to get him cleaned up multiple times. He's harmless as far as we can tell. Just gets stoned out of his mind and spends hours looking at the sky. We usually find him right after dusk, bawling his eyes out because the *beautiful sun* is gone."

"Oh, that's awful. That poor man."

Cyan shrugged and shook his head in a *what can you do?* motion. "We've done all we can for him. He's refused to tell us who he buys from but he's not violent, nor has he tried to sell to anyone else, so we just leave him be. It's sad, honestly."

"I'm sorry," I said. "It must be hard to watch people destroy themselves, knowing you've already tried everything to help."

He rubbed a hand over his head and heaved out a sigh. "You've got that right, Tavi."

I finished off my water, my brain scrambling to fill in the awkward silence. Should I just make an excuse to go? This was the most conversation we'd had in weeks, and Cyan definitely didn't intend to end up in the same room as me. He probably dreaded having to talk to me at all, especially since my *distracting* heart rate had been elevated when I walked in.

"I'll just um—"

"I owe you an apology."

We spoke at the same time, and then stared at each other.

"What?" I said.

Cyan sighed out a long breath, idly scratching the side of his chest where he'd made his vow to me. The scars were completely healed but still looked fresher than the right side.

"I shouldn't have yelled at you the other night when we were training." His hand dropped to his side. "I was frustrated, but not at you. My frustration was...misplaced, and I took it out on you, which was wrong. I'm sorry for how I acted, Octavia."

His use of my full first name was jarring. It felt wrong to not be Tavi to him.

"What were you so frustrated about, then?"

Cyan, also known as Cyanide, the smooth-talking negotiator of the ruling vampire clan, looked absolutely flustered.

"I...ah, huh." He smiled sheepishly, one fang poking his bottom lip. "You really don't know?"

I stared blankly. "No. You said it had nothing to do with me, so why would I?"

"Right, right." He rubbed his jaw, which was starting to grow a layer of stubble. "I—don't worry about it. It was just clan stuff that Thorne talked to me about."

"Oh. Okay." I didn't know what to make of that. Clan stuff was most likely none of my business.

"Anyway." Cyan turned his palms up. "I apologize and accept full responsibility for my actions. I'd love for you to accept my apology, but I understand if you don't."

I crossed my arms, thinking it over. "It wasn't even the yelling that bothered me. But you avoiding me for weeks was really confusing. I thought I had done something wrong. You were like, shunning me and that...that hurt, Cyan."

He winced. "I'm so sorry, Tavi. I'm not good at—" He stopped, swallowed, and tried again. "What I mean to say is I'm kind of, um..." He trailed off again and let out a wry laugh as he looked down at his lap. "I'm not a very good friend sometimes. I fuck up. I let people down." He glanced up at me, his gaze cold despite the warm red tone. "So if you don't want to be friends with me, I would understand."

"What are you talking about?" I asked. "You're friends with everybody in the clan. Everyone I know likes you."

"Rhain doesn't like me."

I snorted. "Rhain doesn't seem to like anybody."

Cyan smirked. "True enough." He set his coffee mug in his lap and stared at it for a few seconds. "I really am sorry, Tavi. I won't raise my voice at you again. And I'll do my best to not give you the cold shoulder, but I...I have some stuff to work out. Vampire-specific stuff that I can't really get into with a human. So if you ever feel like I'm avoiding you, just know that it's me, not you."

He looked and sounded genuine. I wanted to know more about this stuff he needed to work out, but some things needed to be kept private. If the yelling was a one-off, and he tried his best not to be distant, what was the harm in forgiveness? I truly did miss talking to him.

"Apology tentatively accepted," I said. "But I'd appreciate it if you gave me a heads-up before avoiding me for three weeks again."

He gave a small bob of his head and said, "I'll try, Tavi."

With that, I felt ready to bury the hatchet.

"So, is that Bea's coffee?" I gestured toward the mug he'd been drinking out of.

He grinned, actually humored this time. "I like coffee every once in a while. I know you humans drink it to wake up but it actually has a relaxing effect on me."

"How funny. What about alcohol?"

"Same effect as humans." He laughed. "We can actually get a buzz from drinking the blood of an intoxicated person. Doesn't happen often, since they can't really consent to that. But fun if you arrange it beforehand. On that note," he turned toward the cabinets where my fermenters were stashed, "how are your wine projects going?"

"Um." I played with a strand of my hair while figuring out how to answer. People were curious about my wine-making up until the point I started getting technical, which was when their eyes glazed over with boredom.

The process was methodical, full of measurements, and the intricacies required a basic understanding of chemistry. I geeked out about it, but the details were not interesting to most people. They just didn't know that until they asked me about it.

"Pretty good," was what I settled on. "One of them needs to sit for a couple more weeks, but the other two can be racked. I mean, they're ready to be siphoned out and bottled for drinking."

"That's great. Can I help?"

I gave him a long look. "You really want to?"

"Yeah, if I won't be in the way." His fang grazed his lower lip. "Consider my labor an active part of my apology."

"Okay." My breath hitched for some reason. "Sure."

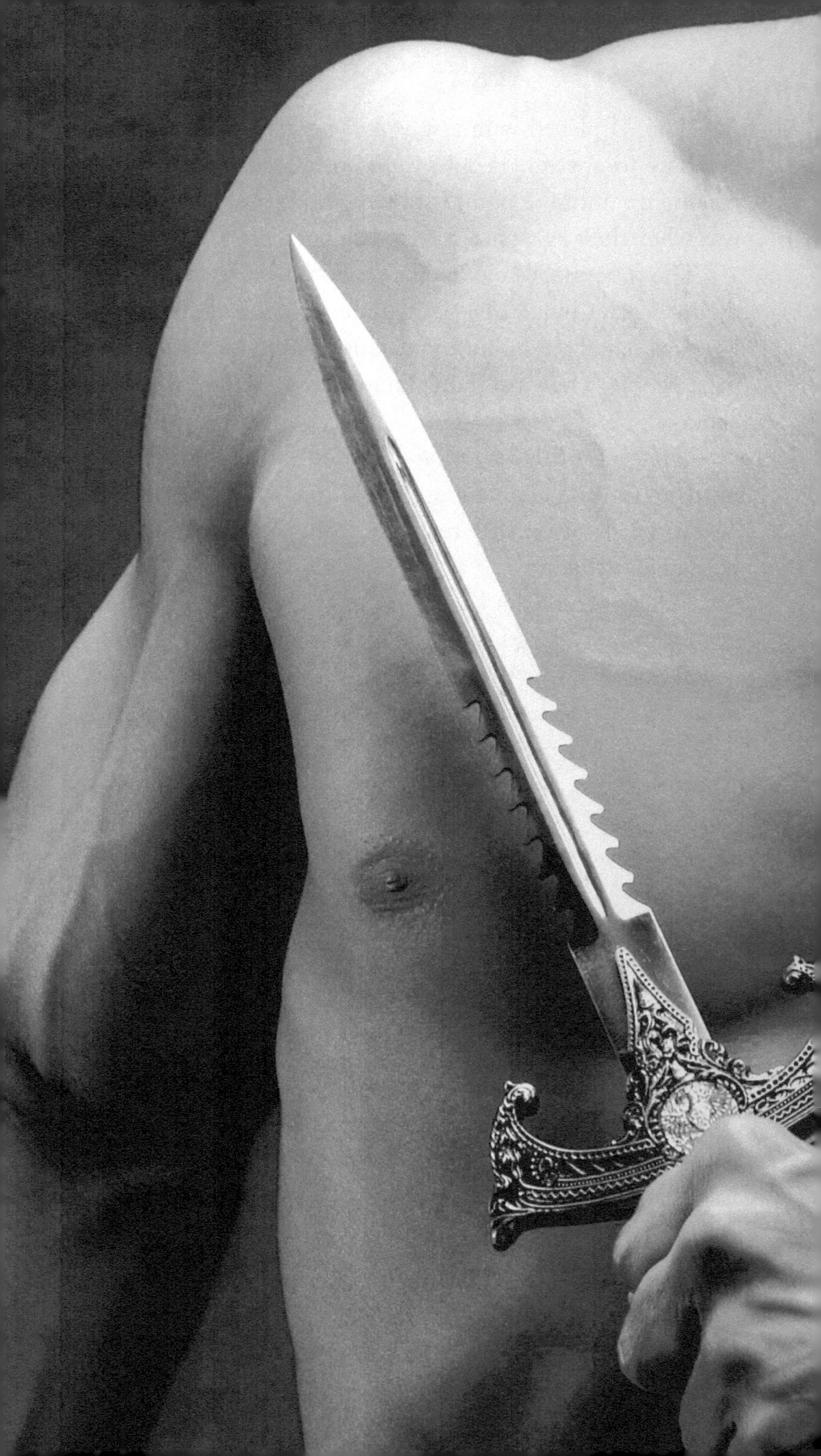

Chapter 12

Cyan

This was a mistake.

I'd done so well with avoiding Tavi for the last few weeks, and it turned out to be all for naught. My fangs throbbed with a dull ache the moment she entered the great room, the sensation running through my upper jaw to my brain. I swore there was a similar ache in my cock, although that could have been due to my recent dry spell.

There wasn't any particular reason for said dry spell, except that I was still feeling off since the night at Pulse Point. I wasn't sick exactly, but all the blood that I'd drank in the past few weeks had tasted wrong. From the blood bank to my favorite necks at the club, all sources turned my stomach a little. A guy had to eat, so I choked it down, but no one's blood really satiated me. I was getting to the point where I wasn't craving anything or anyone at all.

Except for Tavi. I'd never tasted her once and for some reason, my brain was fixated on her. Like her blood was the answer to everything. I knew the fixation would disappear the moment I did taste her, so while we talked in the kitchen, I considered it.

But I promised her, I *vowed* that I wouldn't. And right then, I was helping her rinse out a collection of empty wine bottles.

I didn't know the first thing about winemaking, but there was something fascinating about watching someone else do what they enjoyed. Tavi was in her element, and I could not keep my eyes off her as she held up a length of silicone tubing and a liquid sanitizer solution.

She explained some of the process to me as we worked, but I had a sense she was trying to dumb it down for me. There was a bashfulness about her, almost like she was embarrassed about how much she knew. Naturally, the only logical thing to do was keep her talking about it.

"What's that?" I nodded at the dark sludge sitting in the bottom of her fermentation jar as we siphoned out the wine.

"That," she bit her lip like she was trying not to laugh, "is a yeast cake."

"Doesn't look like a very appetizing cake."

The laugh burst out of her then. "No, it's not. It's the dead and dormant yeast after fermentation is done. I can either throw it away or use it to start another batch."

"Which will you do?" As one wine bottle filled, I swiftly moved the tube to another without spilling a drop.

"I'm not sure. Depends on how this tastes, I guess."

"The yeast affects the taste?"

"Oh yes," she said emphatically. "*Everything* affects the taste. How long it ferments, the ratio of yeast to sugar, the temperature, the quality of the grapes, how long it's mashed *before* it ferments—" She cut herself off abruptly, a blush darkening her cheeks. "Sorry. I get really nerdy about this stuff."

"Don't ever apologize." My voice roughened with the command. "I like seeing your passion."

Tavi's pupils blew wide, her blush spreading to her ears. Saliva filled my mouth and I jerked my gaze away. I had to get a hold of myself before the temptation of her blood literally had me drooling.

"What I mean is," I cleared my throat, "just the fact that you're so into this is what makes it interesting to me." I didn't know if that was any better, but it was the best I could come up with.

Tavi gave a slight smile, her attention returning to her jars. "Thanks. It's actually nice being able to talk with someone about it. Back home, most people didn't want to spend the time helping me, or my explanations just went over their heads. They sure liked drinking the end results though."

It irked me that she still thought of Sapien as "home," but I swallowed that down. "What about your friend? The one you said goodbye to before you left."

She paused, her head lifting to stare at a blank spot on the wall. "Amy um, she would help with bottling sometimes, like you are. But most of my batches were bigger, like five gallons, and it was just too much for her. She'd hang out with me while I racked or mashed but this isn't really her thing. If I talked, she'd listen, but it wasn't really a back and forth. She's more into knitting, quilting, that kind of thing, all of which I'm terrible at."

Tavi blinked tears away and her voice wavered with emotion as she spoke. I could sense her growing effort to keep her composure. This friend was deeply important, to the point of bringing this brave, resilient human nearly to tears in front of me. Being cast off by her own people didn't bring out this emotion, but talking about her friend did. And those tears spoke volumes.

"You miss her." I went to the sink to rinse out the tube and to give Tavi a moment that didn't feel like I was staring at her.

"Yeah." She sniffed and laughed a little. "You could say that. She's like a sister to me."

I opened my mouth to respond, then shut it so hard my teeth hurt. Without even thinking, I had been on the verge of telling her about Kalix. That he was a brother to me and I missed him as well. What the fuck was wrong with me? I hadn't spoken about him in twenty years.

What I had kept locked up tight in a vault had been about to spill out like an overflowing paper cup. Why did this human woman disarm me so much? Because she was adorable, tough, smart, and interesting? Because her pulse and scent had me salivating for her blood?

I hated that she made me want to be real and open with her. The last person who knew me at my core was Kalix, and he ended up nowhere good. Tavi didn't even realize she was doing it. It was bad enough that I just told her I was a fuck-up and a disappointment. It didn't seem to warn her away, and I hated the spark of hope alight in my chest as a result.

Instead of pouring my heart out like a miserable fucking sap, I brought two wine glasses down from an upper cabinet. "Shall we? It's ready, right?"

"Um, yeah. Sure." Tavi's smile brightened as if grateful for the distraction. "The moment of truth."

I pushed the wine bottle closer to her. "I'll let the expert do the honors."

She laughed again, pouring a few ounces of the dark red

wine into each glass with practiced efficiency. Its resemblance to blood was not lost on me. My fangs were pulsing so damn hard that a headache began to throb in my temples.

Tavi and I each held up a glass and paused.

"To friendship," I said.

"To friendship," she agreed with a small nod. "Both new and old."

We each took a sip, and I swore the flavor that hit my tongue soothed the aching pain in my fangs for the few moments it was in my mouth.

"Holy shit." I took another, larger swallow. "Tavi, this is really fucking good."

I expected the wine to be something decent and drinkable, but I was hit with pure, genuine awe. Tavi didn't just know how to make wine, she was fucking masterful at it.

"Not bad." She was less enthusiastic, taking another dainty sip and squinting in concentration as she held it in her mouth. "A little more tart than I wanted, but I should have expected that. The grapes weren't quite ripe enough, but I didn't want to risk waiting too long and having them over-ripen."

"Whatever. This is the best wine I've ever tasted." I drained my glass and helped myself to another.

She laughed as I poured. "It's nice of you to say that, but you don't have to flatter me."

"I'm not. You should absolutely sell this in the human market. I bet vampire bars would love it too. They wouldn't even have to mix it with blood. More?" I held out the bottle to her and she nodded, allowing me to fill her glass.

"I want to tweak some things first, but I'll think about it." She took another small sip, the liquid beginning to stain her pink lips a dark, sultry red.

My fangs went back to throbbing, and now the ache in

my cock was undeniable. I wanted to drink the wine from Tavi's lips, taste her delicious creation mixed with the taste of her. Not even her blood, but the taste of her kiss.

And if I pricked her lip with a fang, would she like it? I knew how to feed without causing pain. The thought of her blood mixing with her wine, with *her,* why did it sound like the perfect cocktail? A trinity of flavors that would feed and sustain me like nothing else could.

I drew my gaze up to find Tavi staring at me. Did she catch me fantasizing about her mouth?

"I wanted to ask you something, Cyan." She seemed nervous again, and set her wine down.

"Shoot." I took another drink, savoring the wine while waiting for her question with bated breath.

"Do you know when I'd be able to visit Sapien?" She laced her fingers together and then pulled them apart. "I'd really like to see Amy soon, if that's okay."

"How about next week? I'll have the night off Tuesday." I set my wine on the counter. "You'll want to stay overday, right? I'll just need to find a spot nearby to crash during that time, but I have friends out in that direction. Shouldn't be a problem."

The joy lighting up her smile and eyes was something I wanted to see all the fucking time. My need to see her happiness was only slightly stronger than the ache for her blood.

"Really? Oh, that's perfect! That would be amazing, Cyan. Thank you."

"Sure. Also it's completely slipped my mind, but I'll get you two phones before then. That way, you can give one to Amy when you visit."

A stab of guilt pierced me. If I'd been taking proper care

of my blood pet like I should have, I would have gotten her a phone when she first arrived. Instead, I'd been avoiding her.

"Are you sure?" She twirled the stem of her wine glass. "You've done so much for me already."

Had I, really? It felt like I'd barely done anything except neglect her. She'd been thrown into this place full of people who were not her species, and what had I done to make the transition easier? Buy her a few tubes and glass bottles while letting her crash at my place?

"It's no issue, Tavi." I savored her nickname like I had her wine. "You miss your friend. It's the least I can do, actually."

The next thing she did was beyond anything I expected. She moved slowly enough that my senses could track it, I just didn't comprehend any of it. Tavi came close to me, reached her arms around my neck, and hugged me.

It was light at first. Tentative. Then she squeezed around my shoulders in earnest.

"Thank you," she whispered.

I remembered too late that I didn't have a shirt on. She was touching me, and fuck, she was warm. Soft. Her breath ghosted over my cheek. I hugged around her waist without thought, pulling her in with gentle pressure. It was wholly unfair that her back curved at just the right angle so that my arms fit comfortably around her.

Her neck was so close too. I could turn my face and my lips would make contact with that delicate, fluttering pulse. Her blood called to me like a siren's song, desperate to break past that soft skin and flow over my tongue. She must not have known how much she was flirting with danger, how fucking hard my jaw clenched to keep myself from ripping into her like a beast.

When I couldn't stand it anymore, on the knife edge of breaking my vow to her, I forced myself away.

Tavi's hold around my shoulders broke abruptly as I stepped out of her embrace, my hands on her shoulders so she wouldn't do something crazy like hug me again.

"I'm happy to help," I told her with a strained smile. "I should probably try to get some sleep before night falls. Thank you for the wine, it really is incredible and you're very talented. I'll get the phones for you tonight. See you later, Tavi."

My feet were moving before the words finished rushing out of my mouth like a waterfall. I couldn't bring myself to look at Tavi's face as I spoke. The risk was too high that I would kiss her, and then *really* taste her.

The aching in my fangs and cock didn't cease when I got to my bedroom. I already knew sleep would not be happening so I turned on the shower, keeping the water cold. When I stripped and stepped under the freezing spray, it barely chased away the heat roaring through me.

My erection would not deflate no matter how much I tried to ignore it and give in to the cold. When I took myself in hand and stroked to ease the ache, my eyelids fell shut with a groan.

None of my usual fantasies came to mind. No memories of past hookups or wild escapades of blood and hedonism had my hips canting into the air, thrusting through my fist while freezing water pelted my shoulders and chest.

No, it was the face of a human woman with reddish-brown hair, a shy smile, and stormy eyes that had me panting and jerking myself faster, desperate for relief.

My teeth gnashed together as I approached the peak, jaws clenching painfully. The chilly, humid air of the shower was a poor substitute for a mouthful of rich, delicious blood. That was the only thing missing, aside from the human woman herself. I needed to be latched at her throat, needed that dark wine from her vein filling my mouth while I filled her.

And when my release shot through my hard flesh, and Tavi's name left my mouth as I painted the shower walls with cum, only then did I realize how fucked I really was.

Chapter 13

Tavia

The next day, I found two brand new cell phones outside my bedroom door along with a brief note.

TAVI,

ENJOY. BEA WILL SHOW YOU HOW TO SET THESE UP. —C

I saved the note and stashed it in my room with the other one he'd left with the key. For some reason, I felt sentimental about his notes and often unfolded them to reread them before I went to sleep. During those weeks we didn't speak, it felt like I held onto a part of him with these notes. A small, private piece of him that was just for me.

I would trace the indent of the words, imagining his hand moving across the page, or sometimes his lips moving with the words as he wrote them. I thought of his fingers and the firm grip he'd held on the pen.

The same fingers that skimmed over my back when he'd hugged me, and that had gripped my shoulders as he stepped away.

His reaction had been such an about-face that my head was still spinning. Before I hugged him, we'd been having a good time. He seemed genuinely impressed with my wine and eager to talk about it with me. No one, not even Amy, had shown half as much interest and curiosity as he had. I had been on cloud nine just over the fact that someone had *wanted* to hear me geek out just because it was something I loved.

When he set a date for me to visit Amy, my happiness overflowed so much that I didn't know what to do with it. I hugged him, and that seemed to ruin everything. He'd said a quick goodbye and ran off like I had the plague.

I was still new to vampire culture, so maybe they didn't touch to show affection or gratitude. He'd probably hugged me back to be nice but the whole experience might have been really strange to him. If I ever actually saw him before we made the trip to Sapien, I'd make sure to apologize.

Part of me hoped his number would have already been in my new phone, so I could just text him an apology, but no such luck.

Three more days passed, and I got the sense that he was avoiding me again. We were supposed to ride out to Sapien the following night, and I hadn't seen him once since that day in the kitchen.

This time, there was no question in my mind that I had done something wrong. He apologized, we were getting along, I hugged him, and now we were strangers again. It was exhausting. I wished he'd just tell me if I was breaking some vampire taboo. Surely that would be better than days of silent treatment.

But on the bright side, I had plenty of wine and freshly ripened avocados to make guacamole with.

A few vampires were hanging around the great room when I entered around seven in the evening, although Cyan was not among them.

"Hey, Tavia." Desmond and Laith sat across from each other at the kitchen island, two wine glasses in front of them and an empty bottle between them. "We didn't mean to finish the whole bottle, but...you're making more of this, right?"

It was my last bottle, but I couldn't bring myself to feel even a tiny bit mad. I felt like a chef who had spent hours cooking a gourmet meal, and everyone I'd served it to had licked their plates clean and asked for seconds. That empty bottle was the highest compliment. Words of praise could never touch the hope in their eyes as they waited for my answer.

"Sure. Twist my arm, why don'tcha." I grinned as I pulled out a cutting board. "But you'll have to wait at least three weeks."

"We live for over eight-hundred years. We're a patient species." Des pulled the bottle toward himself and turned it upward to get the last few drops.

"Hey, don't be greedy." Laith swiped it from him and turned away to drink.

"Fuck you. You poured the biggest glass for yourself."

I chuckled at their antics as I began halving avocados for my highly-anticipated guacamole. They were like an adorable, always-bickering married couple.

Several vampires came and went through the great room as I focused on chopping my ingredients. Rhain and

Thorne never stopped as they walked through, but gave me quick nods of greeting as they headed to the garage. I wasn't sure where Bea was, so I texted her letting her know there would be plenty of guac if she wanted some.

My instincts prickled just as I finished dicing red onions, and I knew before I even looked up that Cyan had walked in. I nearly dropped my knife when I saw who he entered the room with.

Cyan had his arm around a stunningly beautiful woman who was definitely not human. She was tall, nearly the same height as him, with shiny black hair loosely braided over one shoulder. Her eyes weren't red, but a fiery orange with slitted pupils. There also appeared to be scales shimmering on various parts of her body. I almost thought it was makeup, but the scales would disappear and reappear on different areas of skin. Her presence also seemed to heat up the room by a few degrees, like she had some kind of internal space heater. Or fire inside her.

Bea had told me about dragon shifters, including that a few lived in Sanguine, but this was my first time seeing one in person. I didn't know how to picture one when she'd said they were inhumanly beautiful with reptilian eyes, and even in human form, would let their dragon shift come through just enough to show off their scales.

This woman put the human super models I'd seen in magazines to shame. Every vampire turned to look at her, and I knew I was staring too. Just being in the same room with her made me feel like a lesser being. And the fact that Cyan had his arm around her, his smile cocky at all the attention, made me feel even worse.

He didn't even look at me, just led the dragon woman to one of the couches across the room and invited her to sit down, which she did.

I forced my gaze down to my cutting board, trying to figure out why this was affecting me so much. Cyan had told me he didn't want to settle down with anyone. I knew this, objectively. He was doing us both a favor, not forcing the blood pet commitment on me or himself. And not limiting himself to one source of blood must have also meant by extension, not limiting himself to one sexual partner.

I just never expected him to flaunt his partner right in front of me. It had to be considered disrespectful, right? I was still his blood pet, under his protection even if he took no blood from me.

Ignoring him was like trying to ignore a blaring siren. I heard his laugh across the room, the sound of his voice and hers, though I couldn't make out the words.

A presence came up beside me, but I didn't dare look up on the chance that my eyes would fill with tears.

"You alright, Tavia?" It was Desmond checking on me. So the awkwardness wasn't all in my head, but obvious to everyone else. Great.

"Mm-hm." If I used actual words, my voice might choke.

Laith came up to my other side, blocking my view of Cyan and the dragon woman. "It's dickish, what he's doing," the other vampire muttered. "Even if your relationship is platonic, you don't bring someone new to the clan home for everyone to see. It's just messy and fucked up."

"He's looking this way." Desmond sounded amused. "Mind if we stick close to you, Tavi?" He said my nickname loud enough for Cyan to hear. "Cy's looking tense. I daresay he might be jealous."

"Doubt it," I muttered, still focused on my chopping.

"But sure." Honestly, it was nice to have two vampires in my corner when Cyan clearly wasn't.

"Oh, he's fuming." Desmond laughed louder, his head bent toward me like I had made a joke. "Can I tuck your hair behind your ear? I think it'll make his head explode."

That actually made me chuckle a little. "Sure."

"I can feel his eyes like fucking daggers in my back." Laith leaned his forearm on the counter, slouching his upper body to become eye level with me. "So what human food are you making, Tavi? Smells...interesting."

"It's—ow, fuck!"

Desmond had chosen then to touch me, and the graze of his fingers on my ear made me startle. At the same time, I'd been pitting one of the firmer avocados and the knife slipped, the blade sinking into the thumb of my opposite hand.

Blood immediately welled at the cut, and I barely had time to consider the two vampires hovering over me when chaos erupted.

There was hissing, snarling, and commotion all around that was too fast for me to track. Desmond flew backwards, his back slamming into the refrigerator across the kitchen. I turned to see Laith getting up from the floor, like someone had knocked him down. He was all the way in the middle of the great room, closer to the couches than the counter where we'd been standing.

The same couches where the dragon shifter woman sat wide-eyed, but Cyan wasn't with her.

"Tavi." His low voice sounded rough, if even pained. And so close. "Tavi, you're hurt."

Gentle hands directed me to turn around, and there he was. Cyan was shaking and breathing harshly like he was running a marathon. His fangs were the longest I'd ever seen them, and he looked not just pained, but tormented. Tortured.

"Let me see."

Faster than I could comprehend, he grabbed my hands and pulled them apart. The cut I'd been applying pressure to continued to bleed, dripping over my wrist, palm, and onto the floor.

Cyan's grip on my hand became crushing as he hissed a deep inhale through his nose. *"Fuck."*

I was actively bleeding, my hand throbbing in pain, not to mention shocked and confused, and I still couldn't ignore the sexual moan in Cyan's voice as he said that word.

He brought my injured hand to his mouth and dragged his tongue along the trail of my blood. "Oh, *fuck,*" he said again, the curse sensual and reverent.

I almost said the same curse myself. His tongue was a hot caress on my skin, bringing a flush of heat to every part of my body and an aching need between my legs. He continued licking the spilled blood on my wrist and palm, and every stroke of his tongue might as well had been against my clit. My breaths grew shorter, tension and sensitivity winding up in every muscle as this vampire held my hand and licked the blood from my wound.

My confusion only heightened, but that didn't diminish that I was more turned on than I'd ever been in my life. What was happening? Cyan looked like he was in a trance, or drugged. His eyelids were heavy, dark eyelashes fanning over his cheekbones as he turned my hand over, his incredibly soft mouth trapping every drop of blood that escaped my cut.

He reached the wound itself and sucked, sealing his lips over the cut in my skin. The pressure of his mouth drew a moan out of me, along with a full body shiver. I'd never felt anything so, *so* good. If his tongue on my skin started me toward an orgasm, he would get me there in no time now. Each draw of my blood into his mouth hit my clit with a stroke of pressure, the same sweet ache coiling in me tighter and tighter.

And he moaned against my skin as if answering me, as if this made him feel just as good as I did.

"Cyan..." I wanted him to hold me, maybe lie me down or press me against something, because I felt like I was floating away. I needed solidness and purchase, something to hold onto.

His soft, hooded gaze lifted at the sound of my voice. He looked at me as if I were lying in bed next to him, warm and sensual. I felt the flick of his tongue against the wound on my thumb and thrashed at the sensitivity coursing through me. When his mouth pulled away, I wanted to cry out at the abrupt loss of pleasure.

"Tavi." My name came out a low moan as his hand cupped the back of my head.

And when his mouth crashed down to mine, my whole world exploded into new sensations.

The heat and pressure of his lips were intoxicating, an addictive fountain I wanted to sip on for eternity. His tongue swiped across mine and I tasted the coppery tang of my own blood. It didn't bother me, but instead reminded me of the intense pleasure I felt from his drinking it.

This kiss sent pleasure through me in a similar, but different way. I understood it now, how sexual pleasure and blood-drinking were so intertwined. Cyan's fangs added a hard pressure and thrill to the kiss, even though he never cut me. I trusted that he wouldn't, trusted him to hold me here with his kiss and his embrace rather than let me float away.

When the kiss broke, the first thing I noticed was my

thumb. The cut was sealed shut with only a small red line remaining.

"You...healed it." I felt drunk and woozy from that kiss and his brief feeding. My pulse pounded in every sensitive spot in my body and I still buzzed with a need for release. If it felt like that from a tiny cut, how would it be if he actually bit and drank from my neck?

I didn't even mind that Cyan had drank from me when he vowed not to, not when it felt *that* good.

"I'm...sorry."

Cyan's expression was unreadable. He looked angry but also in pain. His chest heaved with harsh breaths, fists clenched at his sides, and he wouldn't look me in the eye.

"Don't apologize, you healed my cut. And I'm not mad that you drank my blood. It actually..."

With each passing second, it became increasingly clear that mentioning how much I enjoyed it would be the wrong thing to say. Cyan's grimace deepened, like every word I said was a silver knife digging deeper into him.

"Cyan, is something wrong?" I went toward him, because no one else was doing anything.

"Don't!" The word was a harsh command, stopping me dead in my tracks.

He then left, running down the staircase leading to the lower level.

As I felt everyone's eyes on me, the vampires in the room and the dragon shifter woman Cyan had left on the couch, confusion wasn't the only thing swirling inside me.

I was humiliated.

Chapter 14

Tavia

Three stiff raps came to my bedroom door early the next evening. As much as I would have loved to keep hiding in the cocoon of my bed, I dragged myself up to answer.

Cyan stood across the threshold, his face a cold, impassive mask. "We leave in an hour. I'll meet you in the garage then." Immediately, he turned to leave.

"Wait, what?"

He paused with his back still turned to me. "We're going to Sapien to visit your friend. Unless you've changed your mind?"

"Oh. No, I haven't. I'll be ready." After the weirdness of last night and this mean robot-Cyan now, I needed my best friend more than ever.

"Good." He started for the door, and I felt my chance for answers slipping away.

"Cyan!"

He stopped stiffly, still not looking at me. "Yes?"

I held onto the doorjamb, feeling crushed under his

coldness. "Is there...can we talk about what happened last night?"

"I would rather not."

The words stung like a slap. He wanted to pretend like none of it happened? He broke his vow to me by taking my blood. Not that I cared, but that had to be important to him, right? Plus there was that giant elephant in the room of him kissing me. I was embarrassingly aroused the whole time but I *knew* I didn't instigate that.

The suite's door opened and I called out in a rush, "You can't keep pretending I don't exist, Cyan! This isn't fucking fair."

The door slammed shut, and I softly closed my own door, wondering how I'd survive riding with him all the way to my former home.

"Twenty-four hours."

That was all Cyan said to me as he pulled up in front of the outer gate of Sapien, let me off his motorcycle, and sped off with a roar. He was so pissed off at me, he couldn't even speak full sentences.

I turned to face the settlement which had been my home since birth, but didn't feel welcoming in the slightest. Amy and Robin were the only ones I wanted to see. No one else sleeping in those quiet cabins and mobile homes cared if I was dead or alive.

It was well into evening now, but I knew Amy would still be awake, probably with her nose in a bodice-ripper paperback. Moving quietly between the homes, I knocked on the door of the single-wide that Amy and I used to share.

There was dim lamplight in the window, and I heard someone stirring right after I knocked.

The door swung open and there stood my bestie in her cotton shorts and the giant, threadbare men's T-shirt that she slept in. Her hair was mussed on one side, like she'd been lying down, and her open-mouthed stare at me was so dramatic that I wanted to burst out laughing.

"Tavia?!" she whisper-yelled, wide eyes scanning me up and down. "Holy shit, what are you doing here? Did you escape?"

I chuckled softly at that. "Hey, Ames. No, just stopping for a visit."

She looked bewildered, like she couldn't tell if I was kidding. I had to remember that from her perspective, I was a sacrifice. A blood meal for the monstrous species who ruled the world we lived in. She might have even mourned me over the past few weeks, believing I didn't live long after Cyan took me away.

"How are you alive? How long can you stay?" Her eyes welled with tears, bottom lip trembling.

"It's a bit of a story, and only for a day." I spread my arms. "Gonna invite in your sister from another mister or what?"

Amy rushed at me with a bright peal of laughter. She was so small that I could pick her up and carry her inside, which was exactly what happened.

The inside of the trailer didn't change much. My side had been largely untouched, the bed still made with one of Amy's knitted blankets thrown over the top. I didn't keep many things in my space, but what little I did have was still there. My clothes still hung on the rack that served as my closet, and the few books I had, science fiction primarily, remained in a neat stack in the cubby of my nightstand.

Amy's side was messy, but in an endearing, cozy way. She had blankets, pillows, romance paperbacks, and unfinished knitting projects piled everywhere. She also loved bright cheery colors—pinks, creams, mint green, and mustard yellow, while my side was more neutral. The blanket on my bed was my favorite that she'd made, a foresty green with small details of red.

"So, what have they done to you for the past few weeks?" Amy pulled me to her bed to sit with her, inspecting me closely. "You look good, healthy even."

"Yeah, I haven't been fed from at all, actually." *With the exception of last night,* I thought, rubbing the base of my thumb where I'd cut myself. The wound was completely healed now, with barely a scar.

"At all?" Amy repeated. "I thought that was the whole point of giving you to them."

"Turns out, it's more complex than that," I said.

"Well, explain." Amy crossed her legs in front of her, settling in for a story.

"A blood pet is significant to vampires, it actually implies a commitment. The protector, the—" I wracked my brain for the word Cyan had used—"the verakt, is responsible for the blood pet's care and well-being. And he's expected to not feed from anyone else."

Amy's eyes narrowed. "So it's kind of like a marriage?"

"No!" I protested loudly. "It's totally normal for the relationship to be platonic, that's what Cyan and I are. We've been becoming friends, kind of."

"And he hasn't fed from you at all?"

"Well..." I couldn't lie, not to Amy. "I cut my finger the other night and he licked a little bit of my blood when he closed the wound, but not like *actual* feeding."

I decided not to mention the kiss or how immensely

turned on I had been, as that would unravel the whole platonic angle. Plus I was still too confused by Cyan's behavior to call us anything but platonic at this point.

"Why not?"

"Cyan didn't actually want a blood pet. I'm guessing none of his clan did, because they drew straws and he got the short one. So he ended up with me."

"Why didn't he want you?" Amy leaned forward, hugging a pillow in her lap. "Scared of commitment?"

"I don't know about scared, but yeah, he said he likes having a variety of blood sources."

"I *knew* it!" Amy pumped a fist victoriously. "He's a rake."

"A what?"

"A manwhore, basically." She held up a paperback and waved it in my face. "Forced into an arranged marriage, but still clinging to his rakeish ways. How long until he realizes his bride is his perfect match after all?"

"Shut up," I groaned. "My life is not a romance novel."

Amy cackled at my reaction. "You have to admit, it sounds like the start of one."

"Well, it's not. The little taste he did get of my blood must have been horrible because he's been all pissed off at me since last night." My mouth slammed shut. Fuck. I must have wanted to get that off my chest more than I realized. At least I didn't mention the kiss, although that too was now a burning weight on my chest.

Amy's expression sobered. "Oh, I'm sorry, Tav. Were you starting to, you know, like him?"

"No, not like that." I shoved back the memory of hugging him, the sensation of his bare skin, and the utter euphoria of his kiss. "We were becoming friends, like I said.

It was his idea to let me come visit, and he got me a bunch of winemaking supplies. Also these."

I swung forward the backpack I'd been carrying and pulled out the two cell phones that Bea helped me to activate. "One is yours. So we can keep in touch."

"Phones?" She took one of the slim black devices and held it as carefully as if it were a gold bar. "Wow, a personal phone! Your vampires must be rich."

"Keep it hidden when you're not using it," I said. "Use the outlet in Robin's place to charge it."

I had already recorded my number into her phone and sent her a text right then and there. She startled when the device buzzed in her hand and I laughed, showing her how to type out a reply on the screen's keyboard.

"I'm *texting*!" Amy laughed in delight as she spammed me with multiple emojis. "This is amazing, it's like passing notes."

"Call or text me any time you can," I said. "Just make sure no one sees you. Any time of night is fine. I'm becoming more nocturnal these days."

She nodded, slipping the phone and charging cord under the pile of pillows on her bed. "So, you're doing okay over there? You're not locked in a dungeon with a bunch of vampires gnashing their teeth at you?"

"No." I laughed. "It's nothing like that. It's...good, actually. I have a friend, a woman named Bea. She's actually a brusang, not a vampire." I quickly explained the difference to Amy. "She's been helping me adjust. They have a market where humans can buy food. Humans can also earn money in exchange for blood at the blood bank, which is totally safe and regulated. The vampires are actually pretty nice. I mean, most of them ignore me, but a couple have been friendly. They're fans of my wine, it seems."

Amy snorted. "Who *isn't* a fan of your wine?"

I grinned. "They drank it all like a bunch of frat boys, but I'll save a bottle for you on my next visit." I grabbed a pillow, hugging it as I relaxed onto my side. "How's everything been here? Same old bullshit?"

She knew I was asking if others were still bullying her or giving her too much work to do. To my relief, she said, "No one's been messing with me much lately. Something else caught everyone's interest a couple days ago."

"Well, don't keep me in suspense, Ames." I nudged her with my foot. "What happened?"

"Someone stumbled in from the human world." Amy chewed her lip.

"Really?" My eyes widened. A human accidentally finding their way to our world wasn't unheard of, but it was rare. "Where are they now?"

"That poor thing," Amy sighed. "They're keeping her in the council room because she kept trying to run. She wants to go home but is completely disoriented on which direction to go. She keeps running straight for the Heart of Sanguine. We would've escorted her to the closest human-world border, but someone let it slip that vampires rule this world. She doesn't believe it, but the council are still worried that she could be a liability if she makes it home and starts telling everyone. So they're kind of...holding her and figuring out what to do."

"Wow," I snorted. "Typical council." Magic was blocked in the human world, to the point where vampires, shifters, and witches were only in folk tales and legends. Even if the woman made it home and ranted about vampires enough so that some people listened, the odds of them finding their way into our world were minuscule.

"Yeah, Robin's going to appeal to the council tomorrow.

The woman should be welcomed in the community and free to make her own choices, not treated like a criminal."

"Have you met her?"

"Yeah, I bring her clothes, blankets, and food. She was really upset and confused, at first. But now I think she's accepting that she won't go home any time soon."

"That's too bad. I wonder if the vampires can help at all."

"Help?" Amy scoffed. "You mean help her leave and lose a potential blood source? Yeah, right."

"I mean, they're just people, Amy." My defensiveness surprised even me. "I'm sure some will love to hear about a human stumbling in their territory with no hope of escape, but they're not all predators. Everyone in Blood 'til Dawn wants humans to be treated well, and I'm sure that would include returning them home."

"If that were true, we wouldn't have to sacrifice one of us every fifty years," Amy said softly. "If they cared so much, they would just let us go to the human world, where they don't exist and we'd be among our own kind." She slouched against the headboard, hugging the pillow to her chest. "But I guess we've been here so long, the human world wouldn't feel like home anyway."

I couldn't bring myself to say it out loud, but sitting here with her no longer felt like home to me either. I'd been gone less than a month and while I missed *her*, I found no comfort in what used to be our shared space. Already I was craving the big, comfortable bed in Cyan's spare bedroom, the spacious kitchen in the great room where I could make my wine, and learning about vampire culture on my friend-dates with Bea.

And I hated how much I missed being on a motorcycle, wrapped around a vampire who now hated my guts.

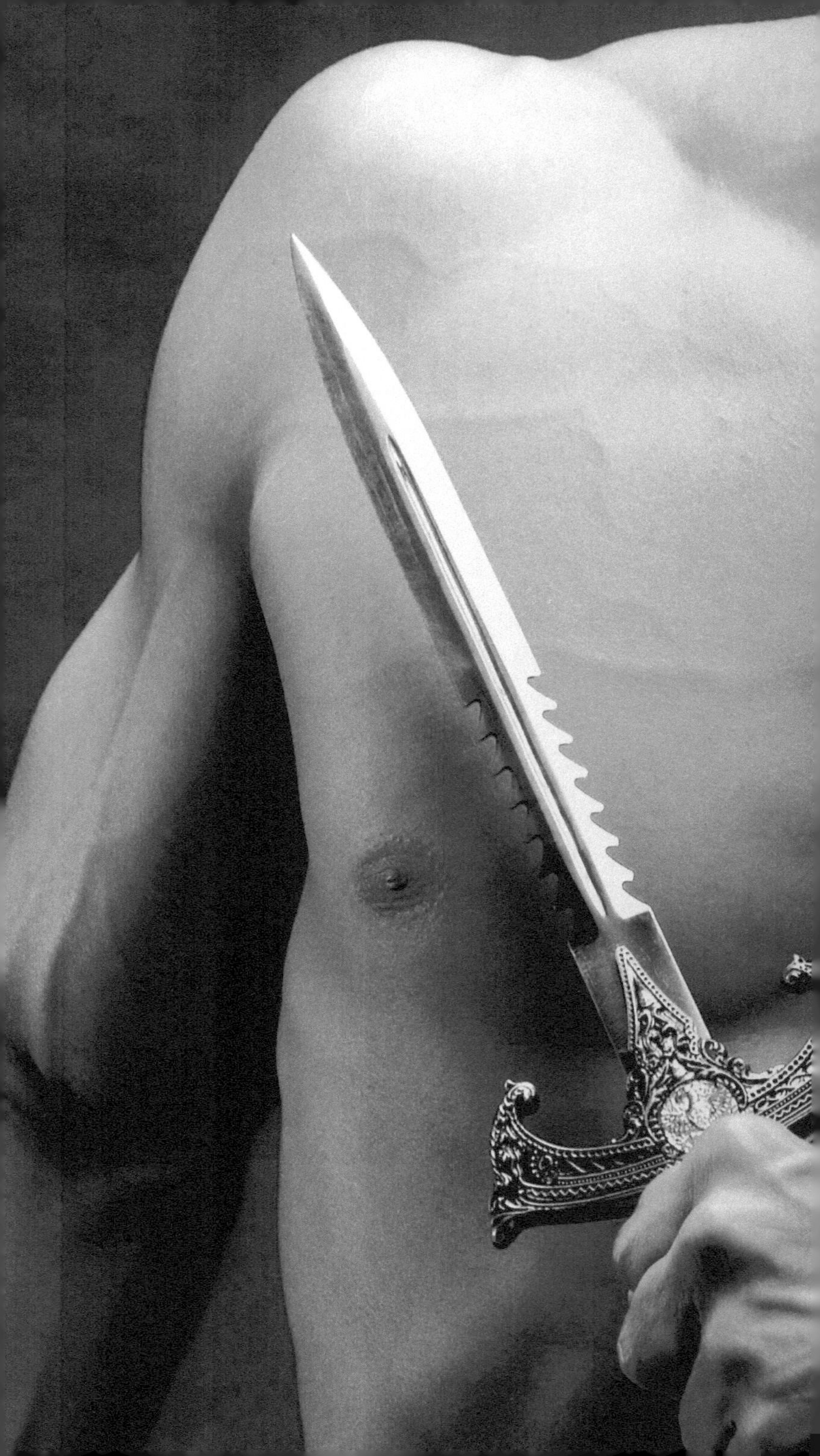

Chapter 15

Cyan

I was so beyond fucked.

Tavi was my blood mate.

I had my suspicions that this was happening when I first met her, but had given it no real thought. The odds, while not impossible, were slimmer than slim. No betting man in his right mind would have taken a chance on this.

But then I tasted her blood and that confirmed it. She tasted better than anything I'd ever had in my life. Her blood was everything my body had been craving because it was chemically perfect for me and me alone.

Everything made sense now, why her pulse and scent had affected me so much. Why all other blood sources had started to lose their appeal. My senses knew on a cellular level what I had been too blind to see.

Drinking any other blood would be nearly impossible now. Since the moment hers hit my tongue, my body would reject any other source. My life as I knew it was over.

I wanted to hate Tavi for this, but she had no control over it either. Fuck, even if she had the power and foresight to orchestrate this, I could never bring myself to hate that adorable, brave little human.

That didn't make this situation any less fucked up or unwelcome.

After dropping her off in front of the human settlement, I headed straight for the neighboring vampire village, Marrowtown. These vampires, called marrowers, were a different sort, and as clearly indicated by the name of the place, they preferred feeding on bone marrow to blood. And I hoped that very substance would help me in my current situation, at least temporarily.

I parked my motorcycle next to a building so small that it could have been an outhouse. While many vampire homes and businesses were mostly underground, the marrowers took it to a whole other level. This little outhouse building was the only above-ground marker of the town. Easy to blink and miss it.

I opened the building's door and proceeded down the narrow stone steps, taking care to not slip on the smooth, well-worn stone. Some believed the marrowers were the oldest clan of vampires, and that may have been true. Some lineages could be traced back to splitting off from the early ancestors of humans over a hundred thousand years ago.

Lively chatter began to echo up the stone walls as I descended deeper into the earth. Darkness gave way to flickering warm firelight. While the marrowers had access to electricity and modern comforts like the rest of us, they preferred a more rustic lifestyle. The air grew warm from torches lining the walls, the old-fashioned ones with an actual flame lighting the end of a stick covered in tar.

The door at the bottom of the staircase was warped and had seen better days, the brass handle polished smooth from the thousands of hands that had touched it over the centuries. I let myself through and the dark, empty underground exploded into a loud, lively dining room.

"What have we here?" The marrower behind the bar grinned, looking sinister with his prominent lower fangs. "A topsider burrowing with the voles?"

The room burst into raucous laughter, all twenty or so occupants turned to look at me from their various tables. The sound echoed against the stone walls and ceilings, bouncing around the room with no escape except for the two tunnels at the far side of the room and the door I just came through.

"Yeah, get a good look at this hot shit," I joked on my way to a barstool. "I'll be the best-looking fucker any of you will see for the next century."

There were chuckles and clapbacks that rose up from the crowd, but nothing truly malicious. Marrowers loved to talk shit about those of us who lived above ground, but it was all in good fun.

"What an honor this is," said the barkeep as I settled across from him, his tone only mildly sarcastic. "What brings you down here, topsoil twat?"

Even in the sour mood I was in, I couldn't hold back my snort. "That's a creative one. You been thinking on it all year, Drace?"

"Only about a month or so."

"Keep telling yourself that, groundhog. Maybe you'll get inspired next time you pop up to see if there's six weeks of winter left."

Drace laughed, leaning on his forearms. He looked like a typical marrower, big and muscular with greyish skin, a large square jaw, and fangs that were bigger on the lower row of teeth than the upper. Apparently, his subspecies had evolved in such a way in order to crush bones and suck the marrow out.

Not that they didn't feed on blood as well, but bone marrow was what they depended on, and was the center of their culture and way of life.

"Seriously, Cy. You look like shit." Drace blinked, his massive pupils like two black holes pulling me in. Marrowers had red irises like us, but they looked like thin red circles with how their giant pupils always stared into one's soul. Probably something to do with how little light there was underground.

"I feel like it," I admitted.

I didn't see Drace often, but I'd consider him a friend nonetheless. As strange as they seemed to some, marrowers thrived on community. They helped each other out, and generally weren't a judgmental bunch. And right then I needed to get some shit off my chest that I wasn't ready to tell the others in my clan.

"Need marrow?" Drace was already grabbing a clean mortar and pestle to work with.

"Please."

"Any special requests?"

"Just the good shit. The best you have."

The big marrower chuckled as he pulled open a slim drawer with an array of spongey bone marrow laid out on a parchment sheet. "I never serve anything less."

I watched in silence as he worked, first crushing the dried marrow with the mortar and pestle, then adding various ingredients as he continued grinding it down into a powder. He splashed in some liquid that made the marrow hiss and bubble, then added what looked like a packet of dried spices, and then a drizzle of some kind of oil. The last thing he did was transfer the marrow mash to a cast-iron pot, which he held over the open flame of a torch for a few minutes.

When he plated up and set the marrow dish in front of me, it looked similar to the mushy breakfast food Tavi sometimes ate when she first woke up. She called it oatmeal.

Tavi, the reason I was here eating bone marrow at all.

I picked up a spoon and brought the smallest possible taste to my mouth. Bracing myself as I swallowed, I waited for violent stomach spasms or my throat closing up, any physical sign of rejection from my body.

But none came. The marrow mash actually tasted good, rich and smooth with a light gritty texture. With a sigh of relief, I spooned a bigger portion into my mouth.

"Good?" Drace grunted, watching with his massive arms crossed.

"You know it is. Thank you for this."

"Sure." He kept watching me eat. "You have some bad blood or something? Gotta flush out from having one of those sunlight junkies?"

"No, worse." I finished my meal first, letting the clean spoon clatter to the stoneware bowl before I sat back and met my concerned friend's gaze. "I'm pretty sure I just found my blood mate."

Drace's brows shot up, his face splitting into a grin. "Are you fucking with me, topsoil?"

"I wish I was."

He barked out a laugh and would have doubled over if the bar wasn't in front of him. "So you're telling me..." He pulled in a breath, started laughing again, then tried once more. "You're telling me you're down here eating marrow to sustain yourself instead of feeding from the one person who's blood chemistry perfectly matches your unique biological needs? Do I have that right?"

"It's more fucking complicated than that but, yeah," I huffed. "I can't feed from her. And now I can't feed from anyone else without wanting to vomit my organs up. So I gotta live on marrow like you fuckers."

"Ah, poor little topsider." Drace finally stopped laughing, leaning in closer to speak more quietly. "I hate to tell you this, but marrow won't sustain you forever. Even among my folk, once a blood mate pairing is found, nothing else satisfies."

"Oh, great." I propped my elbows on the bar and slapped my hands to my face. "I'm extra fucked now, fantastic."

Drace laughed as he straightened. "What are you bitching about, Cyan? Finding your blood mate is a rare and joyous thing. You celebrate it topside too, do you not?"

"We do," I admitted begrudgingly. "And I might've been happier about it in another fifty, maybe hundred years. But I'm not ready to be tied down to one person yet."

"You don't always have that choice."

"Well, I should! Some days I feel like tasting dragon shifter. Other days, a brusang. If I'm feeling vanilla, maybe a human. I should be able to choose who I fuck and feed from, Temkra damn it."

Drace did not look impressed. His arms were crossed again with one eyebrow arched. "And what is so bad about the blood mate you've found yourself with?"

"Nothing."

The word left my mouth before a response had fully processed in my head, because it was the simplest, purest truth. There was absolutely nothing wrong with Tavi. She was the bravest human I'd ever met, sweet with a bite of fire in her, passionate, and beautiful. When I impulsively kissed her, she tasted like the first full breath of fresh air I'd ever had.

She was perfect in so many ways. Which was exactly why I could not have her as my blood mate.

"So, what's the problem?" Drace pressed.

I couldn't think of a way to articulate my thoughts except to say, "Well, she's human, for one."

Drace made a disapproving noise. "So your mate will be near the end of her life, or dead before you feel ready to commit?"

"That's not what I'm saying. She's not the problem, it's me."

"So quit being a fucking problem."

"Marrowers," I groaned, rubbing my eyes. "You all have stones for brains, I swear."

"And you topsiders have done so damn well for yourselves, squabbling over territory and power, that you overcomplicate everything and forget what's important," Drace snarled. "A blood mate is a blessing, one that many don't find in our very long lifetimes. You literally need *her* blood to keep living, so why fight it? Are you gonna waste away, starving yourself while sticking your cock in others because you didn't get to choose *when* you were ready?"

Not many things could truly piss off a marrower, but Drace was getting close. His nostrils flared and he'd begun to pace behind the bar, eyes narrowing as he ranted at me.

He had a point, sure, but there was so much he didn't know. Our clan business never caught much wind underground, so he had no idea about what happened with Kalix, how badly I'd failed him and Blood 'til Dawn. Of all the people who deserved a long, happy life with a loving blood mate at their side, I wasn't even on the list.

"Thanks for the marrow," I repeated, realizing that I

had begun to wear out my welcome. "I'll take another portion to-go. And I'm staying overday, so I'll buy a room if you've got an empty one."

Drace's posture softened just a fraction. "Stay and drink, topsoil. I have beer from that angel brewery. Would hate for you to miss out."

Now it was my turn to raise a skeptical eyebrow. "Don't tell me you dug a tunnel to the angel territory."

"I didn't. My ancestors did at some point." He grinned proudly. "Wouldn't surprise me if we have tunnels going into all the territories, even the forbidden ones. Your border magic doesn't reach this far underground."

"Well, if you're offering." I shrugged. "Might as well."

"Don't tell any of your clan mates about this." Drace procured the bottle with a flourish and started to pour. "I don't need to be strung up by my tusks for having contraband."

"More likely, they'll be knocking down your door for a taste." I brought the small glass of golden, bubbly liquid to my nose. "Do you have a contact with the winged assholes or did you steal this?"

"I've already told you too much." Drace smirked. "Enjoy it for what it is and don't ask so many questions."

"Fair enough." I touched my glass to his. "Thank you for this once-in-a-lifetime opportunity of sampling angel-made contraband."

The marrower grinned. "And it's still not as rare as finding your blood mate."

"Oh, fuck all the way off."

Drace laughed uproariously and poured us more to drink.

Chapter 16

Tavia

"You want to meet our guest?" Amy's voice was full of mirth as we got ready the next morning. "She's feisty. Reminds me of you actually."

"Sure. You were planning on seeing her this morning?" I pulled a brush through my hair and yawned.

We'd been up most of the night talking, and I only caught a few hours of sleep in the early morning. Back at the vampire compound, I would have slept well into the afternoon. Here, I fell back into my human habits and had risen with the sun.

"It's Robin's turn to bring her breakfast this morning, but I like to tag along and give her some company."

"What's her name again? I'm borrowing a shirt, by the way."

"Heather. And sure, help yourself."

"I can't wait to see Robin, too."

"She's gonna flip her shit when she sees you." Amy went quiet. "We never thought we'd see you again. It sounds dumb now but we even had a little memorial for you. We thought…"

"Hey." I pulled her into a hug. "I know. I thought I was a goner too. But the vampires aren't so bad, actually. I might get to visit regularly. Maybe you can even visit me."

Amy pulled away with a cringe. "Visit a vampire clan? That'll be like a lamb hanging out with a pack of wolves, won't it?"

"It's not like that. Everyone's very respectful." Although to be honest, I couldn't be sure. People didn't mess with me because I was Cyan's blood pet. Would Amy be as safe if a vampire didn't have a similar claim on her?

"Whatever you're comfortable with," I tacked on. "Ready to go?"

"Yeah. You hungry?" She led the way out of the trailer and locked up behind us.

"Starving," I admitted. "The market over there has a deli that makes amazing breakfast burritos, but sometimes you want something classic like pancakes, you know? I've been there a few times and have yet to see a basic box of pancake mix on the shelf."

Amy was quiet for a while as we walked. She kept facing forward, ignoring the looks of disdain from others we passed by. Some eyebrows raised and whispers were exchanged when they saw that I was in fact alive and well. I met the eyes of anyone who dared to keep looking, an open challenge to come mess with us. No one held my gaze. Bullies were cowards at their core, after all.

"So they're good to you over there, huh?" she asked.

"Yeah, I would say so."

"Makes you wonder if we're really so much better off here," Amy muttered. "Cut off from the rest of the territory in the name of freedom and independence. But are we, really? Free and independent, that is."

Hope fluttered in my chest, but it was quickly weighed

down by reality. I wanted to say the words, to offer her a way out of Sapien. Cyan would let her come home with me, he would have to. Amy and I would be together, and she'd be safer that way.

But bullying and mob mentality didn't just exist in humans. Vampires were just as likely to push her around because she struggled with some things. Leaving Sapien wouldn't necessarily mean a better life for her, but I would be able to protect her better.

My unspoken thoughts swirled as we caught up to Robin on her way to the council building, carrying a stack of sealed food containers. I called her name and waved, making the poor woman nearly drop her load when she saw me.

"Tavia?" she said in a gasp, her eyes welling with tears. "Holy shit, is it really you?"

"Really me, back for a quick visit. I'm only staying until tonight." I rested my elbow on Amy's shoulder. "I crashed at the short stack's place last night, otherwise I would have come said hello sooner."

"Well, holy hell, you're the last person I expected to see." Robin's eyes scanned over me quickly. "You look well."

"She says the vampires actually treat humans well." Amy's eyes went from me to Robin, making me wonder if they had been talking about leaving Sapien before.

"You'll have to tell me all about it." Robin smiled, and I realized it had been years since I saw genuine joy on her face. "Did Amy tell you about the stray we found?" She angled her head toward the council building.

"Yeah, I wanted to meet her actually." The three of us started in that direction, Robin leading the way.

"She's scared," the older woman said with a look of sympathy. "I actually just got done with talking to Nancy and she agreed to let her out. Keeping her locked up won't help her trust us. We'll prepare a trailer for her to stay in, but what she does from here is her choice."

"Glad old Nancy came to her senses," I muttered.

Amy and Robin both shot me harsh looks. Amy even make a tsking noise, which I ignored. I stopped respecting the elders years ago. And I wasn't part of the community anymore, so there was no point in even pretending to kiss their asses.

The double doors of the council building were held together with a chain and padlock. They were swung outward slightly, as if someone had been pushing against them from inside. A spark of anger ignited in me. The same people who imprisoned this woman allowed my best friend to be mistreated and abused. They would have sent Amy to die if I hadn't stepped in.

I would've tried to run away too.

I held the food containers while Robin unlocked the doors, pulling the chain through the handles and discarding it to the side. Amy walked through first, the warmest and most non-threatening of all of us.

"Hello?" she called out. "It's just us, Heather. We've brought you breakfast and the doors won't be locked anymore."

A bright blonde head popped out from behind one of the desks. Her hair was tangled and her blue eyes were wide. "I can leave?"

"At your own risk," Robin said in her mom-voice. "I highly suggest you stay here, at least until you get your strength up. It looks like you haven't been eating." She nodded at containers of food on a side table next to the door.

"Like I'm going to eat anything you psychos give me," Heather hissed.

I popped the lid on one of the containers in my arms, the smell of cheese, spices, and warm scrambled egg making my stomach growl. "Robin, you got a fork?"

She handed me the utensil from her back pocket, and I used it to cut into the omelet. The blonde's eyes went even wider as steam rose up from the cooked interior. Breakfast potatoes, mushrooms, and cheese spilled out, and I stabbed a generous forkful in my mouth, moaning as I chewed.

If she didn't want it, fine. I was fucking hungry.

"The council are a bunch of assholes, but Maureen sure as hell knows her way around a kitchen." I shoved more omelet into my mouth, thinking I should probably steal Amy *and* the head cook away to Blood 'til Dawn's compound.

"Who the hell are you?" Heather was almost visibly drooling as she watched me eat.

"I'm Octavia. I was actually sacrificed to the vampires by this lovely community about a month ago."

"Ugh, *again* with the vampires," she groaned. "I don't know how they got you people so brainwashed, but it's really concerning."

I waved my fork at her, her eyes following the scrambled egg and potato speared on the tines. "Come out and eat, and we'll talk. Whether or not you believe is up to you."

"Obviously I don't believe." Heather came out from behind the desk slowly, her stomach growling as her gaze fixated on the food in my hands.

I set the container and fork on the floor in the middle of the room and backed away. "A vampire is coming tonight to take me back to their compound. You'll be able to see one with your own eyes."

"Sure." That was all she said before she pounced on the

omelet, inhaling ravenously. She'd forgone the fork entirely and picked the whole thing up to eat like an eggy burrito.

We gave her water and allowed her time to eat as Robin, Amy, and I settled into nearby chairs

"You must know, on some level, that you're in another world," Robin began gently when all the food was gone. "It feels different here, doesn't it? The air pressure, atmosphere, whatever you want to call it. One thing I notice when I go to the human world is the distinct lack of magic in the air."

Heather snorted dismissively before taking another gulp of water. "Sure, okay."

"You felt something the moment you crossed the border into this world," I said. "Everyone experiences it differently, but it's a sensation passing over your skin. It could feel like spiderwebs or a cool mist."

"Convenient," Heather drawled, "that it feels like something you would totally expect to feel while on a hike out in the woods."

"How would you explain that you can't find your way back home?" Amy added. "You retraced your steps, went back the same way you came, and that sensation of passing through never happened again. You kept walking, but never found the trail familiar to you. How do you explain something like that without magic?"

Heather gave her a hard stare. "Are you kidding me? It's called getting fucking lost."

"You don't have to be rude," I snapped. Even with a frightened, hungry stranger, I'd always come to Amy's defense. "This is hard to understand if you're not from here, we get that. We're trying to prepare you in the event that you never return home."

"Why, because you'll kill me?"

"No. Because if you didn't grow up here, the borders

between our worlds aren't perceptible to you," Robin said. "You haven't lived *in* the magic, so how is the magic supposed to reveal another world to you? You're more likely to wander around meeting all the supernatural species before finding your way back home."

"Supernatural species, the fuck?" Heather muttered.

"Oh yeah," I told her cheerfully. "It's not just vampires. The werewolves have their own territory. As do dragon shifters and angels."

She stared at me, blinked, and let out a scoff. "You cannot be serious."

"We are," Amy said. "And there are humans who live in the supernatural territories. Humans who have lived among the supernaturals their whole lives."

"This is crazy. You're all fucking crazy." Heather rubbed her temples.

"You say that, and yet you know exactly what we're talking about," I pointed out. "You know what a vampire and a werewolf are. How is that possible?"

"Because they're in scary stories and shit," Heather cried out, exasperated. "They're in books, movies, TV shows. They're fucking Halloween costumes. Doesn't mean they're real."

"How did they become stories?" I pressed. "How did those legends and folk tales originate? I've read that every major civilization in the human world has their own mythologies about dragons, or dragon-like creatures, despite those cultures never having been in contact with each other in ancient times. How do you think that's possible?"

"I don't know!" Heather's brow furrowed in the silence that followed. She was starting to think about it, starting to see the possibility.

Robin grabbed a piece of chalk from an end table drawer and sat cross-legged on the floor in front of Heather. It reminded me of when Amy and I were kids, and Robin would teach us math problems with chalk and colorful pebbles.

"We can't prove it, but our theory is, our world and the human world overlap a little. Kind of like a venn diagram." Robin drew two circles on the floor with chalk, overlapping them in the middle with a small sliver. She wrote HW for human world inside one circle and SW for our world, which most called Shyftworld.

"We're somewhere around here." Robin drew a small X in the SW circle close to the overlapped sliver. "But sometimes there are shifts." With a finger, she erased the overlapping silvers of the two circles and re-drew them, making the overlapped portions slightly smaller. "Most people believe the human and supernatural worlds were far more over-lapped thousands of years ago. Practically on top of each other." She drew two more circles off to the side, making their shared area much bigger. "It's possible that thousands of years ago, crossing between worlds happened far more frequently than it does now. That's how everyone knows about dragons and vampires, yet they supposedly don't exist in your world today.

"Also, nobody lives in neat little circles." Robin tapped her finger on her drawings. "So what we're probably looking at is more like this." Her arm went wide over the floor, her chalk making a large, random shape with both wavy and sharp edges. She completed the shape with a single closed line, then made a second, equally random polygon slightly overlapped the first one. "You get what I'm saying?"

Heather had been staring intently at the drawings, then

shook her head as soon as Robin posed the question. "You're fucking nuts, lady. Alternate worlds aren't real, no matter what your cult leader tells you."

"Alright, well." Robin gave her a patient, motherly smile. "Enjoy your breakfast. If you'd like to stay, we'll prepare a place for you. You'll be expected to work some kind of skilled trade to contribute to the community. Farming or construction would be ideal, but if you don't have those kinds of skills, come find me. I'll find something for you to do. Otherwise," Robin stood from the floor, brushing chalk dust off her pants, "Best of luck to you, Heather."

She headed for the double doors with Amy and me on her heels. The doors stayed open, the locking chain piled in a heap on the ground.

"You weren't kidding." I rested my arm on Amy's shoulder. "She's a feisty one. I just hope she's not too reckless."

"She's scared," Robin said, sympathy crossing her features. "She's one of those who lashes out when she's cornered." Her eyes narrowed in my direction. "Just like someone else I know."

I stuck my tongue out. "Only to assholes who deserve it."

Robin grumbled something that sounded like reluctant agreement to me.

"Do you think Maureen will make pancakes if we ask nicely?" Amy piped up, bringing her arm around my waist. "I think someone's got a craving."

"Couldn't tell ya. She'll probably ask for some blackberry mead as a bribe."

"Done," I said quickly. "Cyan got me a bunch of equipment and I've done a few batches of wine already. I'll start on Maureen's mead as soon as I get back."

"Well." Robin looked at me with muted surprise on her face. "Sounds like you've got it good over there."

"Yeah," I answered quietly. "I guess I do."

Chapter 17

Taria

The day passed by too quickly. Before I knew it, the sun slipped below the horizon and I stood next to the road outside Sapien, waiting for the roar of an approaching motorcycle.

"I'll text you as soon as I get home." Amy and I had been attached at the hip all day, and while she waited with me for Cyan, I crushed her in another hug.

"Home, huh?" Amy grumbled against my shoulder.

I had no response, and didn't even realize I had said it. Sapien had never been a home to me, not really. Had I really found *home*, and everything that word encompassed, among the vampires?

"You better text me every day," Amy warned, squeezing around my waist.

"You better count on it, short stack." I shook my head clear of the meanings of home, resting my cheek on top of her head as I'd done since we were children.

Amy was quiet for a few moments while we held each other. "I wish you didn't have to go," she whispered.

I hugged her a little tighter. "You could come with me."

Her head shook, her hair tickling my nose. "I can't live with the vampires. I'm not strong like you."

"Shut up." I pulled back to look at her straight in the face. "Are they leaving you alone?"

She shrugged and tilted her head from side to side. "More or less."

"Amy." Her name left my mouth in a low hiss. "You don't have to deal with this shit. You don't have to come with me, but you *can* leave. Go to the human world if you don't want to be among the vampires."

"If I don't stay, people will starve," she argued. "No one will take proper care of the animals. No one else will make big batches of soup in the winter when sickness is going around. People could die, Tavi, and it'll be my fault."

"So?" I was too pissed off to be surprised at the vitriol in my own voice. "It wouldn't be your fault, because their lazy, entitled asses shouldn't put all that on you, anyway. And even if it was your fault, they were going to cast you off to the vampires anyway. Fuck them, Ames."

She kept shaking her head, hearing my words but not really listening. "I can't do that, I don't have it in me. I can't just say, *fuck you all* and walk away. This place is all I have."

"You have me," I reminded her.

"You left."

"I'm *right* here!"

"And I'm so fucking thankful for that, you have no idea." She forced a smile, which she was always better at than me. "But you're not really with Sapien anymore, are you? You've never been happy here. I'm not really surprised that you jumped at the chance to leave."

"What the hell, Amy?" I took a few steps back. "I volunteered to go for *you*. Everyone thought being the blood pet was certain death. I saw it as giving my life for yours. I didn't know I'd be basically moving into a new community."

"I never asked you to go in my place. In fact, I didn't want you to. I was devastated that you made that decision for me. I was scared as hell, but I was willing to make that sacrifice because my fellow humans asked me to. If it kept our kind safe for fifty years, I was willing to do it."

Now it was me shaking my head at her. "Humans are not better than vampires, Ames. You would've been discarded by people who didn't give a shit about you. Chances are, the vampires would treat you a lot better than our own kind have."

"I guess we'll never know." A strange coldness entered her voice. "Because you threw yourself on the gauntlet in my place."

A sigh deflated my chest. "I love you, Amy. I just wish you loved yourself as much as you loved these ungrateful assholes."

"I love you too, Tav." She turned to look at the settlement behind us. "I just don't see it that way. It's more important to me that humanity lives on, that our culture is preserved for future generations. Especially in a world of supernaturals who live ten times longer than we do. If I can contribute to preserving our future, that will have more impact than my own, individual wants. If I abandon our people, then I'm contributing to the erasure of humans."

My lips pressed together in a thin line, fighting the urge to argue. Amy was repeating the same mantra that the council drummed into us since we were old enough to remember. As if humans were some precious, dying out species. There were seven billion of them in the human world. A small handful of them stumbled into Shyftworld every decade or so. Humans weren't going anywhere. And the individual was just as important as the collective. *She* was important to me. Everyone else could fuck off.

A few moments of tense silence passed before I heard the telltale rumbling of a motorcycle. A single headlight floated down the road, growing larger as it raced toward us.

"Your arranged husband arrives," Amy cracked with a smirk. Just like that, we were done arguing.

"Shut up," I grumbled back, trying to ignore the onslaught of nerves.

After a full twenty-four hours apart, I didn't know what to expect from Cyan. Would he continue to ice me out? Or be the warm, flirtatious friend? The stress of not knowing what side of him I'd get sat like a brick in my stomach.

Approaching footsteps had me turning to see Robin and Heather approaching from the settlement.

"You've decided to stay," I observed.

Heather looked much better than she had that morning, with washed and brushed hair, a clean set of clothes on, and a refreshed, hydrated glow to her skin.

She shrugged and the gesture looked like she was trying too hard to be casual. "How could I miss an opportunity to see a real-life vampire?"

Robin smiled at her overly sarcastic tone before approaching me for a hug. "Don't be a stranger, now."

"We'll chat when Amy and I get on the phone," I said, returning her embrace. Quieter, into her shoulder, I whispered, "Thanks for taking care of her for me."

Robin patted my shoulder in response and then released me just as Cyan pulled up. Before I could think any better of it, I decided to make introductions.

"Hey Cyan. I don't think you were able to meet everyone before," I said over the motorcycle. "This is Amy,

Robin, and Heather. Everyone, this is Cyan of Blood 'til Dawn."

"Good evening, ladies." Cyan dipped his head and flashed a quick, polite smile, which was enough to catch a glimpse of his fangs.

"Uh, hi." Amy blinked in wide-eyed fascination.

All vampires were interesting to look at. The differences between them and humans were subtle, but noticeable enough that most people couldn't help themselves. They had a dark ethereal quality that drew one's curiosity.

But Cyan was an especially fine feast for the eyes. Those red eyes, prominent cheekbones, and full lips were on full display in the dim security lights. His long legs straddled the machine under him, hands wrapped around the grips in full, calm control, torso leaning forward slightly. Even though he was relaxed, friendly, he looked like a predator in wait.

I glanced at Heather, whose wide-eyed stare was one of utter disbelief. Her mouth hung open in shock. She didn't start arguing about red contacts or fake fangs because she knew on a deep, instinctual level that Cyan was not human.

Maybe vampires had been feeding on humans since we were little more than primates because our instincts always knew before our eyes and cognitive abilities did. There was something in our DNA that threw up a big CAUTION sign whenever they were around. And you couldn't explain away your deepest animal instincts with hoaxes and brainwashing.

"I've heard a lot about you, Amy. It's good to finally meet you." Cyan's eyes flicked to me before returning to her. "As a friend of Tavi's, you'll be welcome any time at our compound. I understand how hard it is for two close friends to be apart."

Did my ears play tricks on me or did his voice choke a little on that last sentence? Was he talking about Kalix? Also, why was he being so friendly when he'd been so cold to me earlier?

"Oh, um. That's very nice of you to offer." Amy's smile at him was tense. "I'll definitely consider it. Thank you for the phone as well."

"It's my pleasure." Cyan's ruby gaze returned to me and settled there. "Are you ready?"

I nodded and gave one more hug to Amy and Robin, then a wave to Heather, before climbing on behind him.

Cyan's whole body stiffened as I wrapped around him, like my touch was the last thing he wanted to feel. I'd bet anything he'd go right back to freezing me out the moment we were alone.

And I was right. Two long hours later, we pulled into the Blood 'til Dawn garage where he parked, shut off the bike, and waited for me to dismount without a word. Once we both got off, he hurried toward the door leading into the great room. I knew he'd go right back to avoiding me the moment he had the chance, so I called out before he could head inside.

"Cy, wait."

He flinched like the sound of my voice in the echoey garage pained him, but he did stop. "Yeah?"

I tried to swallow the massive lump in my throat, hating that he was facing away, refusing to look at me.

"I'm really sorry if I did anything to piss you off. I feel like I did some massive vampire taboo without realizing it. If this is because of the hug or the..." I couldn't bring myself to say the word *kiss*, not when I was already grasping to find a shred of the connection we'd had before any of that happened.

"You didn't do anything wrong, Tavi." His voice was rough, still facing the door.

Hearing him say that made me immensely relieved but also confused. If that was true, then why the cold shoulder?

"I'm sorry you ended up with me," he went on. "Whenever you're ready, I'll release you from being my blood pet. Just say the word and it'll be done."

The words felt like a slap. "What? Cy."

This time, he did ignore me and went inside.

I realized two things the moment that door closed. One, I was desperate to find out the real reason why he didn't want me as a blood pet. Why he insisted on not blaming me, but continued to push me away so cruelly. I thought he was open to being friends, but now he couldn't even look at me.

Two, I realized with bone deep certainty that I *wanted* to be his blood pet. I wanted to give him my blood, to nourish and sustain him in that way. Ever since he drank from that wound on my hand, it felt like a hidden part of me had unlocked. My blood could do good things for him. *I* could be good for him.

And I wanted to feel that way again. I wanted the pleasure and connection that felt both magical and tangible at the same time. I wanted to feel him ground me before I floated away. And it wasn't even about all the physical sensations. I wanted his smiles and jokes, the warmth and respect in his voice. I wanted the care he displayed when he offered to let Amy and I see each other, and I wanted the fierce vampire warrior who sent that drug dealer running with his tail between his legs.

I was not sorry at all that I ended up with Cyan of Blood 'til Dawn. And I would make sure that he knew that.

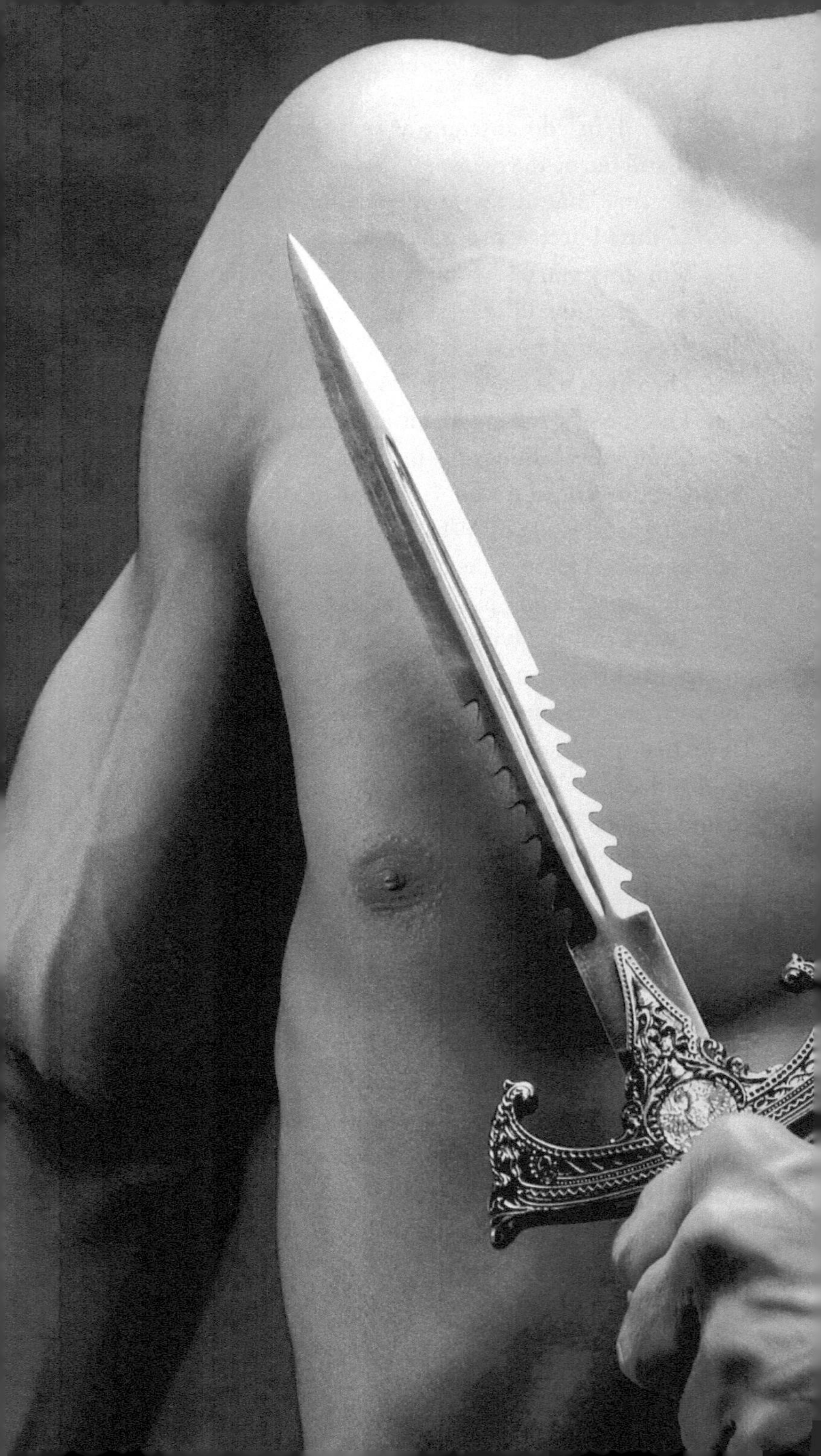

Chapter 18

Cyan

The night after returning from Sapien with Tavi, I had a patrol shift with Thorne, which didn't usually happen. His partner was usually Rhain, and now that Kalix was gone, I was usually paired up with Des or Laith.

Maybe I should have been honored working with our clan leader, but instead I felt like I was put under a microscope.

Part of me wondered if this pairing was by happenstance or design, but I knew better than to voice my questions about it.

We rode to the Crown, the northernmost point of Sanguine. After becoming the ruling clan, Blood 'til Dawn had to seize this region forcefully from the remnants of its previous inhabitants, a clan called Rathka's Order.

Those vampires were something else. Not only did they eat humans alive, but they had begun cannibalizing each other about a century ago. No one truly knew why, though there were speculations of a virus that had eaten through the rational parts of their brain and made them do unnatural things.

Rathka's Order had been doing a decent job of eradicating themselves by the time we stepped in, but there was still a hell of bloody battle. My first real one, about fifteen years ago. The last dozen or so infected members had scattered into the surrounding mountains and forests. Our best hope was that the werewolves had taken care of them for us, but their whereabouts remained a big question mark.

Only one member of Rathka's Order appeared to retain his wits and did not succumb to the cannibalism that ravaged his family. He actually lived near us, right off the Cap in the Heart of Sanguine. Close enough to keep an eye on, just how we liked him. He didn't seem interested in reclaiming the Crown region for himself.

Hence why we continued to patrol the ancestral home of Rathka's Order, in case any of them chose to return and eat the new residents that had moved in. The Crown was popular with dragon shifters due to the cliffs and mountains in the region, but humans and smaller clans of vampires had also moved.

This was a much quieter area of Sanguine with large plots of land for each family. Buildings and roads were made of weathered stone and brick. Only the windows were modernized with light-proof shutters to keep the sun out. Aside from that, the Crown looked like a quaint mountain village from a children's fairytale.

Away from the hustle and bustle of the Cap, I heard crickets and frogs when we cut our bike engines and patrolled the village center on foot.

"How's it going with the new blood pet?" Thorne lit up a darakt cigarette, getting straight to the point.

"Alright."

I felt his eyes on the side of my face, but didn't return his gaze. Tavi would not occupy my thoughts tonight. I had a job to do, and kept my focus sweeping across the street ahead for any sudden movement. At least, that was what I kept telling myself.

"Really?" he mused, red smoke leaving his mouth in an exhale. "Is that why I smelled marrow on you the other night?"

I kept my face and posture neutral, but my fists clenched inside my jacket pockets. Why was it any of his fucking business, anyway? "Was just feeling under the weather. Wanted a little pick-me-up, that's all."

"Is that right." He phrased it like a statement, not a question.

"What about you, boss? Find a new blood pet to play with?" My teeth clenched as soon as the words were out. Just like that, I'd let him know he had gotten under my skin.

Thorne let out a dry laugh, flicking the ash of his cigarette. "Nah. I got enough responsibilities as it is. The last one sure taught me that."

"You mean the angel you had?"

Thorne's expression turned to stone. Only the red smoke drifting out of his nostrils made any movement around his face. "Watch it, pup. Don't go digging for what doesn't concern you."

I held up my hands defensively. "Hey, you brought up blood pets. Not me."

"And I won't make the same mistake again," he huffed, picking up his stride so that I had to hustle to catch up with him.

There had been a rumor going around a few years back

that Thorne had an angel as a secret blood pet hidden some-where away from the compound. Considering angels were one of the species we were forbidden to have contact with, due to their alliance with the werewolves, having one as a blood pet could have ruined everything for us as ruling clan. The dragons could cut off all business with us, and other clans would incite a civil war for a lesser offense.

But Thorne never said a word about it, and neither did his inner circle. Truth be told, Thorne never said much about his own personal history. He was considered young for a clan leader, in the upper three-hundreds. But many older members, Kalix and Rhain included, looked to him faithfully as a leader.

And Kalix's judgment was one that I always trusted, even when I didn't feel like I knew Thorne on a personal level. Maybe that was the issue.

"I didn't mean any disrespect," I said hastily once my stride matched his. "I just...I've been in the clan my whole life, always with you leading us." I took a deep breath, bracing myself for saying his name out loud for the first time in twenty years. "Kalix always trusted you, believed you would lead us to ruling clan one day. And I always looked up to him. So what I'm saying is, I've never had the chance to know you like he did."

Thorne chuckled, tossing the spent end of his cigarette. "So the young Cyanide has a humble bone in his body after all, eh?"

"Just a small one," I cracked. "Let's call it one of my finger bones. Definitely not the important bone."

Thorne paused, inspecting me like he was really seeing me for the first time. "I can see why Kal took you under his wing."

I straightened. "Thank you."

"That wasn't a compliment." Thorne started walking again. "He kept you in check. Without him, you've got a chip on your shoulder the size of Temkra's heart. I can never tell if you're trying to prove yourself or self-sabotage. Either way, you act like you're all smiles and ready to party but your eyes are dead, pup."

I was so taken aback that I stopped in my tracks. I wasn't even offended, just stunned. Here I was, thinking that I barely knew Thorne while he could see through me like I was made of glass.

At my halted steps, Thorne stopped and turned back to face me. "Cyan." He sighed. "What happened to him wasn't your fault, you know."

Yeah, right. He hadn't been there. All Thorne had dealt with was the aftermath, the teetering dominoes of clan politics that he was tasked to keep standing. He wasn't there when I knocked the first domino over.

How much did Thorne blame himself? It was the first time I'd considered the possibility. If we had become ruling clan just five years earlier, Kalix could have been saved. By the time Thorne had consolidated power, it was too late.

I opened my mouth to argue just as I saw lightning fast movement over Thorne's shoulder.

"Behind you!" I bellowed, going for the silver blade inside my jacket. Tavi had my favorite one from our sparring session but I had plenty of backups.

Thorne turned and ducked just in time to avoid a heavy, swinging blow aiming for his head. Long, gnarled claws that had once been fingernails caught the moonlight.

"Stay down!"

I was one hell of a nobody to be yelling orders at my clan leader, but he thankfully did as I said. Taking off at a sprint, I jumped and sailed over Thorne's crouched form with my dagger aimed and ready. With a hard slam, I crashed into his attacker and we went tumbling.

The smell hit me first. The foulest mix of dirt, rot, and body odor that ever hit my senses. We suspected that the remnants of Rathka's Order had taken to living rough in the mountains, feeding on animals and probably each other. Nothing prepared me for that smell, though. And with my silver dagger stabbing in fast, controlled bursts, the scent of burning flesh added to the mix.

He fought me for a long time despite my hitting vital organs and blood vessels multiple times, probably due to the adrenaline and whatever animalistic craze that had taken over his mind. My arms had a few bleeding scratches from those nasty claws but in the end, the life drained out of him and he stopped moving.

"Cy!"

I looked up and turned to see Thorne pulling his own dagger from the neck of another figure covered in dried blood, dirt, and filth. The body crumpled to the ground as Thorne began running toward me.

"Cy, there's more!"

I spun on the ball of my foot, blade covering my throat and facing outward like I'd shown Tavi, but was a fraction of a second too late. How the fuck were they so silent?

My body hit the ground before I knew what hit me. From a sideways angle, I saw Thorne's booted feet dancing as he fought. My arm felt impossibly heavy as I reached for my neck, trying to find the source of blood pooling around me. I felt the gash in my skin, and the steady pump of my heart forcing blood out of my body.

My brain couldn't seem to form any coherent thoughts aside from, *shit, this is bad.*

Some time later, something wrapped around my neck and pulled tight, like it was going to choke me. The sight above me didn't make sense. Thorne with his shirt off? Thorne with his hands around my neck. I could feel my blood pumping against the pressure of his palm.

"Don't you fucking bleed out on me, pup." He sounded like he was underwater. "We're gonna get you back to your blood pet and get you all fixed up, alright?"

My thoughts were sluggish, like I was losing my grip on them as the blood drained from my body. But the words *blood pet* brought a single face to the forefront of my mind.

"Tavi," I gasped through the pain and sensation of life draining out of me.

"Yes, we'll get you to Tavi soon. Just hold the fuck on."

I couldn't see Thorne anymore, couldn't see past the dark blotches obscuring my vision. Vertigo overtook me and I didn't know which way was up. I was being flung and thrashed around, manipulated like a doll. I thought I could make out Thorne's boots hitting the stone pavement, and wondered if he was carrying me.

"Seriously, you better not fucking die on me," Thorne muttered. "Kalix would have my balls if he ever found out."

"Kal..." I groaned out his name, grasping at my final memory of him. He was stoic, determined, resolute, while I had been a mess.

I was always a fucking mess. It was why we lost him.

———

I MUST HAVE PASSED OUT. The next thing I knew, the blurry faces of my clan mates hovered above me. Why did they look so worried?

"Tavi's coming." Thorne's voice sounded close, like he

was near my ear, though he still sounded like he was underwater. "Hold on just a little longer, Cyanide."

A moment of clarity hit me. I couldn't take Tavi's blood. It was too sweet, too good and strong, because she was my blood *mate*.

I would have laughed bitterly if I had the energy. Me, the clan fuck-up with the first blood mate in Sanguine in twenty years. It was a huge fucking joke, and I didn't deserve to take that gorgeous human's blood.

"No," I tried to say, but couldn't even tell if I had a voice. "Not Tavi."

"Shut the fuck up, Cy. Come here, Octavia. Hurry."

Oh fuck. She was here. I must have been truly dying if I couldn't even scent her. I didn't want her seeing me like this. She cared so much for others. I didn't want her to care about me.

And yet I *craved* it. I craved her blood and the scent of her skin, her plush lips against my mouth, my fangs. I craved her arms around me in a hug, on the back of my motorcycle. How fucking pathetic was I, after what I'd done to Kalix, to be dying here and still want the power of this human to save me?

"I'm not sure what to do. We've never..."

"Tavi, get out of here." I moaned at the sound of her voice. Her scent was in my nose now, though I still couldn't see her. "Get her away from me," I said as my fangs descended, throbbing with the strongest need for her yet.

"Ignore him. You're the best chance he has at living. Just put your wrist to his mouth. He'll do the rest."

Before I could protest again, the delicate skin of her wrist pulsed against my lips. I didn't even fight. I was that weak, in spirit and body. Instinct and survival took over, and my fangs sank in.

There was a jerk of her arm but I held fast, and her blood flowing over my tongue made everything right. She was life and vitality, meant to sustain and feed only me in this way.

Her blood, meant only for me.

What a sick, cruel joke.

Chapter 19

Taria

Cyan fell unconscious with his fangs still in my wrist. Thorne and Desmond called it a "deep healing sleep" and said it was normal after a vampire sustained a bad injury.

The two vampires pried Cyan's fangs from my wrist, then eased his limp body to the bed. I was staring so hard at his unconscious face that I didn't notice Thorne had pressed a strip of gauze to my wrist until he spoke.

"Hold that there. The bleeding will slow soon." The clan leader quirked a brow. "Unless you want one of us to lick your wounds closed, but Cy probably won't like another vampire's scent on you when he wakes up."

He wouldn't care, I wanted to say, but the bitter statement remained stuck in my throat. It would feel too real if I said it aloud, even though Cy already said he would release me to someone else. I wasn't ready to give up, and deep down I knew he wasn't either.

And anyway, it wasn't like *I* wanted another vampire licking my skin.

"I'm okay, thanks." Thorne held out a length of tape,

and I allowed him to wrap it around my wrist to hold the gauze in place. "What happens now? Will he be okay?"

Thorne stood, looking weary. "He's already healing. Your blood will speed things along. He just needs to rest. As do you." The vampire gave me a pointed look. "That was a lot of blood you gave, especially for your first feeding. Drink Gatorade or whatever you humans need to replenish yourself."

"I can stay with him, right?"

"You're his blood pet. It would be odd if you didn't."

Thorne and Des left the suite, leaving me and Cy alone together in his bedroom. I'd never been in here before until now. It was almost funny how they left us alone here, like me being in this room was completely routine. But no, I didn't belong here. Cyan had never wanted me here in any intimate capacity.

And yet, I couldn't leave him.

His skin had broken out into goosebumps, so I pulled the covers up to his shoulders and smoothed them out. The wound on his neck already looked much better, no longer a mess of jagged, bleeding flesh. Skin and muscle had already knitted themselves together, the new tissue red and tender.

He looked peaceful now, deeply asleep. His lips were parted slightly, and my pulse fluttered at the thought of our kiss in the kitchen.

Abruptly, I stood from his bedside and left the room. My heartbeat felt too fast, and I had a moment of dizziness as I walked out. The blood loss was stunningly clear in that moment, and I took extra care on my way to the kitchenette. All the physical manifestations of my feelings for Cy were amplified by my low blood cell count. He'd better not wake up too quickly or I'd swoon right in front of him.

I nibbled on goldfish crackers and bits of salami while

keeping an eye on the open doorway of his bedroom. Staying right at his side felt too close, too intimate in a way I had no right to be, but I still wanted to keep an eye on him. I wanted to be available if he needed me.

Or my blood.

I held my own wrist, feeling the tenderness of the puncture marks as I recalled how it had felt. Thinking about that almost made me swoon. It was ten times more intense than when I'd cut my thumb. Each pull on my vein was like a full-body caress, the sensation concentrating the strongest in my nipples and clit. If I hadn't been so worried about him surviving, I might have orgasmed.

Right in front of his clan leader and his friend, which would have been mortifying.

I never wanted it to stop, and that in itself was equally terrifying and thrilling. I wanted Cyan to take it all from me, for my life force to heal him and bring back the vampire who smirked and flirted and made me feel special.

My phone buzzed with a text from Amy, pulling me out of my low-iron induced fantasy. I immediately hit the button to call her, eager for a distraction.

"Isn't it past your bedtime, young lady?" I said when she picked up, heading to the couch with my snacks and a bottle of apple juice.

"Leave me alone, Mom," she snickered. "You would not believe the shitshow today."

"Well, don't leave me in suspense." I reclined and propped myself up with couch cushions so that I could still see into Cy's bedroom. "What happened? You okay?"

"Oh yeah, nothing to do with me. But we all got up this morning to find that Heather disappeared into thin air."

"Whoa." The goldfish I'd just put in my mouth almost fell out. "Did you find her?"

"No, she's still AWOL. Not that she ever had to check in with anybody, but we were all worried since she doesn't know her way around here."

"And didn't believe in vampires until like, two days ago," I pointed out.

"Exactly. So the council had everyone go searching in case she got lost or something. But there's no trace of her. You know what we *did* find, though?"

"Huh?" I took a sip of apple juice and had the random thought that I should make a hard cider soon.

"Another entrance to the human world. With tracks and broken branches like someone had been through recently."

"Oh shit, where?"

"Directly west of the compound. Maybe a mile from where our usual one is."

"Huh, that's close."

"Yeah, there was no blood or signs of distress, so everyone was relieved she's most likely okay."

"So did they keep looking for her?"

"No. They discussed it but she obviously didn't want to stay, so why force her, you know? And even if she talks, one girl rambling about vampires and overlapping worlds isn't likely to cause any trouble for us."

The next goldfish paused on its way to my mouth. "I hope that's true. It's not like she has any proof, right?"

"Right, exactly. She's just another person who's stumbled into our world and then stumbled her way back home. It's like people over there have a mental shield up. No one ever believes them."

"You should still be careful. The vampires don't want any human-led governments or agencies poking around their territory. All it takes is one curious person to bring back proof. Next thing we know, they're invading with tanks and machine guns."

Amy laughed. "How do you know that?"

"I've watched the human-world documentaries on the one channel in Robin's place. It's what humans like to do, discover a new place and invade it."

"You say that like *you're* not human." Amy's tone was teasing, but I didn't miss the slight accusation underneath.

"Of course I am. But you know." I shifted positions on the couch, switching the phone to my other ear. "This place belongs to the supernatural species. They were here first. Humans have been here a long time too but the magic, the land, it's all theirs. We're guests here."

"Well, how nice of them to let us stay," Amy chuckled. "And not feed on us. Some of us, anyway."

I sank deeper into the couch cushions. It wasn't like she actually knew Cy had just fed on me, but it felt like she was teasing about it anyway.

"Anyway, how are you? Is your arranged vampire husband still pissy and brooding? He seemed friendly enough the other night."

"It's...complicated," I sighed. "He was actually injured earlier tonight while out on patrol. He's doing okay and sleeping it off though. I'm keeping an eye on him."

"Glad to hear it. Is he still being an ass, though?"

I almost choked on a goldfish from my laugh. "Well, kind of. Yeah."

"Fuck him, then. I hope he rots."

"Don't be a bitch." I grinned as I said it, because there was nothing like having your best friend always in your corner. Especially when wrestling your complicated feelings for a vampire.

"Too late, skank."

The next thirty seconds were filled with Amy and I trying to suppress our laughter, and making weird snorting and wheezing noises in the process.

"Okay, but really," she sighed as we composed ourselves. "I'm sorry to hear that and I hope he recovers. He's an ass but you care about him, so I wish him well."

"Thanks, Ames."

"Wait." There was a long pause on the phone. "Did you give him blood?"

I bit the inside of my cheek. There was no lying to her. "Yes."

"Are you okay?"

"I'm fine. Got a little dizzy when I stood up fast, but I'm okay. I'm eating snacks and drinking juice."

"So does this change things between you and him? The whole blood pet thing?"

"I don't know," I admitted. "I'll have to wait until he's awake and see if he talks to me."

Amy made a disgruntled noise which promptly turned into a yawn. "I don't like him jerking you around. It was one thing when we all thought he would instantly kill you, but now that he's keeping you alive, he better be good to you."

I wasn't sure how to respond to that. She and Robin were the only people who had been good to me my whole life. It was like I had a lot of experience in that regard.

"Well, he let me see you," I pointed out. "And gave us these phones we're talking on."

And my wine making stuff. And the most electric kiss I've ever felt. I wanted to list out all the ways Cyan had been good to me. But the ways he'd confused me loomed over all the positive things like a dark cloud.

"Not good enough," Amy quipped. "I need to see him

sweep my best friend off her feet. He's gotta put the book boyfriends to shame."

Well, that's not gonna happen, I thought, but smiled at the sentiment. "If anyone deserves being swept off their feet, it's you, bestie."

"Nah." Amy scoffed. "I'm not main character material."

I was just about to argue that when another yawn came over the phone speaker. "I'm gonna let you go, Ames. You're exhausted."

"Fine, *mom*," she chuckled. "Talk tomorrow night?"

"Wouldn't miss it. Love you, goodnight."

"Night, love you." She already sounded asleep when I ended the call.

———

CYAN BEGAN STIRRING about two hours later. I heard his sheets rustling and sprang up to check on him. I still felt a little wobbly but definitely stronger than directly after I fed him.

His eyes fluttered open the moment I sat at his bedside. "Tavi," he croaked, his voice thick with fatigue. "You're here." He sounded surprised, and nothing could have prepared me for his hand reaching to brush against my knee.

"Yeah, of course I am." Throwing caution to the wind, I wrapped my fingers around his. They were stronger, warmer than before. "How do you feel?"

"Like shit." The corner of his mouth pulled upward in the barest hint of a smile. "Weak as a hungover baby rat. That drowned."

I squeezed his hand and felt slight pressure in return.

"Your sense of humor is back, so that's definitely an improvement."

"At this rate, I'll feel like death warmed over in no time." He released my hand, his expression turning solemn as he gripped my knee, fingers stroking gently over my thigh. "Thank you for your blood, Tavi. You saved my life."

My teeth sank into my lip, resisting the urge to spread my knees wider, just to see how far up his touch would tease my skin. "I think Thorne deserves that honor for getting you here so quickly, but I'm glad I could help."

He let out a soft breath of a laugh. "He's a quick thinking bastard, but it was you being here, you willing to do what you never wanted, that is the reason I'm breathing right now." Cy licked his lips, looking conflicted as his gaze drifted over my neck. "And I'm sorry you were put in that position, having to go back on what we originally agreed upon so you could save my sorry ass."

"Cy." I shook my head. "I didn't mind giving you my blood, not at all. To save your life, it wasn't even a question in my mind. If I had to, I'd do it all over again."

He didn't say anything in response, but only stared at me with an expression I couldn't read. It went on for so long that I wondered if he zoned out completely.

"Cy?" I cocked my head. "Do you need more blood?"

His eyes snapped back into focus with a quick lick of his lips. "No, not right now."

"Okay." I forced a smile, wondering why his *no* felt like a rejection. "Okay then, I'll just let you rest—"

"Tavi." My name was a plea from his lips, punctuated by the light squeeze of his hand around my knee. "Will you stay?" I'd never seen him look so raw, so vulnerable, as he did in that moment. "Please."

My pulse kicked up, and this time it had nothing to do

with missing a pint or so of blood. I was all nerves and elated disbelief, my whole body thrumming like a hummingbird's wings as he pulled the covers down and scooted to make space for me.

It was like that moment I first arrived at the clan's compound, that feeling of disconnect from my body, watching myself go through the motions. But there was no fear sharpening my senses, just awe and a sense of wonderment at the closeness he was allowing me.

I nestled into his side, gingerly resting my head on his chest as his arm draped around me. The raised texture of his scars, of the vow he made to me, scraped against my cheek. The rest of him was smooth, like warm marble.

Cyan's mouth brushed my hairline, lips moving as if whispering something. Before I could react, his whole body relaxed into the peacefulness of deep sleep.

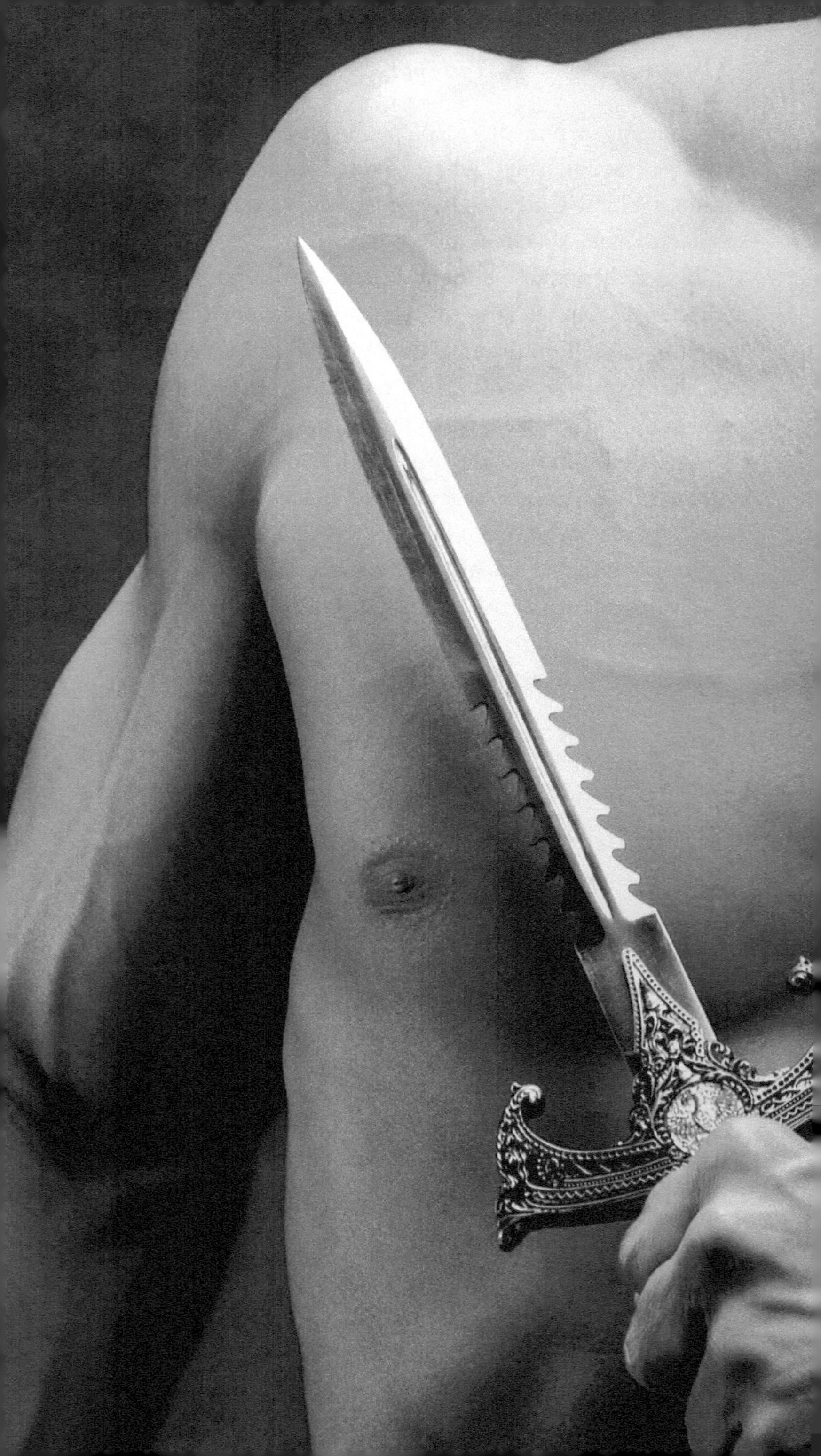

Chapter 20

Cyan

Tavi's heartbeat was the first thing I sensed as I woke up. The rhythmic thumping was steady and grounding, rousing me like the caress from a soft hand. Never before had I been pulled from sleep so gently.

We were in the same position we started in, her head on my chest, my arm running down her back, hand resting in the dip of her waist. Her hair spilled over my shoulder and the pillow. It partially covered her face, so I used my free hand to push it back.

She looked so sweet in her sleep. There was a sharp vigilance about her when awake. I liked that she was hawk-eyed and always aware of her surroundings. It had been especially clear the other night when she introduced me to the other humans. She was protective of her friend Amy, fiercely so. It was evident in her posture and how she always kept one eye on the surrounding humans.

This soft, sleepy Tavi had to be a side of her that hardly anyone knew. It suited her in a way I didn't expect. All the muscles in her pretty face relaxed. Her eyelashes were a medium brown color, slightly lighter than her hair. I felt privileged to be one of the few who saw her like this.

I blew out a soft scoff at that thought. Privileged? More like undeserving. This was me, after all.

But I found myself unable to care anymore. I was too weak, too selfish to do the right thing. Getting injured on patrol was all it took to shred my flimsy resolve, the so-called integrity I'd tried to convince myself I had. It was laughable that I even tried.

Her blood had tasted so fucking good, like utter heaven. And I'd never slept so deeply or well until she crawled into bed next to me.

I wanted to have Tavi. To keep and claim her, even if I ended up breaking her in the end. That was just the piece of shit I was.

She stirred in sleep, her cheek brushing against my chest and a soft breath blowing across my skin. The gentle signs of life sharpened my awareness, and my hunger awoke.

My fangs extended with a dull ache and they pulsed in my mouth. I didn't need to look at myself to know that my injuries were gone without a single trace of a scar. Her blood had healed me, but now I needed it to *feed* me.

The sound of her heart beats echoed in my empty stomach. I shouldn't take from her, not so soon after I'd just fed. But she was here, warm and soft with her skin on mine.

And she was my blood mate. All other blood was quite literally ruined for me. Nothing would sate me but her taste.

My fingers circled where they rested on her waist, then I slowly began to drag them up her back. Tavi stirred again, letting out a gentle sigh.

"Tavi." I brushed my lips against her forehead.

"Hm?" She wasn't fully awake yet, but started to move and stretch. I got harder every time she moved and touched me.

I continued to rub her back until her eyes opened. She gazed at me sleepily, blinking a few times.

"Good morning." I couldn't help but smile down at her. She was so fucking adorable. "Isn't that what humans say when they first wake up?"

"Mm, is it morning?" She rubbed her eyes, and fuck, her sleepy mumbling voice was doing thing to me.

"We slept almost all night, so I think so."

All at once, Tavi seemed alarmed. Her vision sharpened as she pressed herself up. "Is this okay? I'm sorry, Cy. I didn't mean to stay the whole night."

"Get back here." I tugged one of her arms until she flopped down next to me. "It's more than okay. I want you here."

She relaxed, although her expression remained tentative. "How do you feel?"

"Good as new, thanks to you."

Tavi smiled, and I had the fleeting thought that I wouldn't mind seeing her lying next to me like this every morning and evening.

"How about you?" I returned my hand to her waist, pulling her a little closer. "I didn't take too much from you, did I?"

"No. I feel fine." She shoved a hand under the pillow, getting comfortable. "I had some snacks and juice last night. And I think sleeping helped."

"Good."

We said nothing for a few moments, but she must have noticed how long my fangs were. She must have realized how intently I was staring at the long, graceful slope of her neck.

"Cy?" Her pupils dilated and she licked her lips. "Do you need more?"

A part of me wanted to say no, that I could wait. She should have another full day at least to recover from the first feeding. And truthfully, I could wait with little consequence. I was hungry, but it would be another two days or so before I started to feel significantly weaker.

But she was here, now. And I was already so weak to her warm skin, her sleepy smiles, and her heavenly taste.

"You offering?" I drawled, making sure my fangs were revealed in my lazy smirk.

Tavi blushed and I had to hold back my resulting hiss. I knew she couldn't help it but there was no bigger temptation than seeing her skin deepen with color because of that beautiful, hot life force under the surface.

"If you need it, I'm here," she whispered.

I sensed her pulse quicken and her breaths coming in shorter. Oh, she *wanted* me to take from her. My brave, self-sacrificing little human got turned on from it. She was hoping for it, craving it.

How could I deny the beautiful woman in my bed what she wanted most?

I rolled over, pressing up to my hands until I hovered over her. Placing a knee between her legs, I pressed her thighs apart until she straddled me. Tavi stared up at me, eyes wide with anticipation and just a hint of fear.

She was dressed in a large T-shirt and shorts, and I had sweatpants on. None of that was getting removed. I would be drinking from her, not fucking her. Even I wasn't enough of a bastard to use her like that.

But if I was...if we were both naked and I could thrust

inside her while I drank from her, this would be a hell of a view while I did that.

Tavi's hair spilled out over the pillow, blood-flushed lips parted and tilted up to me like the most delectable offering. I lowered my face to hers, hovering a hair's breadth away because I was so fucking weak for her and she had no idea.

"It's not just your blood that I need."

She barely had time to draw in a sharp inhale before I closed the distance with a firm, devouring kiss. I swallowed her surprised little cry with a stroke of my tongue, delving into her warm mouth. She licked my fangs, careful to avoid the points and my cock hardened to steel. I wanted to thrust, to let her feel what she was doing to me, but I kept my hips pulled back.

Tavi's arms went around me as we kissed, and that kind of affection from my blood mate was almost too much to handle. I had to remind myself that she had no idea, and she'd never want me if she knew the truth of what a piece of shit I was. But her soft hands stroking past my ribs, running over the muscles in my back, digging in with her short little nails, felt so good and right. The sweetest fucking torture.

Our last kiss broke and I turned Tavi's face to the side, taking in the sight of her jaw and neck. Instinctively I could sense her vein, knew exactly where it was and how the pulse fluttered under her skin. I kissed the corner of her jaw first, tasting her with my lips despite my fangs aching to sink into her.

"Perfect," I muttered, lowering to my elbows as I kissed the spot under her ear. "You have no idea how fucking perfect you taste."

"Cyan..." She breathed my name so sweetly, her legs sliding up my hips as if to trap me in place. If only she knew she had me hooked with no need to touch me at all. All she had to do was say my name like that, and I'd be on my knees.

"I won't hurt you." My lips were finally at her neck, her pulse thrumming so insistently like the vein itself was trying to kiss me.

My mouth trailed up and down a few times, zeroing in on the perfect spot at this angle, nuzzling into the warmth of her skin. When I found it, I kissed her there and dragged the tip of my tongue over the exact place I'd strike. My saliva acted as a mild analgesic and would dull the pain.

Tavi squirmed underneath me, but not as though to get away. Her thighs squeezed my hips, one foot running down my calf. My blood mate wanted it, wanted *more*.

I struck, sinking my fangs in and sealing my lips over the bite. At the first taste of her on my tongue, I moaned. Everything slowed, and my senses tuned out all but the heady, nourishing wine in my mouth and the soft body underneath me.

Each pull on Tavi's vein thrummed in time to my own pulse. There was a slight pressure on my erection but my hands were on either side of her. Sweet fate, was she touching me through my pants? My hips rolled in lazy thrusts, seeking more of that pleasure. Sharp pricks of pain raked up my back and through my dulled senses, I could hear Tavi's moans and whimpers.

Not too much, some hindbrain instinct told me, the one that remembered I needed to keep my blood mate alive and healthy. *Stop soon.*

I pulled my fangs from Tavi's neck, quickly licking over the puncture wounds to heal them closed. A few drops of blood escaped and I lapped them up, leisurely kissing and nuzzling at Tavi's neck and shoulder even after the blood was gone. She just smelled so fucking good, and she was so warm, soft and beautiful...

"Cy," she choked out, her voice pained. "Cyan, please."

I pressed up, immediately worried at the realization that nearly all of my weight had been resting on her. "I'm sorry. Did I hurt you?"

Tavi's face was in a grimace, her chest heaving with ragged breaths. "Don't stop. I need to come, Cy. Please, please let me come."

Looking down, I saw that my erection rested directly on top of her mound. Through the fabric, I could feel how wet she was, and the firmness of her clit right on the edge of release.

Huh, so that was what had been touching me. Or rather, I had been touching her, thrusting against her heat and the soft, supple pressure of her body underneath me. After being so careful not to at first, I became mindless at the first taste of her.

Tavi trembled so hard, she was practically vibrating underneath me. She needed to come so badly, she was nearly in tears.

"Shh, easy." I moved to the side of her, propping myself up on an elbow. Taking her chin, I brushed another kiss against her shaking lips. She was so flushed, panting so hard. "Of course I'll take care of you. After the incredible gift of your blood, how could I not?"

I released her chin, running my hand down her body. Her hips canted up the moment I slid under the waistband of her shorts, silently begging for my touch. Her ragged, desperate breaths caressed my lips while I hovered above her, watching every reaction on her face.

Tavi whimpered as my palm slid over her mound, bypassing her aching clit. I wanted to feel how wet she was first, feel how much my feeding really turned her on and... oh, *fuck*.

She was absolutely drenched. Delicate skin burned hot and was slick with arousal. Just from *one* brief feeding. My fingers immediately became slippery as they explored, stroking and rubbing everywhere but her clit.

I could only marvel as I gazed down at her, squirming and panting under my ministrations. She was so fucking perfect for me. Not just her blood, but *her*. I had never wished so badly that I was good enough, that I was worthy of this fearless, beautiful human.

At this point, Tavi had walked back from the edge a little bit. She was still desperate to come, but not to the point of pain. Her expression turned to adorable frustration that I hadn't given in to her demands. She rolled to her side, not breaking eye contact as her hand slid inside my sweatpants and gripped my rock solid length.

"I'll make you come first." She said it like a threat. "You wouldn't let that happen, would you?"

My laugh turned to a moan as she squeezed me on an upward stroke. "Go ahead. I'll never leave you wanting, Tavi. Not even after you make me shoot off into your hand. The longer I draw you out, the bigger you'll explode. And I want to see you come apart."

Her brow furrowed. She really didn't expect me to call her bluff. It was so fucking cute, I laughed as I kissed her, swallowing her moan as I inserted a finger into her hot, slick pussy.

"Did you really think I would be out of commission as soon as you got me off?" I slid another finger inside her, relishing in her expression as I filled her. "I'm not one of your human men, Tavi. I don't roll over and fall asleep once I've come. And in case you forgot," I brushed a fang against her ear, making sure she felt the point, "vampires are known for what we do with our mouths."

My two fingers inside her curled as they stroked in and out. I smothered her next moan with another kiss while I swept my thumb over her clit. It wasn't enough pressure to get her there, just enough to ratchet her up to the edge again. She tightened her grip on my cock and found a rhythm, despite being thoroughly distracted. I helped her along, fucking into her tight little fist.

Tavi's scream of anguish when my fingers pulled out almost made me feel sympathetic. Almost.

"Shhh, easy. Relax." I kissed her forehead, grinning while she glared daggers at me. "Just making things a little smoother here."

She watched me grip my shaft and stroke, spreading her wetness all over until my cock was glossy with her arousal. Her eyes followed as my hand returned to her cunt, dipped inside for more of her beautiful slick, and painted my cock with it.

I'd decided I wouldn't fuck her, and this was probably only the slimmest of technicalities, but my selfish mind still tried to justify it. This wasn't sex, just...sexual fun. My cock was coated in her, but it never went inside her. I had been on top of her, kissed her, touched her, but at least our bodies hadn't been connected like that. The air was electrically charged with our passion and heat, but it wasn't *that* serious.

"I swear you're trying to kill me," Tavi groaned as she resumed stroking my freshly-slicked cock.

"No." I kissed the bridge of her nose, smiling.

That simple, two-lettered word could not begin to sum up the maelstrom inside of me. *No, I'm drawing out your pleasure for as long as I can as if that'll make up for how selfish I'm being. No, I'm edging you and building you up to the most explosive orgasm you've ever had because I'm inevitably going to let you down. At least you'll have this as a positive memory.*

"Let me hear you say please again." My forehead pressed to hers while my hand returned to her warm, welcoming pussy. "And my name. Say it, Tavi."

"Cyan, *please.*" Her hips bucked and thrashed against my hand. "Please let me come. Please, please, *please.*"

Fuck, she was so good. So sweet, pliant, and giving. Her hand kept up a steady pace on my cock, twisting around the head in a way that made me shudder. I was close too, and the arbitrary line I'd drawn of sex versus not sex grew even more blurred. I wanted to come when she did. I wanted to tip over the peak of my pleasure because she had reached hers.

My thumb pressed to her clit and massaged around in a tight circle while my fingers dragged along her inner walls. I could almost imagine I was inside her, fucking the slick, hot hold of her cunt instead of her hand. I never wanted anything else so badly in that moment, to feel her in that way just once.

"Cy—"

Tavi's voice choked off on my name the moment she came apart so beautifully. She broke, clenching around my fingers as she shattered into a million pieces before my eyes. It was the hottest, most beautiful sight I'd ever seen, so much that my own release shot through me like a cannon as I watched her. I spilled over her fist, onto the bedsheets. Through her own release, she kept pumping me, wringing it all out of me until I was spent.

Somehow, despite having no bones in my body, I managed to find a towel to place over the wet spot on the mattress. That could be cleaned up later, when I had more than a few brain cells firing.

I collapsed on the towel, drawing Tavi into my arms. Her skin was so warm and her pulse thrummed in a rapid, but gentle beat. It almost felt like she was purring. She nuzzled into my throat, hands stroking over me. Neither of us spoke. There simply weren't words to describe what happened, or this feeling in the afterglow.

Not that it was sex. I didn't get cuddly after sex. This was...us. Me and Tavi, on a whole other level from the debauchery and bloodlust I knew too well.

"Cyan?" Tavi's voice was soft, hesitant. She drew back as if to look at me.

"Mm-hm." My eyelids were heavy as I brushed a kiss over her hairline.

There was more hesitation before she spoke again.

"Are we blood mates?"

Chapter 21

Tavia

Cyan stiffened like a bucket of ice water had been poured on him, and I got a creeping sense of dread that I had said the wrong thing.

"Who told you about blood mates?" His tone was casual but I still heard the iciness in his voice.

"Bea," I admitted. "Something about how one person's blood chemistry perfectly matches the needs of a single vampire, and it makes all other blood taste bad—"

"I know what it is. You don't need to explain it to me."

Cyan started pulling away, and I felt the distance both physically and emotionally. He rolled to his back, hands resting on his stomach, gazing at the ceiling. It was such a startling difference from moments ago. When his hand was between my legs he couldn't seem to stop looking at me.

"I just, it made me wonder since you healed so quickly." I rushed to explain, desperately grasping for the connection he'd severed so swiftly. It was like an on/off switch with him. "And every time you've had my blood, it's made me feel..."

Aroused. Horny. A bundle of nerves and need

desperate for his touch alone. Every way to describe it felt too damn vulnerable now.

Cyan continued to stare at the ceiling as if I wasn't even there. As if he didn't just give me the most intense orgasm I'd ever experienced.

"Blood mates are rare," he said flatly. "Biological match-ups like that don't just happen between two random people."

Is that what we are to each other? Just random people? I was afraid of what his answer would be, and didn't dare voice the question out loud.

"Yeah, Bea mentioned that. She said the last ceremony was fifteen years ago." At Cyan's silence, I seemed unable to keep myself from rambling. "I'm just asking because I don't know, Cy. I'm trying to understand what this is. I'm trying to understand *you*. Why we're so close sometimes, and then I get this complete opposite side of you. I'm always wondering if I'm offending you or turning you off in some way. I'm just confused, that's all."

"Quite the headfuck, aren't I?" He smiled mirthlessly up at the ceiling.

"I mean, if you put it like that, yeah kind of. But I know you don't mean it—"

"And how do you know that?" he demanded sharply, turning his head to look at me. His gaze was just as cold and distant as the rest of his demeanor.

I felt like I was walking on a frozen lake, and each step carried the risk of plunging to an icy, painful death.

"Know what?"

"How do you know I don't mean to headfuck you?" His stare bore into me, harsh and challenging.

"Because you, that's—" I was so whiplashed that I had to stop and start again. "That's just not who you are."

He barked out a harsh laugh. "Right. Because you know me so well." His feet crossed at the ankles while bringing one arm behind his head. He was relaxed, if even enjoying this. All the while, I felt a slow, ripping heartache.

"I *do* know you. You're not a bad person, Cy. You've done a lot to show that you care about me and I...I feel the same way. If I'm your blood mate, that just seals it for us, right? We can be...together. It doesn't have to be more complicated than that."

I wouldn't have felt more vulnerable, exposed, and pathetic if I had taken my beating heart out of my chest and offered it to him right then and there.

Cyan actually sighed and sat up, rolled over to his side table, and took out a darakt cigarette. He leaned against the headboard as he lit up, taking his sweet damn time.

"Here's the difference between you and me, Tavi." He exhaled red smoke and took the cigarette from his lips. "You're selfless to a fault. You care about other people way more than yourself. You'll hurt yourself to make others happy."

I willed myself not to shake. He was right, but he didn't have to throw it in my face like it was some character flaw. I wanted the people I cared about to be safe and happy. Including him. Was that so wrong?

"As for me, I'm the complete opposite." He took another drag, ashing carefully in an obsidian dish on his nightstand. "I only care about myself. And to get what I want, I'm not afraid to hurt others in the process." His brows slashed down over his red eyes. "So you want to understand me? Your blood tastes good and you've got a great body. I'll keep charming you and making you think you're special to me just so I can get a taste. Congratulations, Tavi. You've joined the roster of a dozen other women I rotate through."

I shut my eyes against the tears threatening to spill over. I knew he didn't want to settle down, but I'd never heard him speak this cruelly before. Why was he doing this?

"You're lying. I don't know why you're pushing me away, but—"

"I told you I liked variety. The very first day I brought you here, I told you what the deal was. What I don't understand is why you're acting so surprised."

The words cutting through me didn't match the man who'd helped me bottle my wine, carved vows into his chest, or protected me from a drae addict. Hell, this person didn't even match up with the Cyan who edged me for an explosive orgasm just a few minutes ago. I had reached the point beyond confused and was now awash in a sea of hurt.

"So I'm not your blood mate?"

Cyan scoffed with another exhale of red smoke. "You really think a vampire like me has a blood mate?" Before I could cry out in frustration that I didn't know, he added, "Variety is what sustains me. Not being chained to one boring blood source for the rest of my life."

I allowed those words to sink in, to burrow deeply in my heart so that I would never forget them, and then stood from the bed.

"I can't live in your place anymore." The pain had given way to numbness and I felt oddly detached from the words coming out of my own mouth. "And you can't have my blood anymore. I'm revoking all consent for you to drink from me."

"Fair enough." Cyan lifted one shoulder in a barely-perceptible shrug. "Shut the door on your way out."

A fresh stab of hurt cut through my numbness. He really didn't care. At all.

I left his bedroom, resisting the urge to slam the door

behind me. He already got enough satisfaction of seeing my feelings pour out, and I refused to give him any more. I packed up my belongings and snacks in a daze while every memory of us played like a highlight reel in my mind.

It was surreal to know it was all a lie. Every moment where he'd been protective, tender, or even sweet had been a manipulation tactic. He must have been playing on my desire to help others since the beginning. Getting injured last night probably wasn't planned but it sure was convenient for him.

And fuck my bleeding heart, I still cared about him. I wanted to wish he'd been finished off in the attack, but I couldn't even think that without a fresh wave of tears stinging my eyes.

I had tunnel vision as I left his suite with all of my things. If there were any vampires milling about the hall, watching the pathetic human blood pet with tears streaming down her face, I didn't see them.

My feet and one-track mind led me to one door in particular. Bea opened up seconds after my knock. Black and turquoise eyes widened at the sight of me.

"Tavia! Oh Temkra, are you okay?"

"Hey." I steeled myself with a breath. "I'm really sorry to intrude, but I can't stay with Cyan anymore and don't have anywhere else to go. Can I crash on your couch? Just until I figure things out."

She opened the door wider and immediately ushered me in. "You, poor thing, are taking my bed and I'll be on the couch."

"No! No, I couldn't possibly—"

"Then I hope you love snuggling because we'll be sharing the bed in that case. Looks like you need it."

Bea took my bags of clothes and snacks from me, set

them aside, and pulled me into a hug. That was when the dam broke and I fell apart. My wall of numbness shattered and all the hurt poured through. I sobbed on her shoulder like a child while she rubbed my back and made soothing noises.

"Shhh, you're alright. Let it out." Somehow we made it to the couch, where she continued to hold me. "I don't know what he did, but I'm sorry he's such an inflated monkey's ass. Stay as long as you need."

I half-laughed, half-sobbed while making a mess out of her shirt with my tears and snot. Bea didn't seem to care about her clothes though, and continued to soothe me.

"He was...really fucking mean." I gave her a brief over-view of what happened, then got up to clean myself up. After blowing my nose and splashing some water on my face, I felt a tiny bit better. Still wounded and like the tears would return at the drop of a hat, but not crying right that second felt like a win.

"I'm such a dumbass," I groaned, sinking back onto the couch with Bea.

"You are not," she argued. "Cy's the dumbass. If he's fucked things up for good with you, he's only got himself to blame."

I shook my head, staring at the ceiling like he had been. "You know what's crazy? The shit he said to me isn't even the worst I've heard from a guy. I've been called all kinds of names, been told I wasn't even pretty enough to fuck, you name it. And it never affected me. It all rolled off my back like water on a duck."

"Yup, same." Bea nodded sympathetically. "It hurts a lot more when you think they're different. When you start to trust them and they turn that against you. It sucks really bad."

"Fucking right?" I scoffed and sniffled some more. "Do you think any man of any species is worth trusting?"

"Couldn't tell ya." Bea gave a small shrug. "The last one I was willing to give it a shot with got locked away twenty years ago. And none of the vamps around here have steady partners. So it's hard to say."

I wiped my eyes. "That's pretty much what I thought."

"You know what I think?"

"Huh?"

Bea looked pensive, tapping her chin in thought. "I think Cy developed strong feelings for you too. And he's scared of that. Scared of having a weakness, vulnerabilities. Scared of all the things that falling in love comes with. I bet he thinks he's protecting you in some way. "

"By being an asshole to me? How does that work?"

She shrugged. "Pushing you away into the arms of a more deserving vampire, maybe."

"I don't know," I sighed.

"Well, fuck him in any case."

I huffed out an exhausted, mirthless laugh. "Thanks, Bea. I promise I won't encroach on your space for too long."

"Nonsense, stay as long as you need. Want some chamomile tea?"

"Sure."

She promptly burritoed me in a blanket, then got up to tinker in her kitchenette. It struck me then how this dynamic had flipped from what I was used to.

I was always the fortress that Amy found shelter in. When she needed me, I protected her, no matter what. If I needed something, I shoved it down because I needed to be strong for Amy. She was more important.

This time I was the one who needed a friend, a shelter in a storm. And I was so damn glad I had one.

"Hey, Bea?" I called out.

"Yes, my little chamomile flower?"

I smiled at the endearment. "You're a lovely person and a really good friend. If there is a trustworthy vampire out there, I hope you find him and he treats you like gold."

"Oh stop it," she said over an electric kettle and the clink of tea cups. "Hopefully there's two. Or even three. One for you, me, and your friend Amy."

"I don't think she'd ever go for a vampire, honestly."

"Well if there is only one out there, the three of us will have to come up with some kind of custody schedule."

"Custody?" I laughed. "Of a vampire boyfriend?"

"It has to be fair, doesn't it? Equal time split amongst all of us."

"Makes sense. Then we'll see who's the pet, huh?"

"Exactly!" Bea pointed at me. "That's what I'm talking about. Make him *our* pet."

We shared tea and some more laughs that eased the ache in my chest until the exhaustion became too much. The last thing I felt was Bea covering me with a blanket, and some whispered mutterings of, "if only Kalix could knock some sense into him."

Chapter 22

Tavia

Amy didn't pick up her phone when I called that afternoon, which I thought was strange until I remembered she needed to keep her phone hidden. She was probably finishing up some chores for the day and would call back when she returned to the trailer.

I occupied myself with tidying up Bea's apartment as quietly as I could. It was the least I could do since she was letting me stay indefinitely.

We had slept several hours in the morning, and she remained fast asleep. Her place was much smaller than Cyan's, basically a studio with only a nook for her bed rather than an actual bedroom.

I washed and dried the teacups we'd used in the morning when I came over, which felt like so long ago already. My sleep had been fitful and I was still exhausted from crying and heartache, but couldn't keep lying awake.

My phone buzzing with Amy's returned call was a welcome distraction. Even though I wasn't looking forward to rehashing what happened with Cy a second time, talking to her always lifted my spirits.

I answered the call, keeping my voice low so to not wake Bea. "Hey, Ames."

"Tavia! We need help! Oh God, they're swarming the compound! They just attacked us out of nowhere!"

It took a moment to register that the voice wasn't Amy's, but Robin's. And she was in full-blown panic mode.

"Robin! What's going on?"

"Vampires, I think. I don't know, it's daytime. But they're running around biting and mauling people! They're crazed and out of control, like wild animals!" A sob escaped her and hit me right in the heart. "I think some people are already dead."

My feet moved as if they had minds of their own. I was barely aware of leaving Bea's apartment. "Where are you? Where's Amy?"

"We're in a cellar. A group of us are hiding, but..." Another sob wracked through her. "Amy...Amy got hurt."

I stopped walking and my stomach dropped through the floor. "What? Is she okay?" I realized too late how stupid that question was. "Is she...alive?"

"Yes, but Tavia honey, it doesn't look good. She's bleeding really badly. We need help *now*."

The phone nearly slipped from my hand. With Amy's heart condition, her life was in greater danger than most people's would be.

My best friend in the world was dying while I stood dumbstruck in the middle of the hallway.

I forced my feet to move again, trying to form rational thoughts, basic plans of action through my rising panic.

"I'm getting help right now, Robin. It's going to be okay. You...you're keeping pressure on her wound, right?"

"She has multiple wounds but we're doing our best."

Robin let out a shuddering breath. "Do you want to talk to her? In case..."

I tried to swallow the thick knot in my throat, but it wouldn't budge. "Yes. Please put me by her ear."

There was a shuffling noise on the phone and then the faint sound of wheezed, shallow breathing.

"Ames, it's me." My feet had taken me to a door. I wasn't sure whose it belonged to, but I raised my fist and knocked furiously anyway. "Don't try to talk. I'm on my way, okay? You don't have to worry. I'll be there soon and... and you'll be all better. I promise, Ames. Just hang on."

I pounded at the door again. "It'll be okay, sweetie. I love you, okay? I'll be there as fast as I can. Goddamnit, fucking open up!"

My knocking turned into furious punches and kicks. I was losing it because I could not afford to lose Amy. Finally, a lock unlatched and the door swung open, revealing a disheveled, shirtless Thorne. The vampire leader snarled at the sight of me but I went off before he could tear into me.

"There's an attack on Sapien. People are badly hurt and hiding out. We need to help them. I think it's—it's the drae addicts. Please, the clan needs to go right now."

Thorne blinked at me, then looked at a clock on a side table. Why the fuck wasn't he rallying his people and fucking moving?

"It's another hour until dusk." He didn't even bother to sound apologetic. "We can't do anything until night falls."

"Why?" Another dumb question but I wasn't thinking straight. I was desperate and this was fucking urgent.

"Because we're vampires." He quirked a brow. "Maybe you've heard of the term?"

I felt like a malfunctioning robot, all systems locked up and frozen. Well, except for scream and maybe punch him.

"But...but they need help *now*. My best friend is bleeding out right now. People are fucking dying!"

He crossed his arms and had the decency to look at least a little sympathetic. "I'll rally the clan to ride out the moment the sun is down. But we simply can't move out any sooner. I'm sorry, Octavia."

A beat of silence passed and then I turned on my heel, heading the opposite way down the hall. "Robin, are you still there?" My hand ached from my grip on the phone.

"Yes," she said wearily. "I heard your conversation. Tavia, I don't know if we'll last 'til nightfall."

"You won't be waiting that long." I returned to Bea's room and grabbed a few essential items. Durable shoes, a thick coat, and the silver dagger I'd never had the chance to return to Cyan. "I'm coming right now."

"What? Not by yourself!"

I paused on my way out of the apartment, looking back at Bea still fast asleep. She could withstand pre-dusk light and any backup would help. Just as quickly as I thought of it, I dismissed the idea and shut the door behind me. I'd be wasting precious time waking her up and explaining the situation. Plus, I didn't want to put any more of my friends at risk of losing their lives.

"Yeah, it's just me. The vamps are sitting ducks until it's dark, so what else am I going to do?" I flew up the stairs and crossed the empty great room, heading straight for the garage.

"You'll get yourself killed! There's, I dunno, a dozen, maybe twenty of those things out there."

"I'm armed and I won't pick a fight, I'll head straight for you. I just—" My voice choked and I tried again. "I just want to be with Amy."

There was a long pause and then Robin's panic-laden voice. "Be careful, Tavia. I mean it. Be so fucking careful."

"I will, promise." With the flick of a light switch, the fleet of motorcycles became visible. "I gotta go, Robin. But I'll see you soon."

I hung up before we could get into a drawn-out, emotional goodbye, and headed for the spare bikes that were parked in a far corner. Cyan told me they used these when their main rides needed repairs or were out of commission for whatever reason.

Did I actually know how to ride a motorcycle? No. Did that matter to me when my best friend probably didn't have much longer to live? Absolutely not.

I had driven quads back at Sapien, so I figured I knew the basics. This was just two wheels instead of four. Besides, I'd seen Cyan and the others start these puppies up plenty of times. How hard could it be?

I went for the smallest motorcycle, figuring it would be the most comfortable for my stature, and saw that the keys were still in the ignition. After a quick turn, the bike sputtered a bit only to fall dead.

"No, no. Come on, I need you."

It took a few tries, but she finally turned over, roaring to life. I grabbed the helmet resting on the seat and hopped on, testing my balance before bringing the kickstand up. The gas tank was half full, which was hopefully enough to get to where I needed.

Even if it wasn't, I'd run the rest of the way if I had to.

Once I was confident I could stay on the bike, I hit the garage door button clipped to the handlebars and waited impatiently for the door to rise. Accelerating gently until I cleared the door, I hit the button again to close it, then flooded the throttle with gas.

The sudden movement jolted me, but I kept steady and the bike upright. Wind whipped my hair and jacket as I zoomed across the landscape. The more steady I felt in the seat, the faster I went. Amy needed me and time was not on my side.

To the west, the distant mountain peaks of Vargmore, the werewolf territory, were just touching the bottom of the sun as it lowered. By the time the sun was fully below the horizon, it might already be too late.

I leaned low over the handlebars, my eyes on the stretch of road leading me home. Not so much the place, but the person. I had thought that being with Cyan could be home, but he showed me how wrong that was.

If he didn't need me, I'd give my everything to those who did. I had never failed to be there for Amy when she needed me. And I wasn't about to start now, when she needed a friend at her side more than ever.

Hold on, Ames, I prayed. *I'm coming. Just please, please hold on.*

Chapter 23

Cyan

Putrid, rotten blood that made me want to vomit. Since I broke my blood mate's heart, that was what I had to look forward to at every feeding. And it would be nothing less than what I deserved.

I licked my lips. Moved my tongue around inside my own mouth as if I could lick up any remnants of her. But I had swallowed her blood so greedily, so selfishly, all I had left were memories of how she tasted.

It was nearing dusk and time for me to get up, not that I'd slept a wink since watching Tavi leave.

The hurt on her face played over and over in my mind, cutting me deeply every time. *I'd* done that to her, to my blood mate I was supposed to cherish and keep safe. I made her feel unwanted, unyearned for like she was just an option, when nothing could be further from the truth. No matter how many times I tried to convince myself that pushing her away was for her own good, it felt like a lie.

My instincts screamed at me to chase her down and find her, make everything better. To apologize and own up to my fuck ups, even when I knew she'd never give me another chance. I wanted her to know the truth, to tell her exactly why I was so unworthy of her as a blood mate, but I feared she would still try to see the good in me despite it.

Kalix never blamed me for what happened twenty years ago. He never wavered in his defense of me for a single moment, despite the fact that I'd objectively ruined his life. Tavi seemed like the kind of person to do that too. People like that never stopped trying to help those around them, not even lost causes like me.

Even though I wanted to come clean about why I was so fucked up, I wouldn't. Everyone in the clan already knew, so I was surprised she didn't. Or maybe she did and just never brought it up. Either way, it didn't matter. There would be no trying to win her over. The best thing to do was leave her alone. I'd played with her feelings enough already.

The pound of a heavy fist at my apartment door jolted me out of my wallowing. That kind of knock could only come from Rhain.

"What?" I demanded, not moving from bed.

"Thorne's calling an emergency meeting," he bellowed through the door.

"When?"

"Right fucking now."

His booted feet stomped away, leaving me to wonder if I could skip the meeting. Emergencies usually meant all hands on deck, but in light of what just happened with Tavi, nothing else felt like it mattered as much.

Her blood would sustain me for the next few days, and then I had a lifetime of choking down vile blood that wasn't hers just to stay alive. An emergency could wait for me to have a bit of a mourning period, right? Variety was no longer the spice of life. It was the gross shit I would punish myself with.

I managed to get out of bed and dressed decently, then headed for the great room where a dozen clan members stood around the large kitchen island.

"Nice of you to join us, Cyan," Thorne grouched from the far end. He had an ash tray of two spent darakt cigarettes in front of them, and was already halfway through smoking a third.

I ignored his attitude, because Thorne always had one, and shouldered my way between Des and Laith. "What'd I miss?"

"Sapien is under attack," Rhain supplied. "Your blood pet got a call from someone she knows and she alerted Thorne."

"Seeing as we're the ruling clan and have taken their sacrifice in the Half-Century Selection, we have an obligation to respond." Thorne almost sounded bored.

Shock and disbelief speared through me. "Under attack from what? Who?"

"From the sounds of it, a horde of drae addicts." Thorne drew hard on his cigarette, indicating he was more stressed than he was letting on. "But that doesn't make sense, considering we know how draitrium affects cognitive function and motor skills. Sometimes they act erratic, but most of those on it want to do nothing but lie in the sun all day."

A collective shudder ran through nearly every vampire in the room. Nothing sounded worse than being touched by the light emitted from the giant ball of gas in the sky we were never meant to see.

"The drae could be mixed with something else," Des suggested. "Something that amps them up and makes them aggressive."

"An entire contaminated batch, you think?" Thorne lifted an eyebrow. "Octavia made it sound like the whole compound was overrun with them. That could be anywhere from a dozen to twenty."

"Fuck, that many?" My thoughts reeled. Aside from Tavi, I didn't care much for humans, but they didn't deserve to be slaughtered. And her friend Amy was in that settlement. She was important to Tavi, which meant she was important to me.

"Something else is going on," Rhain huffed. "If a batch got contaminated, there would be random attacks popping up all over the territory. But a bunch of them swarming one location sounds coordinated. Someone set those addicts on the human compound for a reason."

"I agree." Thorne finished his third cigarette. "But we don't have time to speculate on that now. Make sure we keep one or two alive. We'll bring them back here to detox and talk. Be fucking sharp, they will be unpredictable. Any questions?"

"When did this happen?" I said.

"Octavia came to me almost an hour ago."

"An *hour?* What the fuck? Do we know if there are any humans left to save?"

Thorne narrowed his eyes at me. "Since Blood 'til Dawn doesn't partake in draitrium, there wasn't much we could do until the sun went down, Cyan."

Logically I knew that, but panic was settling in at the danger Tavi's friend was in.

"Wait, where is Tavi?"

Thorne shrugged. "Your blood pet is your responsibility. Not anyone else's."

Oh fuck. She wouldn't, would she?

I tore away from the group, sprinting toward the garage. Even freshly fed with the best possible blood, I was nowhere near fast enough. Once in the warehouse-sized, concrete and dry-walled room, I scanned the sea of motor-cycles, looking for anything out of place.

Everything seemed to be accounted for, and I started to relax. She was avoiding me naturally, but she was still here. She had to be. Tavi was smart. Rational. She wouldn't be foolish enough to—

My eyes landed on the spare motorcycles in the far corner, and my relief immediately flipped to dread. One was missing.

"Fuck, Tavi," I hissed through clenched teeth.

My worst fear was true. The brave human woman who sacrificed herself to protect her best friend was doing the same thing. Again.

Only this time, she might actually die.

Fuck, fuck, fuck. What the fuck had I done? She left while believing I didn't care. I thought it was the outcome I wanted, the best possible outcome, but not when she was running straight toward death.

I went for my bike, not wasting another moment. Standard procedure was to ride with the whole group, but fuck that. Thorne and the others could catch up, but I needed to save my mate.

"I'm gonna be so pissed off if you die before I can save you." *And heartbroken beyond measure.*

The bike started with a roar, my fingers drumming impatiently while I waited for the bay door to roll up. The moment I had clearance, I flew like a bat out of hell, pushing my bike to the limit.

Hopefully I would catch up to her on the road. She was an inexperienced rider, and it was a two-hour drive at a comfortable cruising speed.

But if she got there before me...

"Hold on, Tavi. Hold the fuck on."

Chapter 24

Tavia

I reached the settlement soon after dusk plunged into full darkness. Too frantic to find the kickstand with my foot, I killed the motorcycle's engine and tried to lay it down as gently as I could. Every second messing with the bike felt like a second wasted, and I hurried into the village brandishing my silver dagger.

It was too still, too quiet, although it was definitely clear there had been fighting and carnage. Outdoor furniture was broken and strewn all over the place. Windows were shattered, recycling and trash cans dented and overturned, spilling their debris all over the ground.

Blood smeared the ground in long messy trails, as if people had been gutted and dragged away. Bloody hand and footprints covered decks and walkways, all chaotic and with no discernible trail.

No one saw them coming. It must have been madness, people running to whatever shelter they could.

Could draetrium have caused this? Such violence seemed extreme for a side effect. The two addicts I'd seen had been rather mild-mannered and subdued, even if the guy in the restaurant was pushy about it. But this seemed like something else entirely. Like letting a pack of starving dogs loose into a chicken coop. Everything around me showed mindless violence and chaos.

Speaking of chickens, feathers floated on a gentle breeze over all the blood and debris littering the ground. In the animal pens up ahead, I could make out the unmoving bodies of the goats and pigs Amy had taken such good care of. Not even the animals had been safe in the attack.

There were no human bodies that I could see, and I didn't know whether to be relieved or more alarmed at that.

A sound made me freeze, and I held my breath to listen harder. I couldn't place what the sound was, and turned to face it when I heard it again.

That had been a mistake.

Something hit me from behind, crashing me to the ground with enough force to knock the wind from my lungs. Rough hands turned me over, bringing me face-to-face with a creature I'd never seen before.

It looked like a vampire, but also not. Its eyes held the sickly yellow tinge of a draitrium high, but the lower canines were more prominent, jutting up from its lower jaw like tusks. Its skin was gray and mottled with purple veins and bruising around its eyes.

If this was a vampire, he—I could only assume it was male—was unlike any I'd ever seen.

He lunged toward my neck, and I crossed my arms in front of me in an automatic reflex. An animalistic scream erupted from my attacker, and then raindrops fell from my hands and forearms.

No, not rain. Blood.

I forgot that I had been clutching my silver dagger. The

blade had sliced across his face and he scrambled away from me, his skin hissing from where the metal had burned him.

His screams must have alerted others because I spotted movement behind corners and obstacles. More creatures like him emerged, yellow eyes bright as lamplight in the darkness.

I scrambled to my feet, turning in circles to find myself surrounded by yellow-eyed demons. Porchlights threw long shadows, making it seem like there were twice as many as there really were.

I held my knife out as I spun, pausing when I saw the door to the community cellar in the distance. That was where Amy was, where I had to go. All I needed to do was get through this ever-shrinking circle of danger.

They were closing in on me quickly, saliva dripping down their massive lower fangs. Could they even be reasoned with?

"Let me through." I held my dagger out in front of me, injecting as much strength into the demand as I could muster. Cyan always called me brave, but I felt moments away from curling into a ball from fear. "I don't want to hurt any of you, so just let me get past you."

One of them blinked, head cocking to the side. He was large and muscular, looking almost carved from stone with his gray skin.

"...Hurt...?" He mused on the word quietly, like it was familiar but he couldn't remember what it meant.

"Right. This is silver. It'll hurt you." I kept turning in a circle, trying to watch my back at every angle. "I don't want to do that."

"Sill-verr," another snarled before he lunged at me.

His sudden movement startled me so much that I nearly tripped, swinging the dagger wildly as I backed away. It wasn't until my back crashed into something that I realized I lost track of my surroundings.

A fist grabbed my hair and yanked my head back, exposing my throat while pain shot through my scalp. I held my weapon up in front of my neck as Cyan had trained me, my only flimsy defense against these mindless monsters hellbent on tearing me apart.

What was once my worst fear came true, I realized. I thought this would be my fate when I met Cyan. Trapped and cornered while the bloodthirsty creatures dove in for the kill. Feeling everything as they drank my blood, rended my flesh from my bones, only dying when they got past my rib cage and tore out my heart.

Although not in the literal sense, Cyan had certainly done that.

I brandished the dagger as if I were going to cut my own throat, my eyes wide and darting around as the monsters grew closer. With my head pulled back so far, I couldn't see the ground near my legs.

Which was where the immense pain began.

It burned at first, like two hot nails driving into the meat of my thigh muscle. The pain was so blinding and sudden that I couldn't even scream. And then the nails pulled and twisted, trying to rip my flesh from my body.

The horrifying reality dawned on me then. I didn't need my eyes to know that one of them had bitten my leg. My body jerked with the force of the pulling and tearing. The whole limb felt it would get ripped off if I didn't do something.

I stabbed downward blindly with the dagger, realizing too late that the move left my throat exposed. They must have been waiting for me to lower my arm because multiple fanged mouths laughed, and dove in for my unprotected neck.

I was dead.

And I had failed to save Amy.

I squeezed my eyelids shut, afraid to face the gnashing teeth and ashamed of my wasted effort. I'd never even made it to the cellar, never got to be with Amy while she was injured and scared.

So much for being brave.

Someone yanked me so hard, I felt teeth rip through the bite on my leg. Oh fuck, they were going to fight over my corpse like a pride of lions over a gazelle. I was going to end up in pieces all over the ground like the debris when I first arrived.

My body jostled violently, my bad leg aching and dragging. Someone was running as they carried me away, trying to hoard my flesh and blood to themselves.

"I got you, Tavi. Gotta get you somewhere safe, then I'll fix you up."

...Cyan?

My cowardly eyes wanted to crack open and look, to see if that warm, angelic voice was real. But it couldn't be. He'd have to have been right behind me to catch up. And even if he could have reached me in time, he wouldn't. He didn't care enough, and had told me as much.

"You're okay. That's a nasty wound but you're going to be fine."

A hand cradled the back of my head so tenderly, it soothed the pain in my scalp from where my hair had been pulled. Damn, these near-death, blood loss hallucinations hit me right in the heartstrings.

Still not daring to open my eyes, I felt myself being lowered slowly to lie on a flat surface. Pressure on the hot, burning ache on my leg made me cry out, and a warm hand caressed my face as if to comfort me.

"Look at me, Tavi. Are you hurt anywhere else?"

My eyelids fluttered open, helpless to resist. Red eyes, not yellow, stared back at me. The brow that had been so smooth and relaxed in sleep now knitted in concern. For me.

"Cy?" I croaked weakly.

He gave me that familiar, playful smirk. "Can't wait to hear my name like that again, but for completely different reasons."

I was in too much pain to laugh and his smile immediately died. "Are you bitten anywhere else? This blood," he leaned in and inhaled near my neck. "It's not yours."

"I...cut one of them. With the dagger you gave me."

His smile returned, bright and proud while his hand passed over me, checking for injuries. "That's my brave little human."

Once satisfied that I only had the one bite, he pressed both hands over the wound. His fingers were already dark with blood.

"I have to do this fast." He sounded almost apologetic. "You might want to close your eyes again. It'll look weird to you and probably pretty gross."

The pain was so sharp and intense, pulsing up my leg. I clenched my teeth against the sensation and each breath felt like torture.

"What are you—"

Cyan ripped my jeans, exposing the ragged, torn flesh without the bloodsoaked fabric in the way. Fresh blood poured from the open wound and I felt woozy, but I couldn't look away as Cyan lowered his mouth to my leg.

What the fuck, was he going to drink from me while I was a gushing fountain?

But rather than drawing blood into his mouth, he dragged his tongue over my ragged, torn flesh.

Again and again, he licked me. The pain faded to a dull numbness, and then a slight itch. And I realized, with each swipe of his tongue, the bleeding slowed. He kept going until it seemed like I was more or less closed up.

"Thank you," I whispered, now lightheaded from the sudden absence of pain. My leg still ached, but it was tolerable compared to moments ago.

"It's the least I can do for you," Cyan murmured. "You may still bleed a little, but you should be okay until I have time to take care of you properly."

I ignored the implication that he would have anything to do with me at all after this. Now I was no longer on death's door, my priorities were righted.

"Amy," I said. "She got hurt. They're hiding in the cellar across the center of the compound. I need to see her."

To my surprise, Cyan sprang immediately into action, hoisting me easily into his arms like a groom carrying his bride. "There's a way around these buildings, right? All the marrowers seem to be concentrating in the center."

"Yeah, head left around these houses."

I had no brain space to think about why he was helping me so readily, how he got here so fast. The last time I saw him, he'd all but admitted that he was only nice to manipulate me. Amy was the only important thing.

But it still made me wonder. What did he have to gain from saving my life, saving Sapien? It wasn't like I'd ever consent to giving him my blood again.

"The rest of the clan is on their way," he said between my directions to the cellar, not even breathing hard from the exertion of carrying me, running, and talking. "We'll clean this shit up in an hour. Don't worry about a thing, Tavi."

"How did you get here so fast?" My hands clasped together around his neck. Just because it felt more secure, not because I wanted to hold onto him for any reason.

"Rode at top speed all the way here and burned my tires to strips." The corner of his mouth hooked in that smirk again. "Gonna have to catch a ride with someone else on the way back."

But why? I wanted to ask, but was too afraid of what the answer would be.

"Here we are." Cyan carefully lowered my legs to the ground in front of the cellar doors, but kept his arm wrapped around my upper back to support.

"Robin!" I yelled, pounding on the aged wood. "It's me, Tavia!"

I glanced around nervously while waiting for a response, but Cyan seemed undisturbed.

"We'll handle them," he assured with a squeeze around my waist. "I can hear the others' bikes now."

Just as the distant roar of engines became clear to me, the cellar doors cracked open. "Tavia?"

"Robin!"

She pushed one of the doors all the way open to let me through while Cy supported me down the rickety stairs, not letting go until the last possible moment. Robin of course knew him, but I heard a small chorus of gasps from others crowded in the cellar.

Cyan ignored them, his gaze focused on me. "Have them barricade the doors from inside as best you can. Do not open the cellar for any reason until you hear my voice."

"Okay." I nodded. "Be careful."

Again, that smirk. "What's the fun in that?" And then he was closing the doors.

"You heard him," Robin said to the onlookers. "Pull the chain back through the handles and weigh it down with anything heavy. Go!" To me, she said, "Did you get attacked?" and eyed my sore leg that I was favoring.

"Yeah, but I'm fine. Cyan helped." I held onto a shelf of canned preserves for support, not wanting to explain the healing properties of vampire saliva right then. "Where's Amy?"

Robin's face turned grave. "Come with me."

She wrapped an arm around my waist and helped me walk to a small alcove toward the back of the cellar. We turned a corner and I saw a pale figure lying on a cot covered with a blanket up to her collarbones. All around the cot were piles of blood-soaked towels and linens.

"Amy!" I forgot all about my leg and it collapsed under me when I let go of Robin and tried to run.

I felt wetness on my skin, probably my wound splitting open and bleeding, but that didn't matter. I dragged myself to Amy's side, terrified to touch her face that was entirely too pale.

"Hey Ames, it's me." My hand shook as I pet her hair. "It's okay. I made it. I'm here. I made it."

Her eyes were closed and her lips were parted. She was just sleeping, she had to be. They had to give her something to knock her out for the pain, right?

"Dr. Barrow didn't have time to grab anything for a blood transfusion." Robin's hand came to rest on my shoulder. "She's lost a lot of blood, Tavi. And there was...organ damage. I'm so sorry."

I heard everything she said, but none of it registered. They were just words. Just sounds. Meaningless noise.

"It's okay," I repeated. "Cyan can help her. He's...he's helped me so much." I knew I was babbling, the adrenaline wearing off only to be replaced with denial and grief. "Cyan can make you all better, Ames. He closed me up, made me all better. You'll be okay."

Keeping it together felt like a Herculean task, but I forced my eyes to stay on her neck and chest. Did she have a pulse? Was she breathing? Why was it so hard to tell?

I pressed two fingers to the side of her neck and my sanity started to crumble when I didn't feel anything. Then...there it was! Faint and slow, but I felt her pulse.

"That's my girl," I whispered. "You don't let them beat you down, no matter what. You're so much stronger than you know, Ames." I forced out a laugh. "Hell, you don't even need me. Not really."

She didn't answer. I didn't know if she could hear me.

And then her pulse stopped.

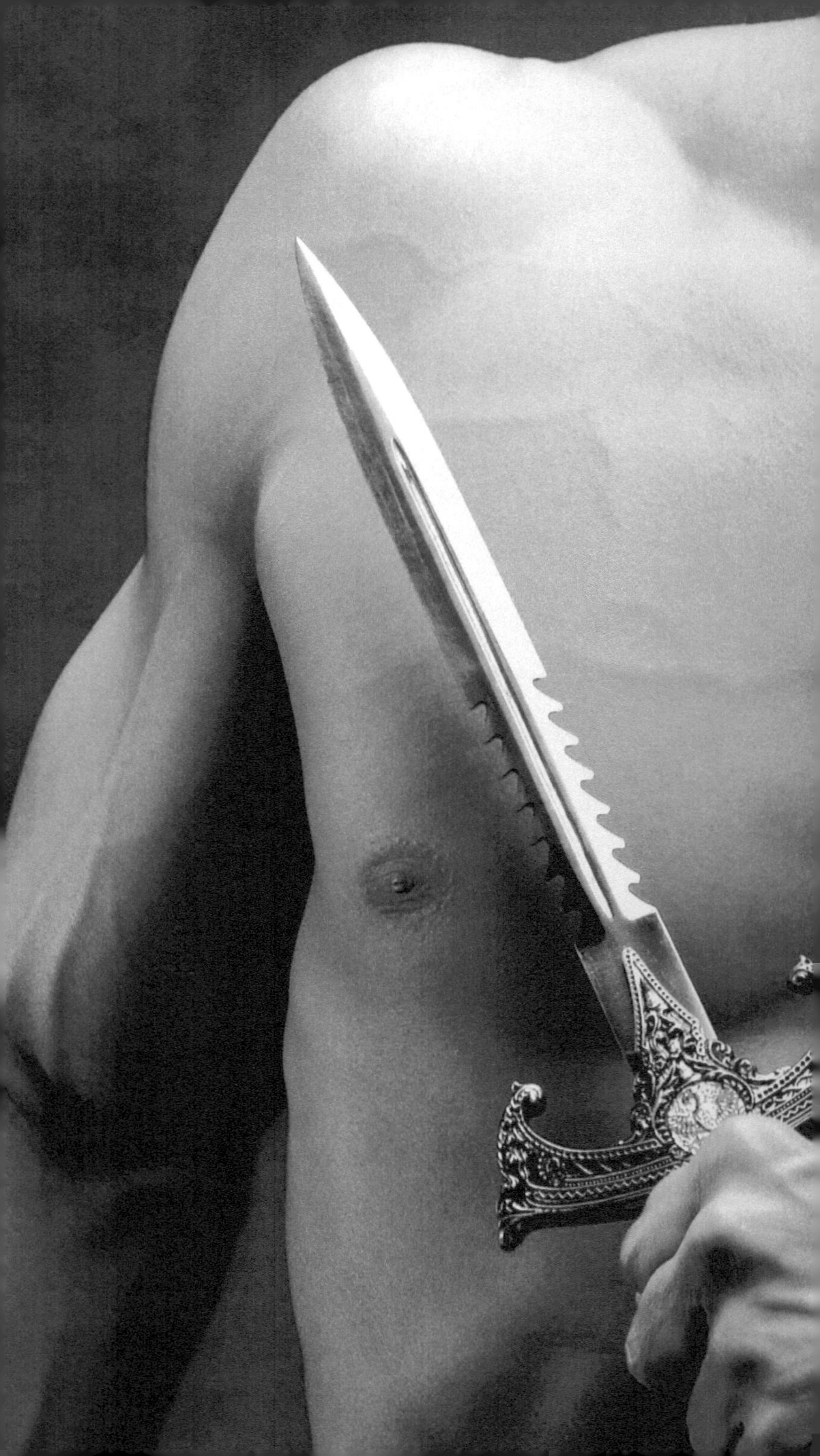

Chapter 25

———

Cyan

arrowers, despite their fearsome appearance, were known as the gentlest of vampires. They largely kept to themselves, steered clear of clan conflicts, and contented themselves with raising livestock for their diet rich in bone marrow.

That knowledge did not help me as a huge, roaring, tusked bastard came at me while swinging fists the size of my head.

"Don't kill them if you don't have to!" Thorne was dodging his own marrower, a significantly smaller one than mine, which hardly seemed fair. "We need information, not more bodies."

"Easy for you to say," I muttered, ducking low to avoid another punch that could have severed my skull from my spine.

My attacker bellowed again, the sound both frustrated and anguished. His pupils were pinpricks, and both eyes had taken on a pale, sickly yellow tinge. Regular, prolonged draitrium use caused the mineral to accumulate in the body, making the user's eyes a deeper yellow over time. This guy didn't have that solid egg yolk color going on. He was a new user, if he was one at all.

From afar, he looked like my friend Drace, the bartender in Marrowtown. I was relieved to find out it wasn't him upon closer inspection, but getting that close got me right up in his punching zone.

I got inside his block and jabbed an elbow into his throat, making him stagger backward and choke. The two silver daggers on me were itching to be used, but if Thorne wanted to keep casualties low, it was best to keep the silver put away.

"They're too fucking aggro, Thorne!" The declaration came from Rhain, who struggled to keep a scrappy, wriggling marrower in a headlock. "We can't keep 'em all subdued until they sober up."

"Do what you have to."

A marrower ripped a fence post out of the ground, lifted it over his head, and ran straight for Thorne. The clan leader's movement was barely perceptible but seconds later, the marrower stopped in his tracks and dropped the post. He crumpled to the ground like a puppet whose strings had been cut, and Thorne's dagger glinted from where it was buried in the marrower's throat.

"Try to keep them from damaging more of the humans' property," Thorne drawled as he went to retrieve his weapon. "We have an agreement to honor with them."

I turned back to the guy who had been on me, only to find him on hands and knees, gasping for breath. He held up a palm in a clear stop motion as I approached.

"Please..." he wheezed. "I...I don't know...where I am..."

I crouched low on my haunches. "Look up. Let me see your eyes."

He glanced up, teeth chattering like he was freezing.

His pupils were more pronounced now, as they should have been. As if on reflex, he wiped under his eyes at the yellow goop leaking from them. He stared at his fingers, brow creasing in a frown.

"What...happened to me? Where am I?"

"You're going to be okay," I told him in my most calming tone. "Looks like you're coming down from the drug."

"Drug? What?" His frown deepened like he was trying to concentrate. "Did I hurt someone?"

He was covered in blood, the dark redness covering from his tusks and chin to his neck and shirt. In his drugged out haze, he had most definitely hurt someone. Or several someones.

"We're going to find out what happened to you," I said. "You will be okay. What's your name?"

"My name? It's, uh." He blinked a few times. "It's Lore. My name is Lore."

"Good to meet you, Lore. I'm Cyan." I offered a hand to help him stand. "You know another marrower named Drace?"

Lore took my hand and the strength I felt as he pulled himself up was unreal. If he really wanted to, he could rip my arm from its socket. "Drace? He's my cousin. Well," He tilted his head. "Fourth cousin, or something."

I nodded, pleased that he sounded lucid. The drug may have had a weaker effect on him due to his size. With a quick glance around, I noted that the rest of the marrowers were now knocked out, dead, or tied up to keep subdued.

Bracing myself with a breath, I asked Lore, "Do you recognize any of the other marrowers here? Are they... family, acquaintances?"

"I...I don't think so. Fuck, I'm so thirsty." He rubbed his

throat and started to turn around with a bewildered expression. "What is this place? How did I get here?"

"Let me take you to my clan leader," I said. "He'll explain, and then we'll get you hooked up with some marrow and blood. Sound good?"

"Okay." Lore looked apprehensive, if even scared. I couldn't say I blamed him.

———

AFTER MAKING introductions between Lore and Thorne, I ran to the cellar doors and pounded on them like it had been weeks since I'd seen Tavi and not just a few hours. "It's me, Cyan. It's safe to come out now."

It felt like an eternity before those doors parted and I found myself staring at the older human woman, Robin, plus a lot of other fear-stricken faces. None of them were Tavi's.

"Where is she?" I barely stifled my growl.

"Are you going to feed on us?" one of the humans called.

"No," I snarled in annoyance. "The agreement between us remains intact. Now where is Octavia?"

Robin moved to the side of the narrow ladder leading down into the cramped storage room. "She's in the very back. Let him through." She gestured for others to move aside as well.

I climbed down into the cramped, musty space, angling my head to not bump it against the ceiling. "Thank you," I remembered to say to Robin. She was important to Tavi, so I'd make sure to show respect.

I didn't have to walk far to find Tavi, sitting on the dirt floor next to a cot where a pale human girl lay eerily still. Only one human heartbeat registered in my senses, Tavi's.

The sight of her made my heart break for my blood mate. Her pain, her loss, was my own. It clamped around my chest and squeezed with a terrible ache. I didn't know if it was seeing her that caused it, or her blood circulating through me, creating an intangible but direct line straight into the core of her.

Tavi didn't seem to know that I was there. She stroked her dead friend's hair and wiped blood and dirt from Amy's face.

"Tavi." Her name left my throat on a strangled choke. I knew her loss too well, even if I hadn't had her blood in me. Kalix may not have been dead, but he was ripped away from me all the same.

"Cyan." Her head lifted, hope brimming in her tear-filled, stormy eyes. "You're here. You can fix her, can't you?"

A knot formed in my throat. "I'm not sure what—oh fuck, Tavi. You're bleeding."

I knelt on the floor next to her, carefully examining one of the seams of her leg injury that had reopened. Wetting two fingers on my tongue, I rubbed the two digits over the split in her skin. Like magic, the two sides restitched together. I would have loved to lick her directly, get a little more of her blood in me, but this moment was not about what I wanted.

"Yes, that!" Tavi grabbed my hand, an excited, but not fully present smile spreading on her face. "Use your mouth to heal Amy."

Fuck me, she was breaking my heart. "Tavi." I caressed her hand, knowing I needed to take the utmost care in what I said next. "I'm so sorry, love. It won't work."

"It might! You have to try. Just please try, Cyan." Her

smile went away, bottom lip wobbling as tears filled her eyes. "Please."

I shook my head slowly. "It doesn't work if...if she's already gone."

Tavi's eyes widened as if in shock. "She's not gone, she's right here!"

The full weight of reality seemed to hit her as soon as the words left her mouth. She drew in a shuddering breath, and then a sob wracked her whole torso as she looked at her friend again, this time *knowing* Amy was dead. I pulled her into my arms as she cried soul-choking sobs with fat tears spilling down her face. It was too fucking much. She had loved this girl so much and her pain was too great to bear.

The unfairness of it all pissed me off. Tavi asked for nothing. She literally placed herself in the path of danger to protect the friend she was now crying next to. She turned herself over to my clan, to *me*, fully believing she would die so that Amy had a chance to live.

Tavi sacrificed herself over and over again. And in return for all that selflessness, her best friend was ripped away from her. It felt like a cruel joke.

This brave, beautiful human in my arms deserved the world because she would never think to ask for it. Never for herself, anyway. And that was exactly why I wished I could give it to her. If only I could pluck a planet or a star from the sky and place it in the palm of her hand.

Not because I wanted her to be mine. But simply because she deserved an extraordinary gift, an extraordinary *life* full of all her wishes granted. All her desires fulfilled.

I would never be worthy of her. But if I could give Tavi a fraction of what she deserved, I'd be content with it.

"Tavi," I whispered into her hair, barely audible over her sobs. "I...might be able to try something."

She lifted her head and looked up at me, her eyes red and filled with so much sorrow. "Yes."

"I need you to listen, love." It was the second time the endearment had slipped out and I cursed my own weakness for her. Especially now when she needed me for strength.

"Yes, yes. I don't care what it is." Tavi swallowed and sniffled. "Try anything. Just bring her back, Cy."

Her faith in me was the twist of a silver knife in my gut, especially after I'd been so fucking cruel to her just this morning.

I smoothed her hair away from her face and cupped her cheeks in my hands. "It might not work. That is a real possibility you need to be aware of. But I can..." my throat tightened with the realization of how much this affected me too. "I can try to turn her into a brusang. Do you understand?"

Tavi blinked and fresh tears spilled down her face. I caught them with my thumbs. Despite the pain in them, her eyes were bright and aware.

"A brusang. Like Bea?"

"Yes," I said. "Her eyes will go black and she'll gain a vampire's lifespan. She will become far less tolerant of sunlight and she'll need blood to live. I need you to think really hard, Tavi. Is that the kind of life Amy would want?"

She looked at Amy's body stretched out on the cot, then smoothed a hand over her friend's brow and hair. Seconds of silence stretched into minutes, and then came the soft sounds of crying. I ran my hand up and down Tavi's back, but said nothing. It wasn't an easy decision, and I would't rush her or try to influence her.

Truthfully, I had my doubts it would work. Every instance I'd heard of a brusang's turning, it had been right before their death as a human or very shortly after. Amy's skin had become deathly pale to the point where she began to look gray.

But for Tavi I would try, if she wanted me to.

Her crying quieted after a few minutes, and then she straightened. She wiped the tears off her cheeks in a rough, almost defiant way.

"Go ahead," she said with a firm nod. "Try to turn her." Her voice was rough, but strong. She was in her right mind and sure about this.

"Okay." I didn't waste time moving closer toward Amy's head. "I have to give her my blood."

Tavi nodded but then quickly held up a hand. "Wait. Does this...bind her to you in any way?"

"No, it doesn't work like that," I assured her. "Human and vampire organs are similar enough that my blood may revitalize and sustain her with some physical changes. She won't be in my thrall or anything like that. Just...changed."

"Okay." She took hold of Amy's hand and rubbed her friend's small, pale fingers. "Go ahead, then."

"Will you hold her mouth open for me?"

Tavi obliged and I bit into my own wrist a moment before pressing it to Amy's lips. She lifted Amy's head and massaged her throat to simulate swallowing.

Please don't be too late. I wasn't much of a praying man, but it seemed like no better time to ask Temkra for a little divine assistance. *Please don't let me fail someone I love again.*

Now that was probably too much of an ask. Failing those most important to me was my number one talent, after all.

"How much do you need to give her?" Tavi asked after we'd been at it for about five minutes.

"Not sure," I admitted. "Better too much than too little, I think."

We kept going until no more blood could be physically forced down Amy's throat. I sealed up my wrist while Tavi fluffed up her pillow and pulled the blanket up higher on her.

"When will we know if it worked?" Her eyes were already bright with hope. It would shatter me if that light were to be snuffed out.

"Let's give it three days," I said. "Brusang usually awaken a day or two after being turned. By three, we should definitely have our answer."

Tavi leaned into me again and I let her, eager and glad to be what she needed even if it were just for right now.

"Thank you, Cyan," she whispered into my chest.

I stroked her hair and her shoulders, the need to be honest weighing heavily on me. "I need you to understand that it might not work, Tavi. The best odds for a successful change is around fifty-fifty. I've never changed anyone before, so I don't think we're looking at optimal odds."

She looked up and actually gave me a small, sad smile. "It's okay. At least you tried."

I was lost for words, and could only hold her a little tighter. Even now, after everything I'd done to her and what happened with Amy, she kept her own desires in check to reassure *me*.

I'd never deserve her in a million years. But if this did work, I wanted to believe that maybe I could deserve her just a tiny bit.

All we had to do was wait.

Chapter 26

Tavia

The cellar had cleared out of people while Cyan and I sat with Amy, which was a relief. I didn't want any of them looming while I grieved. While we attempted to revive her into what was essentially a human-vampire hybrid.

I didn't want to leave her side. If she woke up, I didn't want to miss it. I didn't want her to be confused or scared of what she would become.

I didn't want to fail her again.

Cyan stayed with me the whole time, which was a comfort beyond what I thought I needed. Everything that had happened between us was shoved away, at least temporarily. My mind put his callous rejection in a box, stuck it in a closet, and closed the door. It was still there, but I'd deal with it later.

Right then, I was brimming with a hope that I knew was dangerous. I knew it was a possibility that Amy wouldn't wake up. I also knew I'd be irreversibly broken if that happened.

So I was glad to not be alone. And I shouldn't have been, but I was glad it was him.

I didn't know how long we sat there before he started stirring.

"You should rest," he said. "Do you want me to find some bedding so you can stay with her?"

I shook my head. "There's no way I'll be able to sleep." Exhaustion rode me hard, but my brain would refuse to shut off until three days passed or Amy's eyes opened.

"You should still get some fresh air." Cyan scooted away from me and stood, holding out his hand. "And some food. When did you last eat?"

Stubbornly, I remained on the floor, watching Amy's face for any signs of life. "If you see Robin, could you ask her to bring me something? I can't leave her."

"Tavi." Cyan took my chin in his fingers, making me look at him. There was that warmth, that caring nature that came out when he wasn't cold and aloof. "She won't wake up for a while yet. Hours, if not days. Let me take care of you while we wait."

"Why?" The word came out harsher than I intended, and I suspected that the box in which I shoved my heartache cracked open just a little bit.

Cyan didn't hesitate. "Because the person who never thinks of herself needs someone to make her a priority."

Taking my hands, he pulled me to my feet. I didn't resist and it wasn't forceful, but it was clear he was insistent. He gave a quick glance at Amy and said, "Don't worry. I'll bring her right back," then marched us out of the alcove and up the cellar stairs.

The first hit of fresh, outside air was a shock to my system. I didn't realize how stale it had been down in the cellar. The cool, night breeze held a note of smoke, and I looked around to see activity buzzing around me.

People were burning the trash and debris that had been strewn everywhere in the attack. Others chopped up the mangled furniture into smaller pieces for kindling. Another group brought buckets of water from the well, and tossed it over the worst of the bloodstained porches, doors, and walls before scrubbing the dark stains with soapy brushes.

Aside from the one standing next to me, not a single vampire was in sight.

"Where did the clan go?"

"Took the marrowers to be detoxed and questioned. They'll be back tomorrow night with new tires for my bike."

"Tomorrow night?" I repeated. "So you're spending the day here?"

He flinched. "Is that okay with you? I should have checked first, I'm sorry."

"It's fine but I just—I dunno where it's safe for you here during the day."

"I can stay in the cellar, should be sunproof enough. That way, I can watch over Amy if you fall asleep."

"Okay. Yeah, good. I want to stay with her." *And you.* It felt like Cyan was the only reason I could string a coherent sentence. Somehow, without even touching me, he kept me together. If I was alone or with anyone else, I'd be an inconsolable mess right now.

"Hey, there you are." I turned to see Robin approach me with a dented metal thermos filled with water and a sandwich wrapped in a paper towel. She shoved the items into my hands and gave me a simple instruction. "Eat."

The sandwich was thin, a simple slice of cheese, turkey, and a quick swipe of mustard between two heels of a bread loaf. I took robotic bites and chewed as Cyan turned to Robin. "What can I do to help with the cleanup?"

She and I stared at him aghast. A vampire offering to help humans was unheard of. It completely flipped the notion we'd been taught all our lives. That we were here to serve *their* needs.

"You want to help?" Robin looked at me and then back at him.

"I do." He swallowed and cleared his throat, straightening like he was addressing someone who deserved the utmost respect. "And I know your community must be confused and reeling from this attack. Blood 'til Dawn failed to uphold our end of the Half-Century Agreement when your home was attacked. I will personally make sure we atone for that. We will find out what caused this and I vow to you it will not happen again. It would be my honor to seal this vow into my skin—"

"You don't have to do that," I said, placing my hand on his forearm.

He gave me a sheepish smile, briefly covering my hand with his. Robin's sharp eyes didn't miss the affectionate gesture. "In any case," he went on, "you are my blood mate's people and I feel responsible—"

"Your *what?*" Despite having finished off the water, my throat went completely dry. I stared hard at his side profile, watching the muscle in his jaw clench as he remained silent. He definitely didn't mean to say that.

"Thank you for the offer to help." Robin gave a tight smile, her eyes darting between us. "I'll holler if we need more hands but in the meantime, it seems like you two may need to talk some things out. Tavia, I'll reach out later about Amy's body—"

"Leave her," I said quickly. "I don't want her disturbed down there. Not until I'm ready."

"Of course." Robin mistook my insistence for grief and hurried away. It wasn't like I felt ready to explain Amy's potential resurrection right then anyway. I couldn't get the words *my blood mate* in Cyan's voice out of my head.

"She's right." I turned to face him directly. "We should talk, shouldn't we?"

I expected him to deny it. To shut down and deflect like he always did when we seemed to get close. I braced myself for it but in truth, I wasn't afraid. Losing Amy was the most painful thing I'd ever endured. If she didn't wake up, it would break me. By comparison, another rejection from this vampire was a papercut.

But to my utter shock, Cyan nodded and quietly agreed. "Yeah, we should."

Not five minutes later, we were in the trailer that Amy and I had shared. He dwarfed the small space, gaze floating over our meager belongings like he was trying to find a subject in which to start this uncomfortable conversation.

Only a few seconds of tense silence passed before I couldn't stand it any longer. "So is it true?"

Cyan's throat bobbed with a swallow as his gaze settled on me. "Yeah, it's true."

Emotions thrashed inside me like winds in a storm. Grief. Heartache. Exhaustion. And now a boiling anger.

"Say it, then. I want you to tell me to my face."

He looked calm. But he swallowed again and a vein pulsed in his temple. It was the kind of calm holding back something he didn't want to let out.

"You're my blood mate, Tavi. Only your blood nourishes and sustains me like no other ever has or will."

I stared at him, incredulous. My rising anger crested at a

height I'd never felt before, not even when I saw bullies shove Amy to the ground when we were children. At least that behavior was predictable.

For once I was pissed off on my own behalf. Because I had expected better from Cyan.

"Then why would you lie to me?" I went to sit on my bed but couldn't sit still, so I returned to standing. But standing felt too close to him in this tiny mobile home, so I crossed my arms and tried to force the tears back. "We were in bed together and you just blew me off when I asked if we were blood mates. Why?" I began to shake from the effort of keeping it all together. "Did I...disappoint you?"

"Fucking Temkra, Tavi. No. Nothing could be further from the truth." Cyan's brow furrowed and some of that real, deep emotion shone through his eyes. "You could never disappoint me. I am *awed* by you. From the moment I first saw you, sacrificing yourself for Amy, I have been in awe of you. Your bravery, your strength, your dedication to those who matter to you."

I hated that his words moved me, hated how the rawness and earnesty in voice made me want so badly to believe him. Even after he explicitly told me that I meant nothing, that I was just one blood sample on his variety platter.

But if I was his blood mate, everything else tasted foul to him now. How could this carefree vampire *not* be disappointed that his variety was gone?

I didn't realize my tears had spilled over until I felt his thumbs on my cheeks. I jerked away, fighting the urge to lash out in anger. This vampire didn't deserve my vulnerability. He'd exploited it enough.

"Please leave." I turned away, wiping my face. "Call

someone to pick you up before dawn. I don't want to see you."

"Tavi—"

"No. I'm done, Cyan. I tried and I just can't, okay? Please go before the sun comes up."

I went for the door but he was faster. He darted in front of me, all red eyes and predatory grace. His hands cupped my shoulders and before I could tell him off, he blurted, "I said those things because I don't deserve a blood mate."

The look on his face, raw, open, and even afraid, sank in before his words did. His calm, easy facade had fallen away, and I was staring into the face of an incredibly heartbroken man.

"It's me that's a disappointment, Tavi," he choked out. "I will never, ever be worthy of you."

This was a side of Cyan that I had never seen, except for one fleeting moment. Our conversation from that day in the kitchen replayed in my mind.

"I'm not a very good friend sometimes. I fuck up. I let people down. So if you don't want to be friends with me, I would understand."

Even then, he was trying to warn me away, trying to keep me from getting close.

"I never wanted you to know how fucked up I really am," he went on. Every word seemed to scrape and fight its way out of his throat. "I thought if you got close to me, if you knew, you'd be so let down by me that you'd leave. You deserve much better from a blood mate. That was why I lied, why I avoided you and pushed you away." A mirthless huff of laughter left his lips. "I'm quite the self-fulfilling fucking prophecy, aren't I?"

I backed up a few steps and sat on the edge of my bed, reeling from all this pain and insecurity from the last person

I expected to hear it from. He kept this fear hidden deep underneath flirtatious quips and an easy, charming personality. It was such an abrupt shift that I was completely lost for words.

"Cyan...why do you feel this way about yourself?"

He came toward me and knelt on the floor at my feet. Without thought, I reached for his hand and held it in my lap, finding that my anger had been temporarily deflated.

Staring at our joined hands, he said, "I'm the reason Kalix got locked up."

"Kalix? Your friend who turned Bea into a brusang?"

Cyan nodded. I rubbed his hand and he seemed to draw comfort from it. "We were in a meeting with her boss. The sadistic fucker cut her throat open because she accidentally spilled a drink. She was dying and Kal immediately went to turn her, to save her."

Bea had already told me this, but I didn't dare interrupt him. It sounded like he was getting this off his chest for the first time since it happened.

"That asshole was furious that Kal was trying to save the human he had just murdered, so he lunged to attack Kal. I didn't think, I just acted. I blocked him from reaching Kal, took the letter opener, and stabbed him in the chest with it." Cyan touched his own chest as he seemed to relive the moment in his mind. "It wasn't made of silver, but it went right through his heart. And I'd just made things a lot more complicated for us by murdering the head of another clan."

"Their clan wanted retribution, naturally. And I was terrified. In an act to protect my best friend, I threw Blood 'til Dawn into a conflict we had been desperately trying to avoid. We were negotiating an alliance and I fucked it all up. And then..."

Cyan's voice became even rougher, his breaths shaking slightly. I squeezed both of his hands in my lap, and only then did he seem to find the words.

"Kal took the fall for me. He said he would claim responsibility for the kill and turn himself in. They would get their scapegoat and we would keep the peace."

Cyan's eyes closed on another ragged breath.

"I begged him not to. He was my mentor, my best friend, and I needed him. I was scared out of my fucking mind, but I was willing to own up to what I did. I wanted to step up and take responsibility. But Kal...he wouldn't let me throw my life away. There was no changing his mind. He convinced Thorne it was the right thing to do, and it was done. The only other option was a civil war and we'd worked so hard to avoid that. So Kal went away. The last thing he told me was to look after Bea and to live a good life."

Cyan drew my hand to his right side, just under the vow he made to his clan. The one he'd vaguely mentioned was in remberance of someone when I first saw it.

"I couldn't bring myself to speak Kal's name, so I carved it with a silver blade. I did it slowly, dragging it out to make it as painful as possible. And it still wasn't enough of a punishment."

He looked up, his gaze meeting mine and focusing on me for the first time since he started talking. "I've never been able to forget that I'm the one who should have faced those consequences. Do you understand now, Tavi? I don't deserve a good life. I don't deserve *you*. No matter how much I *ache* with wanting you. You're the most fascinating, brave, and beautiful person I've ever met. I never should have lied. I...I was trying to make you realize that you should hate me."

"I think I knew you were pushing me away," I said after a long silence to take everything in. "I just didn't know why."

"Well, now you know."

"Cyan..." I leaned forward a few inches to rest my forehead on his, and was relieved when he didn't pull away. "Has it ever occurred to you that maybe you *do* deserve happiness?"

He let out a dry, mirthless laugh. "After we woke up in bed together, I never wanted that feeling to end. To spend my days pleasing you and drinking that delicious wine from your veins? Tavi, I would love nothing more than to live in the fantasy that I might actually be worthy of you. But I'm not."

"It doesn't have to be a fantasy," I argued, trying to not get swept up in his words. "This can be real if you'd stop getting in your own way. I'm your blood mate. Biologically, I'm meant for you. And I..." My heart pounded a furious beat, stealing my breath for a moment. "I don't want any other vampire. I want to be with you."

"You deserve bett—"

"Don't tell me what I deserve." I'd cut him off so abruptly that I surprised myself. "Look, I get it. Kal sacrificed himself for you. I know it's a heavy burden to deal with, Cyan, but Kal made that choice. He didn't have to do it, but he did because he loved you. His choice is not a failing on your part, I promise you. He loved you, he wanted you to have a good life, and *that's* the only thing you fucked up. By convincing yourself you don't deserve any happiness because he's gone and you're still here, you're denying your best friend what *he* wanted. And you know what? You're also denying *me* what I want."

I had to stop for a beat, but I wasn't even close to being

done with talking. There was so much to get off my chest, most of which I hadn't even realized until this very moment.

"All my life, I've put aside my own wants. I've been a cog in a machine. A shield that got battered by protecting others. I sacrificed a lot for Amy, so I get where Kal was coming from. And I'm so sorry you lost him. You're entitled to grieve and feel sad."

I pressed a hand to Cyan's cheek, feeling the muscle in his jaw twitch with a swallow. "But don't make his choice your burden. Don't deny what he wanted for you." A shaky breath left my mouth. "I was happy to put aside my wants before. None of them were important as long as Amy was safe. But this," I squeezed our joined hands, "this is important. You are important. You make me feel seen and appreciated for who *I* am. You, Cyan of Blood 'til Dawn, my blood mate, are all I want. I know, just like Kal knew, that you deserve love and happiness. If you need reminders of that, I'll give them to you. Every single day."

There was a long stretch of silence before he spoke. "After what I said to you, how I hurt you, you're telling me you still want this?"

"Well." I measured my response carefully. "Since we're getting so much out in the open, do you regret what you said?"

"Yes." His face was solemn, his eyes flashing with emotion. "Fuck variety, I don't want it. Those other desires vanished the moment I tasted the perfection that was you. Honestly, I started losing my taste for others when I first brought you home. I tried to fight it, but fighting only made me ache harder for you. Being around you brought joy and contentment that I've never had before. When I heard you rode out here alone, I was more scared of losing you than I was of being locked up for murder. It made me realize that instead of pushing you away, I should have been bettering myself."

He swallowed thickly, gaze searing into mine. "You're all that I want, Tavi, and your blood is the only taste I crave."

Despite the elated thrumming in my veins and swooping of my stomach, I stayed firm. "I need to know that you won't push me away again. That you won't intentionally hurt me to create distance. I'll be there for you during low periods, but I will not tolerate having my emotions played with."

"Fuck." Cyan ground out the curse through his teeth, shaking his head in distress. "I was a fucking bastard to do that to you. If you are really blessing me with this chance, I swear to Temkra I'll never say another word to hurt you. And I'll spend the rest of my days making up for treating you that way. I'm so sorry, Tavi."

This vampire, on his knees in front me with his hands in my lap, had no idea he owned my heart already. I was so close to letting go, to leaving all the hurt and confusion in the past and starting anew. But I needed to *know* beyond any doubt that the past would not be repeated.

"I need you to trust me. To be open like this and talk to me," I continued. "I need you to not shut me out. That's how we make this work, Cyan."

He nodded, fingers lacing with mine and gripping tightly. "I've told you my deepest shame and you're still here. I still don't know what you see in me, but if you really want me as I am..."

"I do," I said when he trailed off. "I want the Cyan who helps me make wine and teaches me how to fight with a dagger. The one who came to save me and offered to help us rebuild. Who..." My voice choked, but I forced the words out. "Who offered my best friend a second life because I can't bear to lose her."

More tears fell, all of them caught by the pads of his thumbs. "I will do everything in my power to see you happy and fulfilled. It's not just your blood that sustains me, but the excitement in your voice, and the way your eyes light up. When you are falling apart, I will hold the pieces of you together for as long as you need to heal. I'm no substitute for Amy and I'll never feel truly worthy of you, but I want to be a safe place for you to retreat. I want to be exactly what you need when you need it."

That was when I felt the fear melt away, and the love I'd been too afraid to acknowledge bloomed in full force. From this moment on, I would trust him fully. Deeply. It was on him to trust me too, to be honest and vulnerable in ways he likely never had been before. I had to believe he would choose me every time, and after everything that happened today, and what he'd just told me with all this raw emotion, I was prepared to do that.

"I want you to feel safe with me too," I said. "You are worthy, Cyan. Exactly as you are."

His forehead rocked gently from side to side against mine. "I was such a fucking fool for treating you as I did."

My chin lifted, bringing my nose to brush against his. "You know what I need right now?"

His eyes dilated and I saw the tips of his fangs reach past his lips as he said, "Tell me."

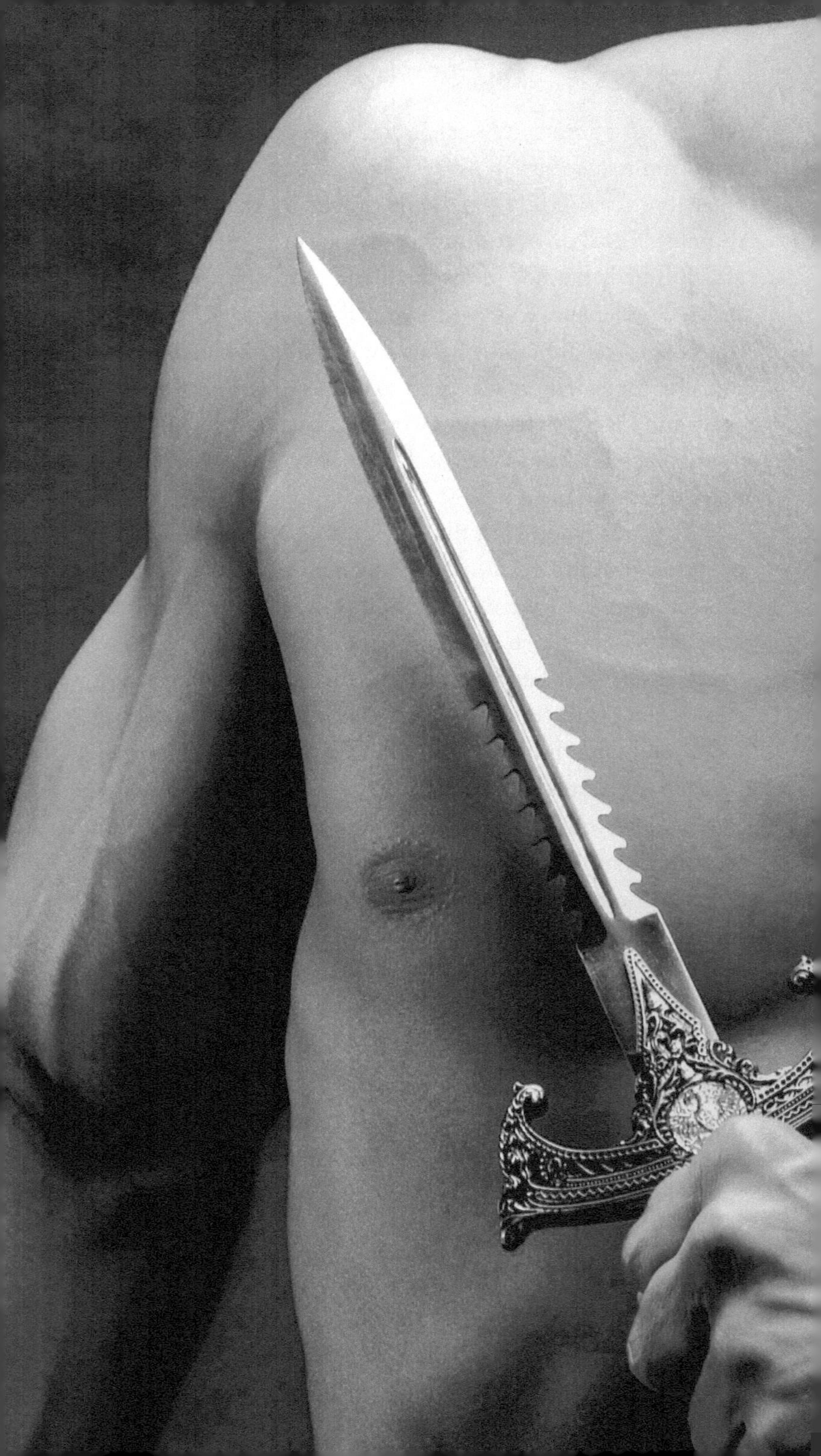

Chapter 27

Cyan

I didn't move an inch. Tavi's breaths ghosted over my lips, her pulse elevating steadily and pounding in time with mine. My fangs ached as she drew closer, the nearness of her, the *safety* of her calling to me more than any lust-based impulses.

Her kiss came hesitantly at first, a shy brushing of lips with barely any pressure. I remained still, not moving even when her mouth grazed my left fang. Only when her tongue darted out to trace it, gliding up the length until the extended tooth disappeared under my lip did I allow myself to tug at her plump lower lip.

Tavi let out a sharp inhale of breath that shuddered through her, and then all shyness was gone. She was in my lap, on the floor with me, arms around my neck and kissing me like she needed me to breathe. If that were ever truly the case, then I would always be her air.

I eased back, giving her enough room to straddle me before I plundered her mouth with the same ferocity. Only the shafts of my fangs touched her mouth, not the points. The last thing she needed was for me to take anything from her now. I needed to *give*. Give her comfort, air, orgasms, anything and all she desired.

On that thought, Tavi's plea came in the rushed, ragged breaths between each kiss. "Take my blood," she said. "Drink from me."

She spoke to my most base instincts with those words. My fangs ached with the pulse of her racing heart. It didn't matter that I was still satiated from the last time I fed from her. Just the offer, the willingness, made my thirst come alive.

My desire to give in wasn't for sustenance or even her taste. There was simply no closer physical connection between blood mates than my fangs inside her and her flavor pouring over my tongue. Only being inside her at the same time would bring us closer together.

But my desires mattered none right now.

"No." I nipped at her with my blunt teeth, careful to keep my fangs away. "You've lost blood from the attack. You still need to heal."

"Please, Cyan." Her begging was sweet on my lips, and I knew she was craving that blood mate connection too.

We had turned a new page, made it to this new place of trust and openness after overcoming obstacles both in our minds and in the physical world. What better way to seal this new era of our lives than with blood?

But it could wait.

"If I feed on you, I could slow your recovery." I wrapped a hand around her nape, applying gentle pressure to the pulses on the sides of her neck. "I'm taking proper care of you now and I won't be fucking around with your health."

"Just take a little?" she pressed. "It feels so good when you do it."

"Tavi," I growled. My pulse pounded everywhere—my chest, my fangs, my cock.

"Yes, Cy?" A wicked smile twitched on her lips. Oh, the little tease.

Before she could blink, I pressed up from the floor and had her stretched out on the bed with each hand pinned next to her head. Her chest heaved with each breath and the pulse fluttered in her neck so sweetly. When I lowered down, it was all I could do to keep my face hovered above hers and not pressed against that sweet vein.

"Be good for me," I said, injecting as much sternness as I could muster. "Or I'll keep you on the brink of orgasm for *days*. That first time was just a small taste of what I'm capable of."

Tavi flushed. Her teeth sank into her lower lip and she writhed underneath me like my warning turned her on rather than struck any kind of fear in her. Fuck, she owned me and she damn well knew it.

"How about just a small taste of me?" Her chin lifted, baring to me the long, beautiful column of her throat.

I lowered and kissed her with a groan, relishing in the softness of her lips and the pulsing of her blood through them as well.

"You're my fate." The lengths of my fangs pressed and dragged over her lips as I kissed her. "I can never have just a taste of you. I will devour you."

Clothes came off in an impatient rush, discarded to the dark corners of the room, maybe shoved between the bed and the wall, I didn't know or care. All that mattered was my naked, breathtaking blood mate. She was hurt, exhausted, anxious to see her friend alive. And she needed me to take some of that away.

I re-pinned her hands in place, pressing her down into

the well-worn mattress with another searing kiss. This bed wasn't as comfortable as mine, but I'd make sure she slept like the dead when I was done with her.

Eventually I had to release her and bring my hands under her, around her back. Our skin sliding together made the most incredible friction. Every point of contact needed to be more. I needed to touch and acknowledge and worship every square inch of her.

Skin on skin was the most exquisite feeling. Tavi was soft and warm everywhere, from her lips to her leg hooking around my hip. A sudden realization brought on a huff of laughter, muffled by my mouth against her shoulder.

"What's funny?" Tavi nipped my earlobe as she said it, one hand dragging over my scalp while the other ran up my back.

"You're the first person I've been completely naked with," I admitted.

This wasn't a quick hookup in a club, a thrilling, but ultimately shallow moment in time with a stranger. This was real intimacy I'd never had before.

"Same here," she breathed.

I pressed up to my hands to take in the full view. She was perfectly visible in the dim lamplight and what a sight she was. Her arms, legs, and chest were golden and freckled from sun exposure, but the rest was a creamy pale closer to my own skin tone.

"So I'm the only one who's seen all this?" My head dipped to pull a nipple into my mouth, the peak taut and stiff from the gentlest graze of my fangs.

"Yes." Her answer came on a soft gasp, her skin flushing red where my mouth teased her.

"I'm the luckiest man alive then, human or vampire." I dragged my mouth over the swells of her breasts, never wanting to lose contact with her skin. "I love how your skin changes color where not even the sun has seen you."

A laugh burst out of her. "You mean my tan lines? You *like* them?"

"Whatever they're called, I love them." My eyes lifted to meet hers. "I love *you*, Tavi."

"I love you, Cyan. All of you." Her knuckles stroked over my cheek. "Even the parts of you that you're ashamed of."

This woman. Fuck me, I would never deserve her. I had no words to respond with, just my body to please her. Every cell and scar down to her name and the vow carved into my chest. I pressed her palm against her name in my skin, over my heart that she might as well held in her hands.

I ravaged her mouth for the last time before making my way down her body. Tavi shivered as my fangs dragged over her skin. Her body tensed, anticipating my bite, but I was serious about not making her recovery longer.

Even so, that didn't mean I completely ruled out having a taste of her.

I grabbed handfuls of her ass, lifting her to my mouth as I kissed the soft curve of her lower stomach. Every inch of her was delicious and I was saving the best for last.

My mouth skimmed over her injured thigh, dragging my tongue for some extra healing to her tender skin. Tavi's breath quickened, her hips shifting from the attention on such a sensitive area.

"You're the bravest, most fearless fighter I've ever met." I skimmed my fingers to the insides of her thighs. "The way you just rode into battle for someone you loved. It's the honor of my life to know I'm one of those someones."

"Well," her breath hitched as my touch teased her sensitive skin, "You might not have been this morning, but..."

I laughed, not in the slightest bit offended. It actually amazed me that I could laugh at the dumb shithead I had been before, rather than mentally beat myself down. Being with Tavi was truly healing.

"What changed your mind?" I asked the question light-heartedly, not expecting a serious answer. "Pulling my head out of my own ass so I could come on a daring rescue? Maybe my tongue?"

"Your honesty." Tavi's hand came down as a gentle weight on my head, nails scratching luxuriously over my buzzed hair. "Your vulnerability. Showing me that you wouldn't run away when things got uncomfortable. That was all I needed. To know you were willing and able to do that." Her hand connected with mine that had been resting on her hip. "And Amy, of course. Trying your hardest to bring her back to me. That's why I love you, Cyan."

Just when I thought I couldn't cherish this woman any more, she proved me wrong. I was lost for words even though there was so much more to say. I wanted to explore and express the depths of my love for her in every possible way. Words couldn't capture all the bursts of emotions happening in my chest, so I decided on something even better. Orgasms.

"Fuck, I love you." I brought one of her legs up to a bent knee and kissed the inside of her thigh. "So much, I think I'll make you come from taking a little blood."

Tavi's legs immediately squeezed around my shoulders with a little moan of surprise. "Oh God, don't tease me, Cyan."

"I never promised anything about that, did I?"

My arms slipped under her thighs, hands clamping onto her waist as I dove for her pussy for the first time. I gave a long, indulgent lick, my tongue sliding her lips apart so I could suck on them properly. The heated taste of her pulled a satisfied moan from deep in my chest. She belonged on my tongue, her blood, her saliva, her come, all of her.

I gave a few playful tongue flicks to her clit, just enough to get her ramped up and squirming. Her growl of frustration when I pulled away made me chuckle.

"Just getting you ready for me, my love." I returned to kissing her inner thigh, finding the pulse of her femoral artery with my lips.

"I've been ready." Tavi's hips lifted, the delectable offering between her legs a feast for my eyes. And mouth. Pity I couldn't feed on two places at once.

My lips curled back and she made a little gasp when a fang scraped the sensitive skin of her leg. It didn't break the skin, but her scent and the rapid thrumming of her pulse made it increasingly difficult not to sink in.

"This might hurt a touch," I said. "My saliva will numb you slightly, but you're so sensitive down here, you might still feel something."

"I want to feel it," she said. "Please, Cyan."

"Hmm." My lips slid back and forth over that thrumming artery, the anticipation almost as torturous for me as it was for her. "Say my name like that again."

"Like what?"

"You know."

"Cyan!" Her voice cracked with blatant, unabashed need that went straight to my cock. "Cyan, *please*."

Her cries did me in, the sounds she made so powerful it felt like my fangs would rip out of my gums if they didn't taste her soon. I found the perfect spot directly over her artery and sank into her flesh.

Tavi jerked from the initial penetration but relaxed the moment her blood flowed into my mouth. She tasted like berries and the sweetest ambrosia. Pleasure and vitality spread throughout all of my limbs. Her blood made me feel like I could conquer the world and give my blood mate the fucking of a lifetime.

I held her leg to my mouth while I drank, my other hand free to caress and explore. I couldn't get enough of her skin, the softness, warmth, and curving lines. Tavi writhed under my touch, pressing into my hand like she couldn't get enough of me either. Her scent bloomed in the air, her pulse accelerating and sending blood faster into my mouth.

My hand found its way back to her pussy, slick and spread open and waiting. I rubbed and stroked her gently, the heat and wetness of her mirroring the exquisite taste pouring over my tongue. She would come from my feeding alone, without any extra stimulation, but I wanted to feel the moment it happened.

She grew closer with every draw of my mouth, her body thrashing as her breaths grew ragged and desperate. I pulled on her artery with a steady rhythm, leading, but not rushing, her directly to an imminent release.

"Cyan...Cy..." Tavi clutched at the sheets as she whimpered my name, her heels digging into the mattress, head tossing from side to side.

I could only moan against her flesh in reply, the sound vibrating against her skin that had to be near painfully sensitive at this point.

And then, she broke apart.

Her whole body shook with release, her leg against my mouth trembling so hard that my fangs nearly unlatched. I held her thigh still as wave after wave of pleasure shuddered through her. Only when she relaxed, limp and spent, did I carefully remove my fangs and soothe the puncture marks with my tongue.

"How was that?" I smirked, my mouth lingering on her inner thigh.

Tavi spent a few moments catching her breaths before her head lifted, a dreamy, blissed out expression on her face. Then she rolled forward and lunged for me.

Chapter 28

Tavia

I shoved at Cyan's shoulders until he leaned back on his elbows, a confused frown crossing his face. "Tavi?"

Planting my hands on either side of his hips, I leaned in and kissed him. My muscles were still shaky from that orgasm, my breathing a little labored, but I was on a mind and body high like I never believed possible.

He didn't just make me physically come. Something about his feeding on me caused a euphoric lightness in my brain that gave the sensation of floating. Maybe that also had to do with the lightheadedness because of my injury. Whichever the case, I felt incredible both in my head and body. Our kiss broke only because I couldn't stop giggling.

An amused smile pulled at Cyan's lips. "Everything okay?"

"More than okay." I couldn't stop grinning, couldn't stop what felt like pure sugar pumping through my veins. "That felt really, really good. I think I'm a little high."

He arched a brow and barked out a laugh. "High? Did you smoke some of my darakt?"

For some reason I found that hilarious and leaned into his shoulder, giggling madly. "Nooo, it was just that good. I feel so...light. I think you sucked my soul out."

His smile grew wider, full of warmth and mirth. "My silly Tavi."

He circled one of my nipples, making my laughter stutter in moans. Everything was still so sensitive. He wouldn't have to do much to make me come again.

"What makes you think I'm done making you feel good?" His voice grew low with want, fingers tugging more insistently at the aching peak until the sensation bordered on pain.

With all the reluctance in the world, I put my hand over his. "Being serious, I need a breather. It won't take much, and if I come within the next five minutes, I'm likely to pass out."

Cyan lowered his hand, but his expression was anything but disappointed. If anything, he looked smug. "Keep making me feel like a fucking king and I'll challenge Thorne for clan leader."

"Hm, before you do that." I kissed him again, hesitating before I spoke. "I want to put my mouth on you."

"You're doing a beautiful job of that." He leaned into me for another kiss, this one long and lingering.

We parted slowly, and I whispered with my lips ghosting against his, "I mean here." I stroked my fingertips along the top of his stiff length. "Maybe suck *your* soul out."

His laugh became a moan as I wrapped my palm around him and gave a few experimental strokes. My fingers squeezed gently, watching Cyan's face as I played and explored just as he had with me. His reactions were adorable, hot, and amusing all in equal measure.

"If you put your mouth on me there," he rasped, "I will not be long for this world either."

"Oh no," I said with mock concern before planting a final quick kiss on his lips. "How will the two of us ever recover from this?"

"I have no idea." Cyan's fingers speared through my hair as I lowered down.

I paused to kiss the scars on the left side of his chest, the symbols depicting my name and the vow he made to me. It felt like ages ago that he'd done it. "What happens to this now? You've gone against the part of never taking my blood."

"I can rewrite it," he grunted, one hand massaging the nape of my neck as my lips went lower. "Make a new vow about my love and devotion to my blood mate. I can do it at our ceremony." His fingers curled into fists in my hair as I traced the top of his hipbones with my teeth. "But your name stays. I love that your name in my skin, that your blood is in my body."

"I love it too."

His cock jumped when I breathed the words along his length, and the reaction would have made me laugh if I wasn't so turned on. I braced one palm against the front of his hip and resumed stroking with the other. Cyan's head fell back with muttered moans and curses. His hips canted toward me eagerly, and my whole body buzzed with arousal and anticipation as my lips slid over his wide head.

Cyan pressed forward a few inches on a sharp gasp, and he just as quickly pulled back. "Sorry, sorry. Just...fuck. Take your time. I'll try not to..."

It felt impossible to smile with my mouth stretched around him, but my eyes must have conveyed my amusement. His grin was full of joy and affection as he stroked my cheek. "Fuck me, you are a gorgeous sight to behold."

After acclimating to the weight and thickness of him in my mouth, I found a rhythm that was comfortable for me and seemed to drive him wild. Cyan muttered curses at the ceiling and praise at me, his hands roaming over me reverently. My confidence grew with each clenched fist in my hair, with every choked, "Fuck, Tavi, that's so good, just like that."

I lost track of time, lost track of everything but the pleasure singing in my body, the sounds he made and his hands on me as I pleased him. He became hard as steel in my mouth, swelling and thickening to the point where it was almost too much.

"You ready to suck my soul?" Cyan hissed through gritted teeth.

I managed an enthusiastic moan before he spilled his release on my tongue. His fist curled so tight in my hair as his cock spasmed, pinpricks of pain in my scalp rippled to my nipples and clit, making my toes curl.

When he finished and I eased my mouth off him, he was just as hard and thick as right before his orgasm. Our eyes met and the look I saw was beyond hungry.

He wanted to consume me.

"Do you um, need a few minutes?" I gestured vaguely toward his crotch.

Cyan shook his head. "I need you."

"I mean, you don't need to recover after...?"

He looked down as if noticing the state of himself for the first time, and shrugged. "Sometimes, but it seems every part of me needs more of you." He grabbed my hands and tugged me forward with a grin. "Thanks to your blood, I bet."

Our mouths connected in a hard, ferocious kiss as he lifted me. My legs wrapped around his waist and his hands supported my ass. He was still kneeling on the bed and seemed content to stay there, kissing my neck and shoulder as he positioned me right at the head of his cock.

As usual, Cyan teased me until I went feral. He thrusted lazily, sliding through my wet, achingly sensitive folds without penetrating. My infuriating vampire mate chuckled and kissed me when I whined and pleaded. I moaned his name, clawed at his back, wiggled my hips, and panted as his heavy length slid over my clit hood but not where I ached for him the most.

"Cyan, if you don't fuck me right fucking now, I'm going to die!" I cried.

"Oh, my Tavi." He chuckled directly into my ear. "Why didn't you say so?"

He made a small adjustment with his hips and pressed inside me in one long, fluid stroke. I didn't know if I screamed, gasped, or made any sound at all, but every solid inch of him filled me in the most exquisite, perfect way.

And when he began to move, the slow drag and press of him through me in a steady, unhurried cadence, that incredible feeling built. Each drive of him into me layering more sensation, more pleasure on the one before.

I clutched his shoulders and my ankles locked together behind his back, thighs squeezing his waist to keep the position. Our foreheads pressed together and I never wanted to stop feeling this.

"Good?" Cyan asked with a light nip to my mouth.

"Yes." I sighed as he pulled back, looking down between us to watch him fill me up again. "So fucking good."

"Do you want more?" His fingers dug into the right side of my ass, his other hand supporting my back.

My teeth traced the shell of his ear. "I want everything, Cyan."

He groaned and muttered something I didn't recognize, maybe something in his vampiric language. The next thing I felt was his grip shifting so both hands held my waist. The next time he entered me, he fucked me.

A gasp left my throat at the impact, at the slamming force of his body against mine. The pleasure inside me intensified, becoming sharper, taking me higher. I didn't just feel him inside me anymore, I felt him crash against my inner thighs. Each thrust struck my clit and filled me deeper.

"Oh fuck, Cy..." I held on for dear life, absorbing every lash of pleasure he brought down on me. If I had any length to my fingernails, I'd be drawing blood from his upper back.

"I know, Tavi. I can feel you. I'm so close too."

His mouth captured mine in a rough kiss and I felt a sharp prick from his fangs. He licked at the resulting blood droplet and moaned, fucking my mouth ravenously with his tongue before breaking away with a growl.

"Can I..."

He was too far gone to speak in full sentences, too lost in the pleasure and the fucking and whatever else his vampire senses picked up. But somehow I knew what he was asking.

"Yes, always." I lifted my chin, giving him full access to my neck. "My blood is only for you."

His fangs sank into my neck without a moment's hesitation, driven by lust and instinct and need. At the first pull, all the layering pleasure in me reached its peak and exploded into release. Only seconds later, I felt Cyan's orgasm follow, his moans deep and animalistic against my neck as his cock kicked inside me.

Every draw on my vein matched his thrusts, striking my clit in shocking jolts of pleasure that gradually slowed until the two of us were so wrung out that we could hardly move anymore.

Cyan eased us down to the mattress, his cock sliding out of me first, and then his fangs. My body felt heavy then, so utterly relaxed without a single tense muscle. It was an effort to keep my eyes open, even as Cyan licked and nuzzled my neck.

With a contented sigh, he rolled me to lie on his chest, his hands tangled in my hair.

"How close is it to dawn?" I mumbled.

"Don't worry about that." I felt a kiss press to my forehead. "I'll get situated and check on Amy while you rest."

Remembering Amy made me want to snap my eyes open and jump out of bed but after everything, including the mind-blowing sex that wore me out, I had absolutely no energy left.

But what I did have was a mate who would take care of things. I trusted and knew that he would.

So I let sleep come without a fight.

Chapter 29

Tavia

I woke up in the same place I fell asleep, nestled against Cyan's chest. My surroundings however felt different, and I sat up to get my bearings.

The first thing I noticed was Amy's cot, where she lay peacefully as if she were sleeping. I leaned in close, inspecting her for any signs of life, but saw none. She remained as pale as before, and her skin felt cold when I placed the back of my palm on her forehead.

Grief rose up like a tidal wave, threatening to drown me. With a hard swallow, I reminded myself that she still needed time. I wasn't sure how close we were to the three-day limit, but there still had to be time left.

I turned to Cyan, who slept next to me on an air mattress. It was a comfortable set-up actually, with a fitted sheet over the mattress, plus blankets and pillows piled on top. He must have set it up with Robin while I was conked out, and then carried me down to the cellar to be with Amy as I requested, all while dawn had been fast approaching.

His care and thoughtfulness lifted the heaviness in my

chest, at least for now. I leaned down to kiss his forehead before standing and stretching my arms over my head.

The physical exhaustion was gone, and my injured leg felt as good as new, if a little stiff. My grief and anxiety over Amy hung over me like the weight of an ocean, but there was a calmness alongside those feelings now. Whatever happened, at least I would have Cyan to lean on.

If Amy didn't wake up in another day or two, it would take a long time to process that, but at least I wasn't alone.

And if she did wake up, well, that would present its own set of challenges. But I'd have the love of my life and my best friend with me.

I walked around the cellar to both kill time and stretch my legs. Someone, probably Robin, had nailed some dark fabric over the light cracks between the boards in the cellar door. The tiny slivers of sunlight weren't likely to harm Cyan badly but it was thoughtful of her anyway.

After making sure I blocked any light with my body, I moved one of the makeshift curtains to peek outside and get a sense of what time of day it was. People milled about, but the clean-up effort looked almost done. The shadows were long and the light looked golden, which meant it had to be late afternoon. I'd slept most of the day away.

If I still had my phone, I'd know exactly what time it was. Maybe even call the council room and get a status report if anyone was in there. But I'd lost it in the struggle last night. And even if there was a chance no one heard what Cyan and I were up to in the wee hours of the morning, no one was likely to talk to me.

I'd made my home with the vampires, and was eager to get back to friendly, fanged smiles over the dirty looks from fellow humans.

Over the next few hours, I passed the time by organizing and cleaning the shelves in the cellar. When dusk fell, I heard Cyan stirring as he woke up, and set down my rag and duster.

"Morning, sunshine," I greeted.

His baffled, sleepy expression made me laugh as I lowered onto the mattress next to him.

"Evening, starlight," he returned with a lazy smile. "How long have you been up?"

"A couple of hours. I've just been puttering around until sundown."

"Have you eaten?" He nodded at a lunchbox-sized cooler against the wall. "Robin brought that down for you."

I hadn't and was honestly starving. Cyan chuckled as I pounced on the cooler and brought it with me to the mattress. "Did she help with this bed too?"

"With some convincing she did." I felt him kiss the back of my head as I dug through Robin's neatly packaged morsels. "She was going to give us two separate beds until I insisted we have one."

I looked over my shoulder, shooting him a playful glare. "You better not have intimidated her."

"Not at all. She intimidates me." His eyes flashed with mirth. "But I wasn't going to be separated from you for any reason."

My inner swooning was buried under my hunger as I wolfed down the sandwich, grapes, almonds, and water in the lunch box.

"How is Amy?" Cyan asked when I finished inhaling my food.

"She looks the same to me," I said.

He moved my hair aside and kissed my nape. "There's still time."

"I know. That's what I told myself when I woke up and

saw her." I leaned back, knowing I would find his chest to rest on. "Do you need blood?"

"Not yet, love." His fingers traced the column of my throat. "Have you given any thought to our blood mate ceremony?"

"I'd completely forgotten, actually. How is it supposed to go? It's a big deal, right?"

"Yes, because a blood mate pairing is so rare. All of Sanguine will turn out to witness." He gave a playful squeeze of my waist. "No pressure or anything."

"I mean, it can't possibly be worse than handing myself over as a sacrifice in front of everyone I've ever known."

Cyan's laugh ruffled my hair. "You handled that extremely well. I was so impressed by you that night. And look where we are now."

"Yeah," I said wistfully, looking at Amy's face. Who knew if she'd be alive and well if I'd made a different choice back then, but I'd never change what I found with Cyan.

"The ceremony can be almost anything we want," he said. "It's a lot like a human wedding, from what little I've seen. Except that it's a more public event. And since you're human, there will be a blood-binding ritual."

"What does that do?"

Cyan was silent for a beat, and his voice was quiet when he answered. "It's a type of blood magic that will share my life force with you. So you and I will live for the same length of time and age at the same rate."

I turned and looked at him, excitement sparking in my veins. "How old are you, anyway?"

"One-hundred and fifteen," he said. "Which makes me one of the youngest clan members. We reach adulthood at one hundred. So I have about seven hundred good years left in me."

My jaw dropped. "Holy shit. You know that's more than seven human lifetimes?"

"Yes." Cyan almost looked bashful, his eyes lowering and teeth gnawing on his lower lip. "Are you sure you want to spend all those lifetimes with me?"

I spun to face him and flung my arms around his neck. "That sounds like a great length of time to come up with new wine recipes." Our laughter came together in smiles that kissed. "And I really can't imagine who else I'd rather spend all those lifetimes with, than the one who picked me up and held me together at the hardest time of my life."

Cyan held my face and kissed me deeply. "You make me wish for an immortal life. Because I'm certain seven human lifetimes with you will never feel like enough."

His words and his lips were a balm on the ache that gnawed deep inside me. If my grief was a tidal wave, he was a sea-facing cliff, strong enough to withstand and protect me during the most furious storms.

When our kissing slowed, I rested my head on his shoulder, and his arms braced in a protective hold around my back.

"So, do you want to make the wine we serve at the ceremony?"

"Hm." Musing on that thought, I kissed his neck with a smile. "I'm thinking hard cider actually. Apple and maybe cherry."

"I like the sound of that. Can I help?"

"If we're really sealing the deal in front of all of Sanguine, you better help."

I almost missed the gentle sound under his laughter. It was barely anything at all, just the rustling of a blanket. Either one of us could have made that sound, but something made me look at Amy.

And I saw her moving.

"Cyan!" I gasped, clutching his arm. "Is that—is she...?"

"Yes." His palm rested on my back. "Be calm, love. She's going to be confused."

My heart pounded so forcefully, I thought it might break through my chest. Amy's arms were pushing her blanket down to her waist. She was still pale, her eyes still closed, but she moved as if waking from sleep.

I stared, unable to blink as she stretched and rubbed her eyes. Her mouth even stretched open in a yawn. After feeling her weak pulse fade to nothing, after seeing how utterly, eerily still she became after her breathing stopped, it felt like I was watching a miracle happen.

I wanted to smother her in a hug and cry out all my relief and happiness on her shoulders. Some instinct was throwing off alarms at how unnatural this was, and that was probably what held me back. The dead just didn't come back to life. Not unless you gambled on fifty-fifty odds and had a vampire willing to help.

Amy rolled up to a seat, rubbing her eyes a final time before she looked at me. Her eyes shouldn't have startled me, but they did. The whites of her eyes had gone completely black, although her irises were the same cornflower blue.

"Tavia?" Her eyes flicked to Cyan for a second, but quickly refocused on me. "Why are you looking at me like that? How long have I been out?"

I swallowed, quickly realizing that, despite how much I'd hoped for this moment, I hadn't prepared for it at all. I had hoped she'd wake up because I was grieving, because I wasn't ready to lose her. But I hadn't actually considered that Amy coming back from the dead was a true possibility.

"Amy." My throat went dry so I swallowed again. "Ames, honey. Do you remember anything?"

"Um, it's coming back." She rubbed her forehead, and when her lips parted on a breath, I saw the tips of small fangs. "We were attacked, right? I got hurt and brought down here to the cellar." She looked around, eyes pausing on Cyan at my side before lowering to the air mattress and mess of blankets we sat on. "It sounded bad, but I guess I pulled through. Sorry if I worried you, Tav. Did Robin call you out here?"

"Uh, yeah. She did." Amy sounded so normal, exactly like herself. How was I supposed to tell her that she was no longer human?

"Did anyone else get hurt?" Amy rubbed her throat. "Damn, I'm thirsty. Is there water anywhere?"

I handed her my water bottle while Cyan pinned me with a hard look. "She'll need to feed soon," he whispered into my ear. "And it can't be from you."

I stared back at him, puzzled by that and wondered if it had to do with the blood mate thing. Whatever the reason, the first order of business was to drop this bombshell on Amy.

"Ames," I said, and steeled myself with a breath. "You were hurt very badly. You...almost didn't make it."

Black and blue eyes widened as she set the water bottle down slowly. "Oh." She gave me a smile with no awareness of her sharp little fangs. "Well, I'm okay now, Tav. No need to look so glum."

It was Cyan's hand making soothing passes over the small of my back that gave me the strength to keep talking.

"You wouldn't have made it if it weren't for Cyan," I said. "You...you died, Amy. I felt your pulse stop. I begged him to bring you back, and...he did."

Amy's expression morphed into fear and disbelief as she looked at him. She clutched the edge of the blanket as she whispered, "What did you do to me?"

Cyan folded his hands together. "I gave you my blood, which your organs recognized as a life source. Biologically, you're still human with some vampire adaptations. We call your kind brusang."

Amy's hand shook as it came to her face. "I'm...what?" She became aware of her teeth right then, and pressed her fingertips against her longer, sharper canines. Horror filled her eyes, and she went eerily still before darting out of bed.

"Amy, wait."

I followed after her, but the vampire blood had heightened her speed. She reached the small, dusty mirror on the cellar wall before I could reach her. There was a shocked squeak, and then a moan of horror that became a deep, chest-wracking sob.

"I should probably go for a bit." Cyan stood, looking concerned but made no move toward the door.

"Is it dark enough outside?"

He nodded. "I'll be fine."

I squeezed his forearm before he could leave. "She'll adjust. It's just a shock."

"I know." He planted a kiss on my forehead, then palmed the side of my neck. "She's welcome to stay with us, of course. Bea will be happy to help too. In time, she'll adjust to her new life."

I reached for his face, finding his mouth for a kiss before releasing him. "Thank you again for bringing her back to me."

His eyes were soft and warm as he ran his knuckles over my cheek. "Anything for you."

We parted with another kiss, and he left the cellar while I cautiously approached a sobbing, curled up Amy.

I went to wrap my arms around her, but to my surprise, found myself shoved away.

"How could you?" she cried, her black eyes now lined in red from tears. "How could you let him do this to me? I'm a fucking monster!"

The words hit me like a punch to the gut and I tried to not take them personally. "You're not a monster. You're still you, Ames. And don't put any of the blame on him. I begged him to do it because I couldn't bear to lose you."

"So you had him, what, Frankenstein me? I never *asked* for this, Tavia! I never wanted to have fangs and black eyes and—fuck." A trembling hand came to her mouth. "I have to drink blood, don't I? That's why I'm still so thirsty. Oh my God..."

"Hey, it's going to be okay. Really." She allowed me to rub her arm and I took the chance to scoot closer to her. "The vampires live really well, you won't want for anything again. There's a brusang I've made friends with, Bea. She's great, and we'll both help you get through this."

Amy let out a low growling noise I'd never heard from her before. "You don't get it, do you? What makes you think I want to be around you or your new vampire family?"

"Amy, what—"

She pulled away from me and stood, leaving me speechless on the ground. When she turned to face me, her expression seething, I had to admit she did look more monstrous than human.

"I told you I wanted to stay with humans, to preserve our culture and our way of life. You made your choice and I made mine. I thought we respected each others' choices, Tavia. But now you've gone and turned me into *this*," she gestured at herself, "and my choice is gone. Now I have to live in the vampire world, something I never wanted. You *knew* that and you forced this on me anyway!"

"I..." A sob choked off my response. Of course, I hadn't thought of it that way. I was too out of my mind with grief to think of any real consequences. "Ames, you were *dead*."

"You should have let me stay dead!"

"I couldn't." A harsh, shaky breath escaped me and tears blurred my vision. "I'm so sorry. I just couldn't."

Maybe it was selfish of me. Maybe I should have given more thought to what Amy would have wanted, but the simple truth was that I couldn't let her go. Not when there was another option.

The grief might have slipped away, but now guilt overtook me. Had I doomed my best friend rather than saved her?

"I'm sorry," I repeated, blinking to let the tears fall. "I'm so sorry." The words were inadequate, but so was everything else I could have said. "I should've...fuck, I'm sorry."

Eventually, Amy's arms came around me. She was still so much smaller than me, and I rested my cheek on top of her head as I hugged her back.

Wrapped up like that, my best friend and I cried together.

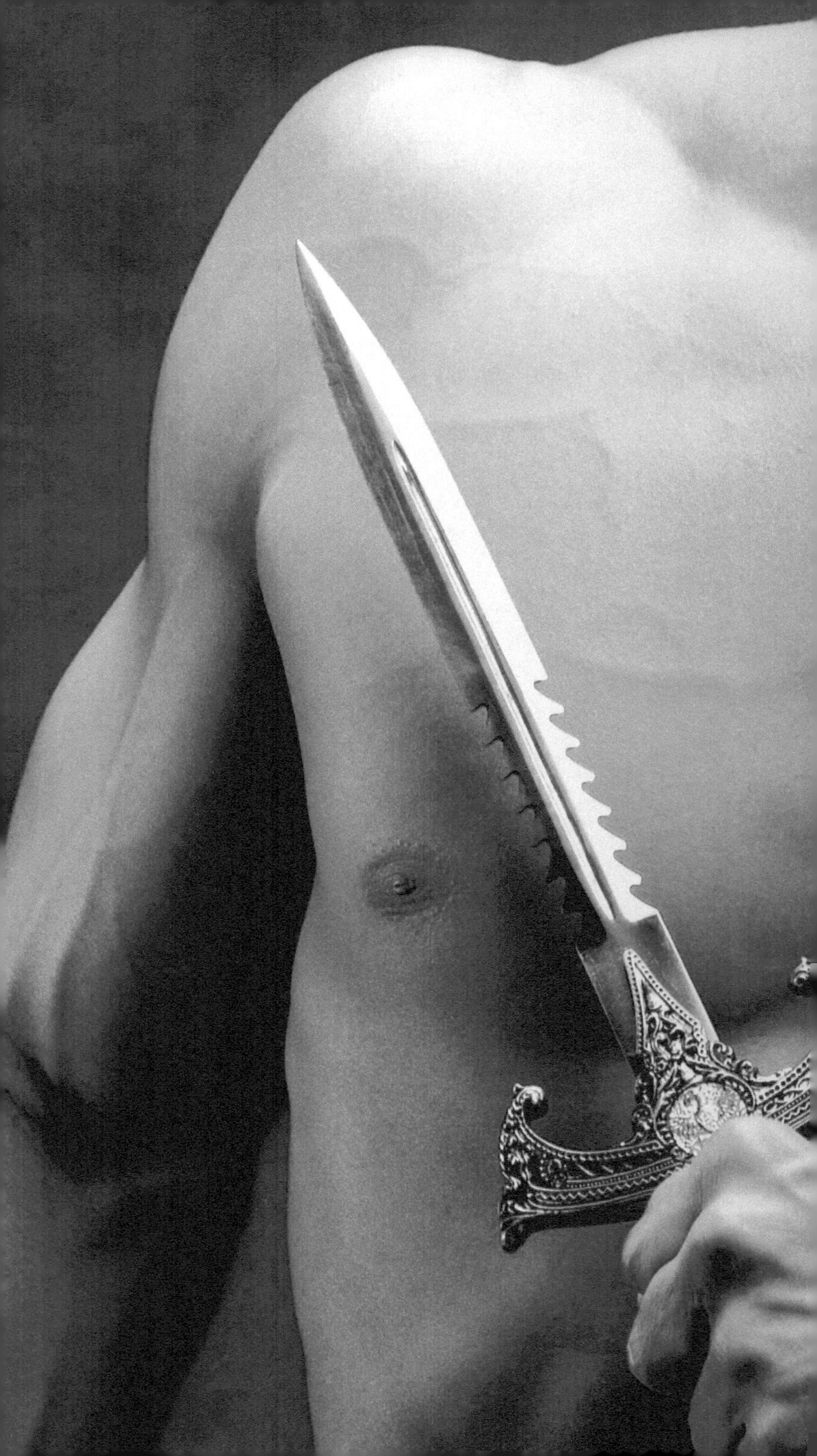

Chapter 30

Cyan

I lit up a darakt cigarette, tapping my foot while I listened to the phone ring on the other end.

"What's up, Cyanide?" came Desmond's greeting.

"Hey," I said on an exhale of red smoke. "Any marrowers talking yet?"

"Oh yeah. We're not getting anything substantial though. Detox is a bitch and they're in a world of pain. All of them say the same thing, they don't remember anything."

I pondered that, taking another drag. "You believe them?"

"Thorne and Rhain seem to. They want to get your opinion, I think. Since you're cozy with the marrowers."

I blew out a breath. "I mean, Thorne knows better than anybody they've never gotten involved in any of the clan conflicts. As a whole, they're a peaceful bunch and would rather hide underground than get into that mess. I've never heard of them having issues with humans, either. But every species has bad apples."

There was a pause on the phone and some staticky

rustling. It sounded like Des was lighting up a smoke of his own.

"I think they're telling the truth," Des confessed. "The big guy, Lore, he seems genuinely horrified at what happened, and swears up and down that he's never touched drae in his life. And if you were here, seeing him coming down from this shit, I think you would believe him too."

"Withdrawal is that bad, huh?"

"The guy says his skin feels like it's on fire. I feel bad for him, to be honest."

"Yeah, marrowers and drae just don't make sense." I rubbed my chin. "They like sunlight even less than we do, for fuck's sake."

"Right. So the feeling here, and I would agree, is that someone drugged these people and set them on the humans for some reason."

"If that's true, it could be anyone." I sighed. "At least half the clans hate that the humans have their independent settlement here."

"Sure, but like you said, marrowers hardly have beef with anybody. Who would use them to do it?"

"Anyone who hates humans badly enough. Or it could be a tactic for all we know. Pin it on the ones with no known enemies while keeping their own hands clean."

"Bloodless pricks," Des hissed. "I'll bet you it's one of the big clans. Carpe Noctem, probably. They're the only ones dickless enough to do some underhanded shit like this. The humbler ones would have just attacked the humans themselves and claimed responsibility proudly."

Both options had me clenching the phone until my knuckles ached. I would never be the biggest fan of humans but these were Tavi's people. They were only trying to live and survive, to exist as everyone else had a right to. They didn't deserve to be attacked just because of that.

"Listen, Des. I'm coming back soon, but can you bring up a nightly patrol around Sapien to Thorne? We should be vigilant in case whoever did this tries again."

"Sure." Des' voice held a note of surprise and there was a hesitant pause before he spoke again. "Is Tavia coming back with you, or...?"

"Yes, she's coming home with me." Never had a sentence felt so damn satisfying leaving my mouth.

"She's still your blood pet then? Laith is going to be disappointed."

I knew he was teasing, and still failed to suppress the growl rising up my throat. "Actually, she's my blood *mate*. So Laith ought to keep his hands and his fangs away from her if he knows what's good for him."

Des coughed like he inhaled too much smoke. "Blood mate? Are you serious?"

"Dead serious." A grin stretched my mouth wide. "I've told Tavi about the ceremony and we're starting to plan."

"Well, congratulations, Cy. Temkra's blessings to you."

"Thanks, Des." I poked my fang into my lower lip. "I'm pretty sure we're bringing home a friend of Tavi's as well."

"A friend? Well, any friend of Tavia's is a friend of Blood 'til Dawn."

"We'll see," I hedged. "She was badly injured in the attack and, well, she's a brusang now. She may have some trouble adjusting. Give Bea a heads up, will you?"

"Sure thing. She'll be thrilled to have someone like her around." Des's voice lowered. "She's never said anything but I get the sense Bea's always felt a bit outcasted from the rest of us. I mean she's always been clan, but it must be tough being the only non-vampire."

"She won't be for long." At the sound of door hinges and then approaching footsteps, I looked over my shoulder to see Tavi heading my way. "Gotta go, Des. I'll let you know when I need a ride."

I ended the call, lifted my arm, and Tavi immediately tucked into my side, nestling there. My arm wrapped around her shoulders, holding her close while I wondered why I'd ever prefer meaningless sex and feedings over this. Simply this, having her at my side, eased all the tension inside me.

"How's Amy?" I planted a kiss on top of her head.

"Physically? Fine." Tavi laughed humorlessly. "She's so upset and yelled at me a ton. It makes me wonder if she no longer has asthma and a heart murmur now. She would've felt faint and out of breath if she yelled and swore at me like that before."

"Our blood has healing properties too, not just our saliva. It's possible the changing process fixed those issues for her." I smoothed back Tavi's hair until she looked up at me with those stormy eyes. "But she's not happy."

Tavi shook her head and her pained expression killed me. "Was it the wrong thing to do? Was it...selfish of us to bring her back?"

"No, my love." I took her face in both hands. "Her life would have been cut short far too soon otherwise. She would have died too young, with her whole life ahead of her. And you gave that life back to her."

Tavi drew in a shaky breath. "Amy was proud to be human in a world full of supernaturals. She never wanted to be anything more or different, she was content with what she had. She wanted to continue preserving human culture for future generations. And now I've taken that humanity away from her."

I pulled her into my chest, trying to comfort her as best I could. Her arms went around my waist and squeezed.

"I don't know what it's like to be human, or anything other than a vampire," I said. "But I know *you*. I know your heart and that you don't have a selfish bone in your body. You would never take anything from Amy. You give to her endlessly. With this second chance at life, you gave her the greatest gift of all. I'm sorry she doesn't see it that way now, but with time, I'm sure she will."

Tavi pulled away from my chest to wipe tears from her face, sending a weary smile up at me. "How do you always know exactly the right thing to say?"

"You are my sole source of nutrients and vitality. I don't have any other choice."

Her laugh came with a swat to my chest, but there was brightness and hope in the sound.

"Amy is lucky to have you as a friend," I said when her laughter died down. "She'll have Bea too. No matter what, she won't be alone in this. And when she's ready, she's in full control to do whatever she likes with her life. She can still be involved with humans if that's important to her."

My phone buzzed with a call, and I swore at the interruption as I checked it. "Speak of the devil." I answered with a frown. "Hey Bea. Everything okay?"

"Yeah!" the brusang chirped through the speaker. "Is Tavia with you? She's not answering her phone."

"I lost my phone," Tavia said, able to hear her clearly. "But I'm here. I'm okay."

"Oh, great!" Bea sounded relieved. "Glad you're alright. I'll just text Cy then until you find yours. Thanks, bye!"

She hung up before I could respond and I frowned at the phone.

"What was that about?" Tavi wondered.

"No idea."

A flurry of text messages came through, and I spent the next few seconds scanning them before laughing out loud.

"What?" Tavi stood on tiptoes to look at my screen.

I handed her my phone. "She's sending over a brusang beginner's guide, including meat-based recipes to slowly acclimate a new brusang to drinking blood."

My beautiful blood mate scrolled through the incoming messages, tears filling her eyes once again. "Oh my god, this is..."

She trailed off and brought a hand to her mouth. I was about to ask what was wrong when a bright laugh bubbled out of her, followed by a smile full of relief and gratitude.

"This is so sweet of her. It's..." She laughed again, wiping her cheeks. "It's like she was waiting to share all this knowledge. Oh Bea, you're amazing."

I wrapped an arm around her shoulders and pulled her close again with a kiss on her forehead.

"Everything is going to be fine, my love."

Tavi lifted her face to mine and accepted the kiss I gave her with a smile.

"I actually do believe that," she whispered.

Epilogue

Tavia

Four weeks later

"How the fuck is *he* allowed to be here?" Des hissed over Cyan's shoulder, glaring at the figure seated in the crowd below us.

Cyan didn't miss a beat. "Because he's Amy's guest, which means you'll behave yourself during the ceremony."

"But why'd she have to bring *him* as a guest?" Laith echoed Desmond's disdain.

The vampires' eyes fell on me for an answer.

"I don't know," I admitted. "She said he kept her safe that day she went missing. Apparently they've been in touch."

Des and Laith grumbled at that. "He's using her to get to us," Des bit out. "Why else would the last sane member of Rathka's Order have anything to do with a freshly turned brusang? How do we know he's not a cannibal like the rest of his kin?"

"Maybe he actually likes her," I shot back.

Des' expression was one of bewilderment. "Nothing against Amy, of course—"

"Can it," Cyan growled, his fangs long. "Do your gossiping after the fucking ceremony. He's here. We have eyes on him, and so far, he's minding his own business. Why can't you do the same?"

Des lowered his chin, mumbling an apology. "You both look great, by the way. Congratulations."

A flurry of nerves rose from my stomach to my chest. This was it. I felt like a bride on her wedding day.

This was so much more than getting married, though. I was about to become blood-bonded to Cyan, my lifespan connected to his. Instead of hoping to survive to my seventies, or optimistically, eighties, I had about *seven hundred* years of life to look forward to. A typical life expectancy for a vampire, but unfathomable for a human.

The entire blood mate ceremony, including the blood-bonding ritual, would be performed by a high priest from the clan Temkra's Blood. They considered themselves direct descendants of the vampire's main deity, and dedicated themselves to preserving the history and teachings of Temkra. For that reason, they were the ones usually called on for ceremonies such as this.

It was also rumored that the high priests of Temkra's Blood were truly immortal, most of them being thousands of years old.

Human wedding tradition had nothing on blood mate ceremonies.

I looked out at the crowd from our place on a raised dais. The last few invited guests were finding their seats, while the public drew as close as they dared to the Blood 'til Dawn clan members posted around the perimeter as security.

We were in the main square of the Cap, and people were also watching from windows and rooftops in the surrounding buildings. The moon hung full and round in the sky, and while vampires didn't have particular affinity for the moon phases, I found it beautifully poetic that our ceremony was being performed on a full moon night.

I spotted Amy near the back of the seating area, a handsome, well-dressed vampire at her side. He was Novak, and the one Des and Laith grumbled about being here. He had pale, silvery-blonde hair to his shoulders that contrasted with brown skin. His arm rested on the back of Amy's chair, his gaze sweeping the crowd as if checking for any threats.

Apparently Novak belonged to a clan that was a longtime enemy of Blood 'til Dawn's. I didn't know the full story, nor how he ended up as Amy's plus-one. She'd only met him two weeks before, and scared me half to death when she'd gone missing for most of a day. It turned out she'd been with him.

Amy's expression was blank, her eyes vacant like she was lost in thought. Adjusting to life as a brusang had been hard for her, to say the least. Our friendship felt strained since her turning. She argued with me more than she ever had as a human, often yelling at me to leave her alone.

It hurt, but I tried not to take it personally, as Cyan and Bea often reminded me. Amy was mourning the loss of her old life, and the transition to her new one would take time.

She showed up for my mating ceremony, which I appreciated. For a while I wasn't sure if she would.

Novak placed his hand in her lap, angling his head down to speak to her in a low voice. Amy immediately cocked her head to listen, her gaze sliding toward him with a slight smile. They seemed close, and I had to admit it worried me. In Sapien, guys would pretend to like her just to ridicule her and break her heart.

But no matter how deeply protective of her I was, she was her own person making her own decisions.

A figure ascended the short staircase on the back of the dais, and my breath stuttered at the sight of the priest. He was shirtless and covered from neck to waist with ritualistic scars that looked very old. I recognized a few characters of the vampire's ancient language. Stripes of black and red paint also covered his forehead, cheeks, and torso.

The priest had long, straight black hair to his waist. He was barefoot with loose-fitting pants and a wide leather belt around his hips. There was a presence to him, a low humming vibration in the air surrounding him. I didn't know if it was his connection to Temkra, his magic, or his age, but he radiated something that was unique among all the vampires in attendance.

"Hello, I'm Ruslan," he said with a slight bow of his head. "It's my honor to join two blood mates before Temkra and all of her children." He looked at Cyan and then at me, his eyes such a dark red they were almost black. "Are you ready to begin?"

Cyan and I only needed to glance at each other for one heart-pounding moment before nodding. "Yes, we're ready."

"Excellent." Ruslan gave a slight smile. "Octavia, do you renounce your human lifespan and accept the blood bond to this vampire? Your lifespan will directly connect to his, and as such you will live for centuries. When Temkra carries you to eternal rest, you will both go together. Do you accept this?"

I looked at Cyan, who was biting his lower lip as if he was nervous. As if there would be any doubt in my mind.

"Yes," I said, a little breathless with emotion. "I accept the blood bond."

Ruslan turned to my mate. "And are you, Cyan of Blood 'til Dawn, willing to make a vow in silver to this woman as well as a blood bond, before Temkra and and all of Sanguine present?"

"I am," Cyan said solemnly, his gaze locked onto mine.

"Do you have a silver blade with which to make your vow?"

"I do."

"You may proceed with your vow."

Cyan removed his loose-fitting shirt and placed it on the small altar next to us. He picked up the silver dagger next to the shirt and unsheathed it. With his eyes on me and without a single beat of hesitation, he held the sharp tip to his skin right above where my name was carved. On his next breath, he spoke his vow as he carved it into his skin.

"I vow to honor, love, protect, and cherish Octavia..."

A sharp breath escaped me when he carved out my name, cutting into the scar tissue that was already there. Why wouldn't he just skip over it?

"My blood mate," Cyan continued. "Only her blood will fuel me. Only her embrace will hold me. Only her love will sustain me."

His breathing labored slightly, and his entire left side was swollen and red, but his gaze and voice never wavered. "Octavia has my devotion, my body, my love." The vow was long enough to be going under his chest now, cutting across his ribs which had to be horrifically painful. "Until we die in each other's arms, and Temkra carries us to eternal rest."

Cyan sheathed the dagger and placed it calmly on the table, although I found it difficult to see through the tears blurring my vision. He reached for my hand, rubbing his thumb back and forth over the back of my palm while I blinked rapidly and composed myself.

Ruslan gave me a gentle smile when I looked his way. "May I take your arm, Octavia?"

I held my free hand out to him, palm up.

"Cyan?"

Cyan did the same, mirroring my pose while our right hands stayed connected.

"I need to draw a small amount of blood from both of you for the blood bond ritual." The priest's gaze passed over us. "Do you consent?"

"Yes," we said together. Thankfully I'd been prepared ahead of time and knew exactly what was coming.

Ruslan picked up a sharp, glinting blade from the altar. With a quick, definitive slice, he made a shallow cut across the inside of my forearm. He then moved my arm over an ancient-looking wooden bowl, turning my arm and squeezing gently to coax some blood from my wound. After he had roughly a tablespoon's amount, he offered me a clean cloth to press over the cut, and then repeated the cut across the forearm with Cyan.

He had to cut Cyan quite a bit deeper to mitigate his fast healing, although my mate never flinched. Since feeding on me regularly, Cyan seemed to heal from surface wounds even faster than normal.

Our blood mixed in the bowl and the priest released Cyan's arm. He didn't offer a cloth, as the wound was already closing.

The hum of magic in the air grew more intense as Ruslan gently swirled our blood in the bowl, whispering words in the vampiric language. He pinched dried herbs of some kind and what looked like salt from a dish on the altar, sprinkling it into our mixed blood.

Visually, nothing happened. No spark or *poof* of magic that I could see, but I knew as soon as Ruslan stopped speaking that something had happened. It wasn't just our blood and a few herbs mixed into that bowl. Whether it was Temkra accepting me for one of her vampire sons or some kind of chemical reaction, I knew it was a concoction that would transform me.

Ruslan picked up the bowl with both hands and held it out to me. "Whenever you're ready, Octavia."

I accepted the bowl and looked directly at Cyan, the cocky, flirtatious vampire with a deeply hidden vulnerable side. Even now, his brow furrowed with mild worry, like he feared I might not complete the ritual after all.

"Cyan." I took a steadying breath. Saying vows of my own weren't in the original plans, but it felt important to say something as I did this. "I love you so much. And I can't wait to spend the next seven hundred years at your side, supporting you, loving you, and putting you first like you've done with me. You were always worthy and I'll remind you of that every single day."

His eyes glittered with unshed tears as he mouthed, "Fuck, I love you."

I brought the edge of the bowl to my lips, tipped it up and drank.

The mixture didn't taste like blood, but like liquid fire. It was hot, almost scalding, and somehow tasted *alive*. It didn't move like liquid as I swallowed, but seemed to stretch out in all directions until it was absorbed into my organs and even my cells.

The sensations would have been fun to sit with, but

everyone was cheering and Cyan pulled me into a bone crushing embrace.

"Congratulations." Ruslan ducked his head with a warm smile. "In the eyes of Temkra and her children, you two are officially mated and blood-bonded."

My arms went around Cyan's neck, but he turned his head before I could kiss him. With a smirk and a mischievous glint in his eye, he ran his tongue along the cut on my forearm, sealing the wound closed.

"Only my fangs will draw your blood from now on," he whispered, leaning in.

"Hm, I dunno." I couldn't suppress my grin as our noses and foreheads touched. "That avocado knife might give you some competition."

His laugh was full of elation and mirth.

And his kiss? Full of love and tenderness with an undercurrent of passion that only my blood mate could give.

———

Thank you so much for reading **_Taste of Fate!_**
Curious about Amy and Novak, the mysterious man who sat with her at the ceremony? Those two will soon be main characters in their own book! In the meantime, get a sneak peak of how they first met in the **_Taste of Fate_** bonus scene!

Download the free bonus scene here:
https://BookHip.com/WBMFBWG

———

If you're wondering what the werewolves are up to in their territory, those characters have books as well! You might even seen some familiar vampire faces. ;) The Howling Death MC series starts with ***Traitor Wolf:***
http://books2read.com/traitorwolf

Glossary

Clans of Sanguine and Vampiric Terms

Vampire Clans

Blood 'til Dawn: Current ruling clan of Sanguine

Carpe Noctem: A previous ruling clan, longtime rivals of Blood 'til Dawn

Marrowers: Clan and subspecies of vampires with a diet rich in bone marrow and preference for living underground

Rathka's Order: A near-extinct clan that succumbed to an unknown illness causing madness and cannibalism

Temkra's Blood: Clan and religious order with a strong focus on the vampire's primary deity, Temkra

Vampiric terms

Blood mate: Someone whose blood is considered chemically and nutritionally perfect for the recipient. Once tasted, a bond is created in which all other blood tastes foul and rancid. Can be one-sided or between two parties.

Blood pet: Someone who provides their blood to a vampire in exchange for care and protection. Generally expected to be an exclusive arrangement on both ends, unless both parties agree otherwise. Can be platonic or a sexual/romantic arrangement.

Brusang: A human who has been given vampire blood

near or soon after their death. They awaken after 2-3 days with blackened eyes and adopt vampire traits such as the need for blood, accelerated healing, an 800-year lifespan, and an aversion to sunlight.

Darakt: A mixture of dried blood and herbs crushed to a fine power, usually rolled in paper and smoked like cigarettes. Provides a brief, euphoric high like nicotine to humans.

Draitrium (drae): A mineral found in the dragon shifter territory that allows vampires to walk in daylight unharmed. Also a highly addictive drug with terrible side effects.

Half-Century Selection: Event in which the human community of Sapien gives one of their own as a blood pet to the ruling vampire clan every fifty years. In exchange, no vampires are permitted to feed from Sapien citizens.

Rathka: Temkra's younger brother, an impulsive trickster deity prone to violence. Patron deity of the clan, Rathka's Order.

Sapien: The last remaining human-only compound in Sanguine

Temkra: primary deity of vampires, thought of as the mother of the species. The territory of Sanguine is believed to be the remains of her body when she laid down to die. This is why the regions of Sanguine are divided into body parts (the Heart, the Ribs, etc.)

Verakt: A vampire or brusang who claims a blood pet. Responsible for the blood pet's care, comfort, and protection. Generally expected to be an exclusive arrangement on both ends, unless both parties agree otherwise. Can be platonic or a sexual/romantic arrangement.

Also by Sophie Ash

Gods and Myths

The Minotaur

Howling Death MC

Traitor Wolf

Enemy Wolf

Cursed Wolf

About the Author

Sophie Ash is a USA Today bestselling author from Northern California, writing paranormal romances with plenty of bite, as well as passionate retellings of myths and folklore.

When she's not writing, she's probably reading, gardening, vacuuming up cat hair, or enjoying a craft beer in the sun.

Sign up for Sophie's email list and get a free standalone novella as a thank you gift: https://BookHip.com/KBRCFWN

facebook.com/Crystal.Sophie.Ash.Books

instagram.com/crystalsophieash

amazon.com/author/sophieash

bookbub.com/profile/sophie-ash